Praise for *The One Hundred*

"With a sensibility that's as compassionate and quirky as those of her two indelible heroines, Marianne Cronin offers a deceptively light-hearted response to life's heaviest questions. As Lenni and Margot leave their mark on one another, so too does this tearjerker of a book leave its mark on the reader."

—Kathleen Rooney, author of
Lillian Boxfish Takes a Walk and *Cher Ami and Major Whittlesey*

"Graceful, intelligent, beautiful writing. Full of wisdom and kindness. It is just the kind of book I adore."

—Joanna Cannon, author of
The Trouble with Goats and Sheep

"Sharp and funny, warm and wise, a remarkable friendship sparks two lifetimes of shared stories in one unforgettable book. I loved it."

—Jess Kidd, author of *Himself*

"Gorgeously poignant novel . . . unexpectedly funny, touching, and so uplifting."
—*Good Housekeeping*

"A gorgeous, heartbreaking story readers won't soon forget."
—*Elle* (a "Most Anticipated Book")

"With its uplifting message, the story is both poignant and also comical."
—*Cosmopolitan* ("Twenty Books You're
Going to Want to Read This Summer")

"A beautiful debut, funny, tender, and animated by a willingness to confront life's obstacles and find a way to survive. . . . It celebrates friendship, finds meaning in difficulty, and lets the reader explore dark places while always allowing for the possibility of light. Lenni and Margot are fine companions for all our springtime journeys."
—*Harper's Bazaar* (UK, Author of the Month)

Eddie Winston Is Looking for Love

Eddie Winston Is Looking for Love

A NOVEL

Marianne Cronin

HARPER PERENNIAL

NEW YORK • LONDON • TORONTO • SYDNEY • NEW DELHI • AUCKLAND

HARPER ● PERENNIAL

Also published in the United Kingdom in 2024 by Penguin Random House UK.

HarperCollins books may be purchased for educational, business, or sales promotional use. For information, please email the Special Markets Department at SPsales@harpercollins.com.

FIRST U.S. EDITION

Designed by Jen Overstreet

Library of Congress Cataloging-in-Publication Data has been applied for.

ISBN 978-0-06-338351-7 (pbk.)
ISBN 978-0-06-338350-0 (simultaneous hardcover ed.)

24 25 26 27 28 LBC 6 5 4 3 2

for my girl
i love you to the moon, to the pink sky,
to the top of the tallest clocktower
and back to mama

Part One

Eddie

And so, we come to the end.

The remnants of a life don't add up to much, really. Not once the big things—the fridge freezer, the three-piece suite, the body—are all boxed up and gone.

What remain are the little things. Odd bits and pieces. Books and records and jumpers and wellies, rusted jewelry all a-tangle. Cards and letters and Snakes and Ladders games where the dice have gone missing and the snakes are shedding a skin. Pajamas and photographs and seashells and postcards.

Life in all its mundane glory.

The trouble with all these objects from all these moments in all these lives is that they arrive all at once. Packed together in a bin bag. And there is no telling if the shoe brush (£3) or the pink enamel mirror (£7.50) are pieces of historical importance, of meaning and metaphor, or if they are just bits of old junk. Things picked on whims that eventually become the bones of a house. Maybe it is in fact the game of Mouse Trap (50p, missing its boot piece) that is the thing that this poor deceased person treasured so dearly. And yet, here in the back room, sitting on my floor cushion because the chair hurts my knee, my hands ensconced in the gardening gloves that Marjie has made me wear since the "Incident with the Human Tooth" (root hanging off it, covered in crusted blood, £0), that I sort through the donations made by the living and the dead and I put a price tag on the souvenirs of someone else's life.

Mr. McGlew's life arrives in a black bin bag packed by a stranger.

The young man who works for Birmingham City Council's house-clearing team comes in every few weeks with the belongings of those who have died alone in the council's care. The squelchy sound of a wet piece of gum being pressed between his molars comes in with him. Today, he's wearing a high-visibility waistcoat over a filthy gray Nike sweatshirt and a pair of joggers that are hung way too low.

When I close the Mills & Boon I've been reading about a rascally stable hand and the wealthy middle-aged countess who loves him, the young man jumps.

"*Jesus*," he says, putting his hand to his chest, "I thought you were a mannequin."

This is absurd for three reasons. First, there are no mannequins on earth as wrinkly as me. Second, this gentleman (though that term is a stretch) has handed me a bin liner of items scooped from a council house hundreds of times in the last few years. And third, we have just the one mannequin and she stands lonely in the window in whatever terrible outfit Marjie and I have wrestled her into, hoping it is fashionable enough to entice someone inside.

"Here." He hands me the black bin bag that has "Mr. McGlew" written on a piece of paper taped to its side.

"Do you happen to know the first name of Mr. McGlew?" I ask, taking out a donations form.

"William, I think it was, bud," he says, checking the name written on the back of his hand in black felt-tip—he knew I would want to know. That's sweet. Then he shuffles out of the shop, pulling his black jogging bottoms up over his Calven Kine boxers and inviting me to "Have a good one."

The council flat that was once the home of this Mr. McGlew

will already be being cleaned by the housing maintenance team. It will be back in the council's database tomorrow and someone else will be living in it by the following evening, all evidence of Mr. McGlew having been wiped and dusted and vacuumed away.

"You want a tea, Eddie?" Marjie calls from the back room. I can hear her skirt bustling about as she fills the kettle. She's wearing her favorite one today, made of purple and magenta scraps of fabric that are all patchworked together. I am relatively certain she makes them herself because I've never seen anything quite so Marjie for sale in a shop. A few months ago, Marjie cut her hair. She used to wear it in two long silver plaits that snaked all serpentlike down her back, but last month she had it chopped and cropped into a pixie cut and it suits her so well. Neat, no nonsense, and usually adorned with a clip to match whichever Frankensteinian skirt she is wearing. What I love about Marjie is the paradox of her—she is orderly, plainspoken, doesn't suffer fools gladly, and yet she dresses like she plays the accordion in a traveling circus.

"No, ta," I reply.

Marjie has decreed that we are only allowed to shout back and forth to each other when there are no customers in the shop, which, late in the afternoon on a gray Thursday, is inevitable. As I fill in the donations form, I hear the kettle click off. Mr. William McGlew, *"posthumous donation."* Rest in peace, good sir. There will be other forms being filled in about him now. A death certificate, perhaps, an application for a cremation done as cheaply as possible on behalf of the city with a funeral-less goodbye.

Marjie rattles through the bead curtain that divides the front of the shop from the staff room (£12.50—we took its tag off and kept it because Marjie and I enjoy rattling through beads). She walks carefully, stirring the Oxo that she always drinks in her dancing-fox mug. Her Foxo.

"What is Oxo?" I had asked Marjie when I started working in the charity shop, shortly after my retirement began making me feel restless. "I mean, I recognize its smell, but what is it *really*? What's it made of?" She replied, as though this were a completely normal thing for a human to want to drink, "Concentrated beef."

"Well, no time like the present." I haul Mr. McGlew's bin bag off the till and rattle back through the wooden beads.

"You're a star," Marjie calls, knowing that it always makes me sad when the city council is in charge of discarding someone's final earthly possessions. Usually, a crying relative will drop them off, or at least an old friend, even a neighbor. When the council does it, it means the person who died was completely alone in the world.

Mr. McGlew has very little that will be of use to us. Which makes me feel even sadder for him. What makes it into the "sell pile" is a wooden carriage clock, a vintage radio, and a cross-stitch of a lamppost next to a barrel of flowers on a cobbled street.

And for the recycling bin is the rest of his life. Moth-eaten jumpers, a tea-stained ordinance survey map, a butter pot with buttons inside, and a broken badminton racquet.

And that is it for poor Mr. McGlew, everything he owned is now dispersed to be sold or burned or recycled. All, that is, except for five sun-yellowed envelopes addressed to "Elsie Woods, 33 Church Lane, West Dean, Chichester, P019 3QX." I place these precious epistles into the "Eddie Pile."

I hear Marjie clip-clopping across the shop floor in her low-heeled shoes like a well-dressed horse and I quickly stuff the contents of the Eddie Pile into my jacket pocket.

"Home time!" she sings.

"Mm-hm," I reply, trying not to move, lest she hear the telltale crunch of someone else's words against my chest.

I pop on my hat and check the train times on my phone. There's a train in eight minutes and another in thirty-eight, so I decide not to be too cruel to my knee and walk slowly down the hill towards New Street Station.

I love the bustle of New Street. All the busy people in their smart clothing with their laptops and lunch leftovers in heavy backpacks. I do get bumped into a lot, particularly by men in suits who have conducted an assessment and found themselves to be the most important creatures on the crust of the earth, but I love it nonetheless.

As I make my way to Platform 10a, I feel Mr. McGlew's letters crunching away in my pocket. *Bet you can't wait to read us*, they whisper with every crinkle.

And they are right.

Mr. P

———◆———

It began on my second day of volunteering at the charity shop.

His name was Michael and he had died in his sleep in a retirement home for army personnel. He had the usual things, of course, books and trinkets, knitted sleeveless jumpers, and strong aftershave, but nestled between these things, I found a small sliver of paper that in gorgeous lilting handwriting listed:

wool (cream), card for Harry, wrapping paper, flowers, black thread

And across the top, in an entirely different hand, in boxy navy letters, were the words "Gwen's Last List—March 1995."

He held on to that list for nineteen years. What better evidence of a love that never wavered could I find? This list was worth everything to Michael. How could it now be worth nothing simply because he had died? It couldn't be sold in the charity shop, of course, but I couldn't bear to throw it in the recycling bin. So, Gwen's Last List and Michael's enduring love for her came home with me.

Next came the rusty locket. When I first chanced upon it, my heart took a little break from beating, as I have been looking for one just like it for nearly half my life. Though it wasn't the one I was seeking, the two sweethearts inside, a young woman with curled brown hair and a man in naval uniform, certainly didn't belong in the bin. *They can stay a little longer*, I thought. Then came Evelyn's bouquet, 1911, pressed and framed and tied with a pink ribbon with "Evie's Wedding Flowers" written on the back of the frame. And below that, "Granny's bouquet" and below that still, "Great-Granny's bouquet." Her pink roses didn't deserve to die just yet, so I snuck them home tucked under my jacket. They look nice propped up against the box of photographs that were left in a bag outside the charity shop one winter in which a brother and sister named Andy and Sue cross what looks like North America sometime in the late '80s, having a whale of a time, dancing in discos and driving an open-top car, drenched in an orange sun made more orange by the Polaroid and the passing of time. The wedding certificate of Ada Akintola and Walter Smith from 1961, where the witnesses were both unrelated to the bride or groom and the ceremony was held at the registry office, couldn't be bound for the bin and so I framed it in gold and placed it on the top corner of the dresser.

The dresser I keep my treasure in is old too. It's from 1905 according to the inking on the inside of the right drawer. It does look a tad out of place in my modern city flat, but it comes with ghosts of hands that have touched it, of plates that have been stored in it, of bits and bobs that lived within the drawers. The woman in the Red Cross shop said it was one of the oldest pieces of furniture they'd ever had. And I snapped it up, thinking we could be old together.

Mr. McGlew's secrets are still crackling in my blazer pocket as I ride the lift up to my flat. I love my flat. I love seeing all the young professionals with their tired eyes and their travel mugs full of coffee in the lift in the mornings and hearing their pounding bassy music on the weekends. I love how they don't mind a more senior gentleman such as myself living among them. Or if they do mind, they keep it to themselves.

"I'm home, Mr. P!" I call as I pop my keys into the bowl by the door (shaped like a goose, slight scratch on the beak, £3).

He squeaks his reply. He is such a clever fellow.

The young woman arrived in the charity shop about six months ago, carrying the cage and looking like she needed a hug. Scarf half wrapped around her, cheeks chapped from the wind, dark bruise on her chin, lip split, eyes raw. "Can I donate this?" she asked, placing the cage on the till.

Outside the shop, two little boys in matching coats were waiting for her, standing beside a huge suitcase and a stack of bin bags. Each boy was wearing a superhero backpack and they were bundled up in what looked like all the cold-weather clothing they owned.

From the look in her eye as she noticed me noticing them, I sensed that I had surmised what was happening correctly.

I turned the cage around and peered in between the bars—nestled among the sawdust was a creature. He looked like a toupee come to life, with long white and orange hair flowing down his sides. I could only just make out which end was the front.

"Hello there!" I said to him. "What's your name?"

"Spiderman," she said, with evident embarrassment. "They named him." She gestured to the boys.

"Ah." I looked down at the little living wig. "Well, hello, Mr. Spiderman."

"Guinea pigs are supposed to live in pairs," she said, "but he's a bit vicious, so the vet told us to keep him alone."

"And you're sure you want to part with him?"

She nodded. "The place we're going doesn't allow pets and I don't know—"

"It's okay," I told her. "Leave him with me."

"It's allowed?" she asked.

"It's probably not," I whispered. "But if you leave before Marjie gets out of the loo, I think we'll get away with it."

Thank you, she mouthed, and she hurried out of the shop. I watched her through the window as she and the little boys gathered up their luggage and bin bags as best they could and hurried off towards the train station and, I hoped, a better life.

Marjie came out of the loo, cistern hissing, picked up her half-drunk Foxo from the till, and stopped dead.

"What the hell is that?"

Sitting on the dining table in my open-plan living room, the guinea pig I rechristened Pushkin Spiderman Winston squeaks with the happiness of a guinea pig who loves his human and is pleased to see him return from work, *or* an animal who associates the opening of the door with his food bowl being refilled (who can say?). He scurries over to his bowl in anticipation of the bounty of crunchy veg I am about to provide.

I attempt to ruffle his fluff through the bars. "Good afternoon, Pushkin." He whips around to nip my fingertip, but I'm far too quick for him. "These sausages are mine, old boy," I remind him.

Once his bowl is filled with cucumber sticks and he's munching away with a thousand tiny nibbles and not a hint of an apology, I take off my jacket, descend into my comfiest armchair, and place my latest treasure across my lap. Mr. McGlew's letters. All addressed and yet not one of them bears a stamp, which means none of these words ever made it to Elsie. From the first envelope, I unfold a delicate piece of unlined paper. It is skin-thin. In the top corner is the date; February 8, 1971. And in slanted inky writing are the words:

All of the best moments of my life involved you. I miss you, Else.

On May 29, 1974, he wrote:

I still have your white gloves. I can't bear to throw them away.

In October of that same year, he wrote:

I will wait for you, Elsie.

On February 8, 1975, he wrote:

Do you remember the first time you kissed me? On the pier while your mother was at church? I knew then that I would never love another.

And in the last envelope, from 1981, his final words to Elsie:

Even if you never speak to me again, I will die happy, thinking of that kiss.

I hope he did die happy, thinking of her, of their lips meeting for one perfect moment.

I wonder what I shall think of when I go.

The Girl with Pink Hair

———◆———

I'm collecting my post from the basement. I don't do this often because I'm forever losing the little key. But here I am, and what do you know? Beneath the bank statements and local election paraphernalia in my postbox is a piece of junk mail for Thitima from number 515. Apparently, she is entitled to twenty percent off her next pizza so long as she orders a medium with no extra toppings on a Tuesday in May between three-thirty and four o'clock. I am almost at the point of letting the flyer drop into her postbox when I realize that an opportunity for mischief has presented itself. And mischief is not to be ignored.

You see, it is not uncommon for me to find myself in the lift with the young folk of the building, and I have spotted, more than once, the way that Daniel from 518 looks at Thitima from 515. The way he holds his breath when she gets into the lift as though he might accidentally say something about his love out loud. He told me a few months ago that he's homesick. I'm relatively certain the young ones think of me as the grandfather of the lift. Perhaps they think I'm haunting it. But either way, they tell me things. So I know that Daniel is in the third year of his post-doc in engineering and Thitima is in the fourth and unfunded year of her doctorate in English.

Given how much I enjoyed her recommendation of *Gilmore Girls*, I know that Thitima can be trusted. Given that she said she watches it every day, I know she's lonely.

The flyer is shiny between my fingers and the gooey cheesy pizza slices on it do look tempting. *Go for it, Eddie,* the flyer says to me. *Maybe they can share a slice.*

I'm smiling about it all morning, thinking about Daniel standing at Thitima's door, checking and rechecking his hair, hoping and not hoping that she will open the door . . . her smile when she sees that it's him. And all it took was a misdelivered pizza coupon and a little chicanery from an old elevator gremlin to make that happen.

"No guinea pigs," Marjie says to me with a pointed finger as she pulls on her cardigan, leaving me in charge of the shop while she goes in search of something for lunch less disappointing than the Marmite and cheese sandwich she brought from home. It had a big blob of green mold along the crust. "Ugh, bread," she said to me as she threw the sandwich in the bin. "I never feel more alone than when I'm confronted with the fact that I can't get through a loaf of bread before it goes moldy. If my sons still lived with me, it would be gone in a day. They eat like horses."

"Do horses enjoy bread?" I asked, but Marjie didn't know.

I imagine Marjie will go to McDonald's. She likes McDonald's, but for some reason is rather embarrassed about it. Throws away the wrappers in the bin outside the shop before she comes in and then pretends she went to Greggs. I bet she orders something beefy at McDonald's, like a burger with extra beef dripping (I've never been, but I imagine that's the kind of thing they serve).

Just after she leaves, a man comes in, browses the hats, tries one on, looks at himself in our wall of mirrors for sale, takes a photo of himself in the hat, puts the hat back on the shelf, and then leaves.

And then nothing. Nothing for so long that I pick up Marjie's *Good Housekeeping* magazine and flick through to the "March styles to put a spring in your step." There's a jumper I think I might look quite good in. It's a pastel blue fluffy number from Dorothy Perkins for the wholly unreasonable price of £59. I think it would bring out my eyes.

I don't notice her standing there until I hear her sniff. I lower the magazine to see a young woman with candy-floss-pink hair, dressed all in black and holding a huge cardboard box.

"Here, please, let me help." I move the magazine and my cold cup of tea out of the way and I help her lift the box up onto the till. It's such a big box that I can't see her now.

"I'd like to donate these," she says from behind the box. Her voice is a lot softer than I expected it to be.

"Thank you very much for the donation." I take a donations card from the stack under the till. "May I ask the name of the person donating?"

"Um, it's on behalf of . . . you can just put 'Jake.'" Her voice cracks when she says his name.

I write "Jake" on the donations card.

"And what's in the box?" I ask. "Just a general category helps. For example, toys, shoes, homewares, et cetera."

"It's, um, it's mostly clothes," she says, her voice giving way at the end and making it sound like a question.

I lean around the box and look at her properly.

Her eyes are red raw, but she isn't crying.

She looks small.

And scared.

And so incredibly sad.

"Are you okay?" I ask.

She nods even though she is very clearly not okay. "He," she says, "he doesn't need them anymore, so . . ."

I come around the till table and, without thinking, I open my arms. For a moment, I regret it and fear she's going to think I'm some sort of deplorable. But she steps into my hug.

I offer her some tea. I offer her some Foxo.

But she doesn't stay.

The Box

—————◆—————

Sometimes, they come back.

Did you sell that Pink Panther jumper yet? My mother knitted it by hand.

Has the gold clock gone? I hated the thing, but it reminded me of Grandad.

I donated an emerald ring. Is it still here?

Once in a while, the item will be on my "Eddie Shelf" and I tell them we will search the back rooms after closing so that I can scuttle home and bring it back and then "find" it in our nonexistent store-room. Sometimes they are so relieved that they make a big donation to say thank you. If the item has already been sold or sent to the tip, I fumble for the words. I offer them tea. But they rarely take it.

The girl with the pink hair didn't stay and I have a heavy sense of dread as I heave the box she donated onto the floor of the back room.

Among the neatly folded T-shirts with what seem to be skate-boarding brands printed on them, I find a notebook. It is full of scribbly drawings of the girl with the pink hair, from the side, laughing, asleep. All in scritchy-scratchy black biro and with a liveliness to them. There are also song lyrics and poetry, but I don't stop to read, I just enjoy turning the pages and the crinkle they make from being so laden-down with black ink.

I'm closing the notebook when out slips a collection of glossy photographs.

Everything about the girl with the pink hair changes from photo to photo. Her hair color, her makeup, her clothes. But in every picture, the young man beside her is the same—tall, slim, dark-haired, and wearing some combination of T-shirt and jeans and a pair of white Converse trainers that appear to be covered in writing. It seems he never took those shoes off.

Yet at the bottom of the box, here they are, worn to the shape of his feet and absolutely covered in love.

And no longer needed.

On the right shoe is a drawing of the two of them, which is quite good considering it's on a shoe. "I love you" loops around the laces beside a date—12.12.18—and across the back of the heels in black writing that has been gone over and over are the words "Bella and Jake Forever."

I will keep them safe, until she's ready to come back.

Night

———————————

Mr. McGlew is whispering and it's keeping me awake.

I will die happy thinking of that kiss, he whispers from the shelf where he sits, in paper-and-ink form, his self-penned epitaph.

That kiss, that kiss, that kiss.

He is not Resting in as much Peace as he should be.

I wonder about his kiss with Elsie. On a pier, he said it was in his letter. I imagine their hair whipping around in the cold seaside wind, as they found themselves closer than they had been before. Her neat Sunday gloves as he took her by the hand. What words must they have spoken to each other when it became clear that they were about to kiss? Perhaps it was his first kiss and he was a nervous teenager, sweaty palms resting on the small of her back, having no idea if he had done it correctly. Perhaps it was the best kiss either of them ever experienced, and they parted different people.

I turn over and pull the quilt up over my ears to try to quieten him.

I will wait for you, Elsie, he whispers. *I will wait.*

What happened to William and Elsie that they could not recover and why couldn't he find it within himself to feed his words into the grinning open mouth of a postbox?

I peel off my warm covers, pad into the living room, and turn on the lamp. It is far too late or far too early for the big light.

Pushkin is sleeping with his paws out in front of his face, fluff rising and falling with every quick breath. He's probably never had to worry about such a thing as love, has never had his little heart broken. If his disdain for all humans is anything to go by, I doubt he misses the small boys who named him Spiderman. He isn't really a people person or a pig's pig. It must be nice to not have to worry about being alone.

I take Mr. McGlew's envelopes from the Eddie Shelf and spread them across the dining table. What would he make of a stranger reading the words he meant only for Elsie all these years after he wrote them? Whatever his opinions, Mr. McGlew has fallen quiet.

I open the first of the envelopes and reread his words. Then the second, then the third. Only this time, I notice that the envelope of the last letter he wrote contains something else. A strip of paper, no bigger than a receipt, and on the back in pencil he has written:

> *somewhere, out there,*
> *grows the tree*
> *that will be the tree*
> *that will make your coffin.*
> *you must hope it is small*
> *only a seedling, only sap*
> *but it might be tall by now*
> *stretching its branches like arms into the sky.*
> *if I knew where it was, I would chop it down.*
> *I would return to the forest*
> *again and again with my axe,*
> *never resting,*
> *so that you might live forever.*

It is four by the time I have finished rereading it and there is a pink tinge to the sky. A promise of morning. I will not sleep now. Carefully, like the curator I like to imagine myself to be, I return the letters to the warm embrace of their envelopes and place them back on the Eddie Shelf.

He really loved her,

I sit and listen to the tick of the clock.

Oh, how he loved her.

And, I decide, she deserves to know.

I retrieve my spiral-bound notepad and attempt to pull out a few sheets. They rip right in half. More carefully this time, I try again and I find a pen.

I try to picture Elsie, a woman in her seventies now. She was beautiful then. She is beautiful now, her hair wispy and white but neatly combed, her blue eyes diluted yet still twinkling. Old. Just like myself. Just like everyone eventually becomes, if they're very lucky. I picture her sitting in a faded pink wingback armchair, hair neatly curled, eyes on mine, head tilted to one side, listening.

Elsie,

I'm a pirate.

A thief.

A crustacean collecting pieces of seabed detritus to stick on my shell.

Except what I collect isn't debris, it is precious.

Unfortunately, the value of the item exists only as long as the person who values it lives on.

And you see, Elsie, I have come across something that belongs to you. That is meant for you, or that was.

Perhaps you would like it back?

It consists of five letters written but never sent by a Mr. William McGlew.

The letters were donated to the charity shop in which I work, because (and I do hope I am not the first to share this sad news) unfortunately Mr. McGlew is no longer with us.

Please write to me at the address below and I will gladly return his words to where they belong.

Sincerely,

Eddie Winston, Donations assistant

The Heart Trust Charity Shop, 24 Corporation Street, Birmingham, B2 4LP

I copy her address from the envelopes. And this letter *does* make it into the eager open mouth of Her Majesty's postbox. Landing with a faint *flap* upon all the other words bound for better places.

I hope it's not too late.

Shoes

———◆———

I'm lining up dead men's shoes on a rack.

How strange that for all their lives, the men who wore these shoes walked a path that would lead to me. At any point, through their childhood or in their teenage years, we were destined to be linked. The intersection of our timelines was always to cross here, with me kneeling on a cushion in front of the men's shoe shelf, sorting their brown brogues and scuffed trainers, hoping that these shoes, now useless for their dead feet, might be of interest to someone still living.

Jake's shoes are not here, of course. They're on my Eddie Shelf in a box to keep the dust away. Alongside Mr. McGlew's love letters and his poem, which I can't quite get out of my head.

Marjie rattles through the bead curtain, crunching on some pork scratchings.

She holds out the packet to me and I shake my head.

"Would you mind popping those orange bags in the window?" she asks through a mouthful of scratching.

"Certainly can, dear." I rise, my knee crunching as I go.

The shop window is our constant source of exasperation. We have no idea what will entice young, stylish people in to browse, so Marjie likes to select a color to guide us. This week, the mannequin is dressed in various shades of orange. It doesn't look terrible. But it doesn't look good. As I stack up some orange bags ready to place beside our poor neon mannequin, Marjie flicks on the radio from Mr. McGlew's donation and a Latin dance song crackles out, as though we have our own samba band with us on the shop floor.

"Ooh," Marjie says, bopping to the music and popping another pork scratching in her mouth. I join in with what I imagine is a salsa step. *Taka taka taka.* I dance towards the window and Marjie twirls, her purple hippy skirt flaring out around her calves. She puts down her scratchings and holds out her hand towards me. I spin her around as the music gains some drums and shakers. The energy of the song rises and Marjie spins me around too, and we are just doing a little two-step when the song stops, rather abruptly. At the very same moment, I spot a face at the shop door. The girl with the pink hair has been watching us dance with an expression I can't quite place. How odd—I was just thinking about destiny and shoes and there she is.

When our eyes meet, the girl with the pink hair turns and hurries off down Corporation Street.

Marjie, still a sway in her step, heads back behind the till and resumes her crunching. If she noticed the girl with the pink hair, she doesn't say.

"I'm just going to pop out for a minute," I tell Marjie, pulling on my hat. I never "just pop out." I usually wait for her to tell me when I can take my break. That's just what good employees do.

"Lunch?" she asks

"Er, yes, I'm in search of lunch," I tell her, and off I go.

I reach the crossing where New Street intersects with Corporation Street, the people flowing all around me, and look left and right, desperate to see a flash of pink. The shrill alarm of a tram goes off and I realize I'm standing in the road. I step onto the pavement and as the tram sails by, I ask a few passersby if they have seen a young lady with pink hair, but they look at me oddly and walk on. Despite my hat, the sun is bright and glaring in my eyes. I put my hand up to shield my face. She might have run down to New Street Station, might already be heading to a platform now, getting onto a train. She might have followed Needless Alley up towards the cathedral and Pigeon Park and onwards to the Jewellery Quarter. She could be anywhere, but I have to tell her! I have to tell her that I saved Jake's things — his crinkly notebook and the photographs and the white shoes that are covered in love.

But she's gone.

A Visitor

———◆———

I'm sitting on the floor cushion, organizing the bookshelf. Yesterday we received fifty-two Mills & Boon books posthumously donated on behalf of a Mrs. Hill. As I shelve them, I wonder if Mrs. Hill was embarrassed about owning these books—perhaps her family members found them stashed under her bed after she died. Or perhaps they were on display in a nice cabinet in the dining room for all her friends and family to see as they supped their tomato soup from the sides of spoons, the blue spines barely containing the big bosomed duchesses and handsome dukes within.

All done, I dust my hands together and begin to think about the multistage process of getting up from the floor.

As I'm halfway up, I put my hands on the windowsill and spot her outside. Beaking at a piece of loose paint. She raises her head. Eyes sharp and clever. Staring into mine. An almost imperceptible wink.

"Hello," I whisper. "So, you're a blackbird today, are you?"

Crow

———◆———

May 19, 1954

Bridie Brennan is nineteen years old and standing on the steps of a church dedicated to Saint Expeditus, the patron saint of procrastinators.

Saint Expeditus is dressed like a Roman soldier, with a metal breastplate and a pleated skirt. He has a red cloak wrapped around his shoulders, a quill in his hand, and a halo of gold around his head. Beneath his foot is a dead crow, the form the devil took to convince him to delay his conversion to Christianity. But delay he did not. And look where it got him. Murdered.

The crow is holding a flag in its dead mouth that says *"cras."* If Bridie could read Latin, which she cannot, she would know that the inscription means "tomorrow," but she enjoys the crow's act of defiance all the same and likes to imagine he has written "fuck you" to Expeditus for squashing him.

Bridie is dressed like a bride. Which is fitting, given the circumstances. In a floor-length ivory satin gown that is too tight at the hips. A bouquet of wilting cream roses in her left hand, she carries an upturned horseshoe threaded with blue ribbon for luck in her right. She has a garter made of matching blue ribbon on her thigh and it is making the flesh bulge at either side. Her mother's short veil of white lace with a yellow stain she couldn't get off is circling her wild brown hair and her feet are squished into heels that are pinching at the toes. She feels absurd to be dressed like this while waiting for a painted saint to send her a sign.

Bridie looks at Saint Expeditus, rendered with care on the church sign, his dark hair waving in a breeze only the painter knew about. Saint Expeditus does not look back at Bridie. He is staring into the middle distance, cross of Christ held high.

Beyond where the church railings would be had they not been stripped to make stretchers during the war, a red bus sails past. If she took the bus to Acton, she could sit on the top deck and rip the bottom half of her dress off, making it into a tea-length dress, which would attract much less attention. Then she could walk to Saint Michael's graveyard and leave her bouquet on her mother's grave. It would be nice for Bridie to pretend that her mum would have known what to do. Would have known whether to advise her daughter to go inside the church or to run. But Bridie's mother would not have known what to make of Alistair with his handsomeness and his cleverness and his somewhat surprising interest in her dumpy daughter any more than Bridie does. Not that her mother would have said that Bridie was dumpy, she would have told her she was beautiful. But Bridie fears that the truth is that she is dumpy even on her very best day and even in her very best dress.

If you were going to run away, you would have run already. The thought arrives as though it has come from outside herself.

But if she were going to go in, wouldn't she already be inside?

Inside. They're all waiting for her. The organist has cycled through the list of hymns. They are back to "The Magnificat." Bridie's favorite. She had to battle the organist to have it and now she's had to play it twice.

A bike bell rings from far away. *Focus, Bridie. You said you would marry him.* Alistair Bennett. Tall, good-looking, charming. Exempt from fighting for the shape of his foot. Exempt from the rules of society for the shape of his handsome face. Exempt from her questions for his pinpoint intelligence. He doesn't want to wear a wedding ring when they marry. *If they marry.* But isn't it a gift just to be chosen?

After all, it was unlikely at best, unbelievable at worst, that Alistair Bennett should have any interest in Bridie Brennan. Which was why when he started flirting with Bridie as she took his orders, pulled his pints and replenished the crisps at his table of rowdy academics, that she did not believe it herself. Alistair approached finding a wife in the way that one might approach hiring a maid, assessing her suitability from her amenability to his needs. Would she mind moving to Birmingham, if he were to secure his first lectureship position there? he had asked over a drink, and when her answer was no, she felt that she had pleased him. Did she ever want a dog? No, again. Was her heart set on children? And when no came her answer, she anticipated judgment, but found only relief in Alistair's expression. When he proffered an old gold ring from a knee bent in the frosty grass of the local park, Bridie realized that the assessment was over and she had been found suitable. They would move to Birmingham and have neither dogs nor children.

"The Magnificat" plays on. As Saint Expeditus is silent on the matter, she supposes she must ask God. She closes her eyes. *Lord, what should I do?* A breeze blows, making the roses in her hand shiver and jiggle to keep warm.

The church door opens and, for a moment, Bridie thinks it is a sign from God telling her to go within, but then out comes Father Rawlings. He is a whiskery man. Dark tufty eyebrows growing too long from his face and stubble on his cheek and chin that betrays a razor that needs replacing. There's a sour note of a heavy tea drinker on his breath. He is new. Came to conduct the funeral for the previous priest and then never left.

"Bridget?" he asks. "Are we ready to get married?"

We? she thinks.

For a moment, it seems like an absurd marriage proposal. But Father Rawlings got off easy: he married Jesus, who probably asks for very little on a day-to-day basis. Doesn't need his food cooked or his clothes cleaned, would never dream of making snide comments about how your hips look in your Sunday dress. Doesn't look handsome and ugly all at once when he is laughing. Doesn't embarrass you down the pub by calling you "piglet" when you've asked him not to. Doesn't touch you on the knee and erase all the unpleasantness with the way he runs it up your thigh and makes your breathing stop. Doesn't make you tingle in places an unmarried woman ought not tingle. Though, perhaps Jesus *does* make Father Rawlings tingle and that's why he married him.

"Now then," Father Rawlings says when she does not speak, "shall we go inside?" He asks it in the tone one might use to coax a child or a goat into doing something it didn't want to do.

A deep and sad thought settles in Bridie's mind.

It is already too late.

The priest beckons her closer, and smelling his breath on her face as he tucks her hair behind her ears makes her feel sick. "There," he says. "Pretty as a picture."

This is not actually the case, and the way he has tucked Bridie's hair behind her ears looks lumpy and strange. Several years from this day, she will throw away all the photographs that were taken until her hair fell back into its usual place.

"He looks very handsome," Father Rawlings says.

Bridie twists the locket around her neck back and forth. Her mother gave her the locket just before she died. It is gold, filigree, and has "B.B." engraved upon the back. It is fortunate that her initials will remain unchanged when Miss Bridie Brennan becomes Mrs. Bridie Bennett even if all else about her will. Bridie wanted to put a photograph of her mother in the locket for today, to keep her close, but she doesn't have any photographs of her mother small enough to fit in her heart and she doesn't dare cut one up.

Bridie wishes she had the courage to run. She wishes Alistair wasn't so handsome. She wishes she was that crow, dead under Saint Expeditus's Roman sandal but waving a flag from her beak as a final act of defiance. And she wishes she could have chosen a more original song than the "Wedding March" as, flanked by the Father who is not her father, she begins her walk down the aisle.

Noodle Day

———◆———

I'm wearing my new blue jumper from Dorothy Perkins while taking my lunch in Pigeon Park. I've already had two compliments on it—one from Marjie and one from the *Big Issue* seller who works outside Superdrug. I would have bought his magazine anyway, but it is nice to know that my jumper looks "sick."

Pigeon Park is not really a park so much as a large graveyard around the cathedral with a path cutting through the center that connects the offices of Snow Hill with the much more fun shops and restaurants in the city center.

It's nice that the pigeons have a park for themselves. There are certainly more of them than there are people, but it is the people that I like to watch the most. I like seeing the smartly dressed office workers at ease, even if only for an hour, top buttons undone, ties loosened, faces turned to the sun. Eating their lunches and scrolling on their phones to see what the world has been up to in the three hours since they sat down at their desks.

It's Noodle Day and I'm spinning a wooden fork in my ginger chicken udon when I hear a small voice.

"Thank you."

I look up and she half smiles, but it's not a real smile, it can't be.

"It's yourself!"

She's wearing a Sainsbury's uniform that looks all wrong on her, pink hair catching fire in the sun.

"Thank you for the hug." Her badge that tells me that her name, as I suspected, is Bella.

"Would you like to sit?" I ask.

And sit she does. We are both quiet for a brief moment.

"You came back," I observe.

"You're a very good dancer," she says. I can't tell if she's teasing me or not, but I enjoy the compliment either way.

"I do love a bit of salsa music. It always feels like a party."

"Was that your wife you were dancing with?"

"Good lord, no. Marjie is my boss. Well, she's my friend now too. I think. I've never been very good at telling when someone becomes a friend."

"Me neither," Bella says.

"Oh I'm sure a young thing like yourself has plenty of friends."

She looks as though she is about to say something, but she closes her mouth.

"But you returned, to the shop . . ."

She breathes in. "I thought I wanted something back."

"I assumed as much."

"But then I realized, it's probably too late."

Oh how I love to tell her. "It is not too late at all, my dear. His clothes are still in our back room."

"It wasn't the clothes I wanted, it was . . ." She looks out across the park as a group of office workers in suits walks past, shouting over one another to be heard and laughing. "Well, it doesn't matter anymore."

"You don't want his shoes back?"

"You didn't throw them away?" she asks cautiously, seeming unsure of whether to allow herself to feel hope or not.

I place the lid on my noodle bowl and turn to her. "Would you be so kind as to indulge me if I told you a little secret?"

She lights up at this and says, "Try me."

Bella is the first person I have told about the Eddie Shelf. I certainly couldn't tell Marjie, she might be forced to sack me, or report me to the police. I've never really known whether I am rescuing or stealing the items I take from the shop. Whether I am an archivist or a thief.

"So, there you have it," I finish.

"You kept them," she says.

"I've never seen shoes quite like them."

"But you kept them," she says again. "Why?"

"In case you changed your mind."

On a bench on the other side of the path, a young couple sit down, their legs crisscrossed over each other's, tangled up together. *Look at me*, their love whispers. They talk for a moment, though we can't hear what they're saying, and then she puts her hand on his cheek and kisses him.

I turn and spot that Bella is watching the young couple too.

She looks so sad.

"I wish I had something wise to say," I tell her.

"You don't?" she asks.

"I haven't had a lot of experience with love."

She glances down at my unclaimed left hand.

"Intriguing."

The couple on the bench untangle themselves from each other and stand. The young man stretches his arms up and then puts one around the young woman's shoulders, as though they are in a cinema. She laughs and they walk in step together towards the Jewellery Quarter, and I wonder if they are off to buy a ring.

"You can keep his clothes. But the shoes, the notebook, I . . . I don't know what to do."

"There's really no rush."

"Isn't there?"

"I'll keep them safe," I promise her.

"For how long?"

"Until you're ready."

Crus

Bridie Bennett is nineteen years old and standing on the steps of a church dedicated to Saint Expeditus with a gold ring on her finger and a frozen smile. And she is twenty-seven years old, holding her beloved tailless cat, Ferris, in front of the Christmas tree, and she is thirty, standing on the banks of the Seine in a hat she had no idea was so unflattering until she collected photographs. And she wore that hat the entire weekend. There's not a photo of her without it. Why didn't Alistair tell her? The answer is a simple and eternal one: because he wasn't looking. And in front of all these memories held in matching silver frames, Bridie Bennett herself is sitting in her uncomfortable office chair, staring into space with a pen held just above a purchase requisition form.

She doesn't need a degree to see that academia is something of a scam. Her husband writes the books, they cost a fortune, and then he designs the course and examination such that his textbook is essential. Many of the students have complained that there's only one copy in the library and so Bridie must now order more. Alistair isn't pleased because when he last checked, there were six copies of *Exploring Prose through an Applied Linguistic Prism* waiting unsold on the campus bookshop shelf and "They shouldn't be getting them for free."

Bridie hasn't the time to explain to Alistair how libraries work. But how would he know how libraries work? Alistair is never in one; she has to collect his books for him. "Imagine a student seeing me on my hands and knees looking for a book," he'd said. "Mortifying."

Bridie has been staring at the purchase requisition forms for twelve minutes. It is still another two hours until lunch. She sighs and slides the biscuit tin closer.

She's halfway through chewing a Ginger Nut biscuit when he appears. Tall. Thin. Gangly. He looks to be in his late twenties and yet he is wearing a bow tie. He knocks his elbow on the doorframe.

"Ooh, got my funny bone," he says with an embarrassed smile.

In he comes, though she did not invite him in.

Rubbing his elbow with his other hand, he reads the name plaque that rests on her desk and says with a bright smile, "You must be Birdie."

The first peal of her laughter sends a little piece of Ginger Nut shooting out from between her teeth. She claps a hand over her mouth.

He seems pleased that she is laughing, despite his confusion about what might be so funny. He glances back at the sign and the *i* and *r* must dance back into their correct positions, because his face crumples into another smile.

"Oh," he says, a hand to his hair to ruffle it. "I'm so sorry, you must be *Bridie*."

"Please," she says, gesturing at her chair.

He sits. Palms up. Entirely at ease.

"Bridget," she explains of herself. "But Bridie stuck when I was a girl."

He extends a hand. "Eddie Winston. Lovely to meet you."

Birdie

September 19, 1965

Bridie shakes his hand, and because she isn't sure what to do next, she offers him a cup of tea. Nobody stays for tea. Not her husband or his fellow professors, not the girls from the assistants' office, not the students. She has offered and been politely declined so many times that she doesn't remember the last time she cleaned the guests' mug that sits upturned on the tray beside her forbidden electric kettle.

As the kettle begins to boil, she opens her window to let out the steam. Beyond the hedge, they can see students milling to and from their lectures.

"I like it," he says.

"The kettle?"

"Your name."

"Oh, thank you. 'Birdie' would be more interesting, though, wouldn't it?" she asks, blowing the dust out of the guest mug.

He thinks about this. "No. I like it as it is. There is something of the bluebird about you."

She keeps her back to him so he cannot see how much this has made her smile. "Are you the new Semiotics lecturer?"

"No, sorry. I'm a final-year PhD student. I've just transferred here from Lancaster, I'm one of—"

"Professor Leech's students. Yes, there are five of you coming over, aren't there?"

"Actually, it's just me. The others submitted early to save moving. I think Professor Leech might be a little disappointed."

He takes the cup of tea, offering his thanks, and Bridie slides the biscuit tin between them. As they sit in pleasant silence for a moment, Eddie selects a digestive biscuit and dips it in his tea. It immediately crumbles and begins to sink. He tries to fish it out with his fingers with little success, which makes him giggle.

"Did I ask how I can help you?" Bridie asks, handing him a teaspoon so he can scoop out the wayward biscuit.

"I'm looking for the key to the postgraduate office," he says, and he nods to a carrier bag full of textbooks and ring binders that have pierced holes in the bag and are protruding shiny corners. "I don't really know where I'm going," he says.

This is not her job. And yet.

"I'll show you," she says, and she pulls open the key drawer to take out the master key.

"Oh, that's too kind," he says.

As they make their way down the corridor, mugs of tea in hand, he asks, "Would you mind if I call you Birdie?"

In he comes, though she did not invite him in.

Lunch

———◆———

It's supposed to be a sausage and egg sandwich but the sandwich maker (or sandwich robot, I don't know how sandwiches are made these days) has calculated the ratios terribly. It is nothing but slimy egg whites and cold, congealed ketchup.

"That looks horrible." I look up and there's Bella.

"It is turning my stomach," I agree, and she points to the spot on the bench beside me.

"May I?"

"You certainly may."

Out of a Sainsbury's bag, she pulls a ham and cheese roll and a barbecue chicken wrap. "Want one?" she asks.

We tuck into our sandwiches in companionable silence.

Pigeon Park is uncharacteristically quiet. A woman with a tiny fluffy dog walks past and then a man who looks like he's had a few too many heads in the direction of the Jewellery Quarter.

"I realized," she says, "that I didn't ask you your name."

"What do you think my name might be?" I ask her, and she grins and appraises me, takes in my beige cardigan, bow tie, gray slacks.

"Ernest," she says.

"Not far off, actually!" I say. "It starts with an *E*!"

"Erving?"

"Erving?"

"You know, like Irving Layton. But with an *E*."

"Do you like poetry?"

"I like the good stuff," she says as she takes a big bite of her chicken wrap and a slime of lettuce slips out of the bottom and lands on her work slacks. "Balls," she says.

She unpins her name badge from her fleece and then pinches the fabric of her trousers and slides the safety pin in. Now midway through her thigh, her trousers declare that her name is Bella and she is a sales associate. "There," she says. "Nobody'll notice now."

A scruffy pigeon lands at our feet, his long neck inclined with interest at an old sandwich wrapper beneath our bench.

"Here." I offer him a quarter of my unwanted sandwich and he takes it in his beak and flaps away in case I am about to rescind the offer. Within seconds, three or four gray pigeons and a white and brown fella descend on him and an intense tug of war for the crust begins.

"How are you?" I ask Bella. "I bet everyone is always asking that."

"They did at first," she says. "Not so much now. My mum keeps saying I need to get 'back on track.'"

"On track?"

"Stop working in Sainsbury's. Use my degree."

"Perhaps she's right."

"I don't want to do anything," she says, watching the melee of pigeons fighting over the egg-white sandwich.

"Then it is not a career change that you need," I say to Bella, "but a little fun."

Arrows

———◆———

I'm in the lift on the way down to the basement bin store, clutching a bag full of Pushkin's sawdust, which I've just replaced. He loves running about on the carpet while I change it.

The lift stops on level 5 and the doors slide open and there is Thitima. She looks ravishing. Hair in a bouffant of sorts, red lipstick, red dress. She's carrying a red clutch bag and when she sees me, she smiles, but the nerves are evident.

"Please." I gesture beside me for her to enter.

As the lift begins to descend again, she fiddles with one of the pins holding her hair at the back.

"It looks first-rate," I tell her.

"Really?" she asks.

"Not a wisp out of place."

She shifts from foot to foot in her red strappy heels. She smells nice too. A sweet plummy perfume. I hope that seeing me in my slippers with my bin bag full of guinea pig excrement and sawdust isn't ruining the beginning of her elegant evening.

As we reach the ground floor, the lift clunks and the doors slide open and there is Daniel, hair combed neatly to one side, holding a red rose wrapped in cellophane. I can't hide my grin.

For a moment, Thitima doesn't move. "Go get 'em," I whisper

to her and give her a gentle elbow in the right direction. She smiles and whispers, "Thanks, Eddie."

Off she bravely goes, a little unsteadily in her heels, and Daniel beams at her. The doors slide closed and I descend into the basement. Like an ancient, subterranean refuse Cupid.

Treasure

———————◆———————

"Eddie, my duck, these had to go to you."

Bhav heaves two shopping bags onto the till with a thud. The bags sigh and slowly expand.

I peer at the necklaces writhing within. The beads and chains and the tiny bits of sparkle glint in the shop lights. *Do you suspect you might find what you seek?* they hiss at me.

"I can only apologize for the state of them," Bhav says. "What a shambles! But that's what you get when you accept teenagers doing the Duke of Edinburgh Award into your donations room."

I met Bhav on one of my many visits to the shop she runs in Selly Oak on behalf of a homeless charity. Or was it a cat charity? I can't remember. Perhaps it was for homeless cats, but it's closing down now, anyway. Bhav says *supper* instead of *tea* and *greetings* instead of *hello*. We shared one energetic dance last year at the Birmingham Charity Gala when she was covered head to toe in black sequins and I was wearing my snappiest suit and my hedgehog bow tie. My knee let me know about it in the morning, but oh, what fun we had.

"This is very kind of you," I say, not quite sure where to begin with separating the serpentine chains to see if I can find it.

"I always kept a lookout," she says. "Whenever a locket was donated."

"Thank you, Bhav."

"I assume you haven't found it yet?" she asks, her eye caught by an orange scarf that hangs on the stand by the till.

I shake my head. "I got very close once. But there was a name engraved on the back. 'Ingrid M.'"

"And inside?"

"It was empty."

I have never wondered what I might feel if I finally find her locket and it is empty.

"I do like a treasure hunt," Bhav says, picking up the orange scarf and running it through her fingers. "So exciting to be searching for something. It gives us purpose, don't you think?"

She buys the scarf and implores me to let her know if I ever find my treasure. She is on her way down Corporation Street before I realize, I have no idea how to reach her even if I do.

Bella and I place the bags of snaky necklaces across our knees on the bench and work quietly, detangling wooden beads from rusted gold chains, separating silver hearts from pearl strings.

"We're looking for a locket, then?" Bella asks.

"A locket," I confirm.

"A gold locket," she says.

"That's right." I manage to untwist a gold dolphin pendant that's wrapped around a purple friendship bracelet.

"It's always in the last place you look," she says. "When did you last see it?"

"Nineteen sixty-eight."

"Hm," she says. "We probably can't look there." And she pulls out a pink beaded necklace with the name "Emily" written on it and pops it around her neck.

one

—◆—

fuck fuck fuck
   i absolutely fucking hate this
   why do you have to be dead?
   the doctor put me on the waiting list for counseling when you died and look at that, just thirteen months later, i found myself sitting opposite a woman dressed head to toe in beige who kept smiling at me, like we shared a secret. and she kept using my name. how are you feeling, bella? thank you for coming to see me today, bella. *it's every other tuesday morning at 8.30 am in sparkbrook which is convenient for literally no one.*
   she said i should write you a letter
   thirteen months of waiting just for her to tell me to write you a fucking letter
   i asked her where i should post it
   and she didn't seem to think that was as funny as i did
   i might as well laugh because i can't cry
   it doesn't mean i don't love you
   it's just that i want to scream more than i want to cry
   and I'm trying to hold it in
   the therapist said there are places you can go to scream, like the top of a mountain or a roller coaster. there were screaming clubs during the pandemic, she said. she told me i could probably join one if i wanted
   but what's the point in sanctioned screaming?
   i don't want to scream when it's okay to scream
   i want to scream in the middle of new street station at rush hour as loud as i can and for half a second have everyone stop and stare at me and fear for their lives that something terrible has happened

i want to scream in the library all the way down the
escalator, ruin everyone's train of thought
    i want to scream in people's faces when they look happy
    i'm not going back
    she's trying to fix something that can't be fixed
    fuck her
    fuck everyone
    fuck you for dying
    i'm so fucking furious with you
    but still. i love you

                                                    bells

Pushkin

———◆———

If I'm very still, Pushkin forgets I'm here, comes out of his little igloo, and scurries around in the sawdust. He comes out now, stops still, breathing fast, black beady eyes darting about the cage.

"It's just you and me, buddy," I whisper. But I don't think "buddy" suits him. "Old chap," I correct. "Little fella?"

If he can hear me, he doesn't let it show.

"It's not so bad, really, is it?" I ask him. "We gentlemen against the world."

He doesn't reply. Perhaps he doesn't agree.

It is a quarter past two and the night is low. The taxis that line up across the road have fallen quiet, except for the occasional *whoop* or *beep*. It is time for sleep.

Off I creep.

"Goodnight, my friend," I whisper.

He seems to like that one.

Old-Fashioned

———◆———

"Eddie," Bella says, popping up in front of me as I am tucking into the peanut butter sandwich I made at home, "shall we go somewhere proper for lunch?"

I don't need asking twice. There's something to be said for eating at a table. I'm up like a flash. The pigeons descend on my sandwich the moment I set it down on the ground.

"Not too shabby," Bella says, looking around the Italian bistro we have found ourselves in. We are the only patrons here. It is very fancy.

"And not a pigeon in sight," I agree.

Since I met Bella, I've been eating my lunch in Pigeon Park a lot more frequently. But I haven't told her that. Partly because I like to give Marjie some time in the shop to eat her beefy wares in peace. But mostly because I think Bella and I might be friends, but I'm not sure yet.

"Well, then," I say, unfurling my linen napkin across my lap, "what are we celebrating?"

"It's Jake's birthday."

Oh.

"Oh," I say.

She tries for a smile, but it betrays her and shows how sad she is.

The waiter places a carafe of water and two teeny glasses between us. He hands us a heavy menu and leaves. Bella looks up at me.

"He would have been twenty-five today," she says.

"He *should* have been twenty-five today," I agree.

"Yes. He fucking should." She begins pouring the water, but her hands are shaking. I take over for her and once we both have full glasses, I look at her, wishing I could help.

"We had our first kiss on his fourteenth birthday," she says. "So it's the anniversary of that too."

There is a pause and then I have an idea.

"What was Jake's favorite drink?" I ask.

Bella doesn't look up. "An Old-fashioned."

The waiter reappears and looks from Bella to me. He must notice how sad she looks because he asks, "Are you okay?"

Bella sits up straighter, fluffs her fringe, shakes herself like a cat. "I just got fired," she lies.

"Oh, man, I'm sorry," the waiter says. "What did you do?"

"Investment banking," she says, and I try very hard not to choke on my sup of water.

"Sorry to hear it," he says.

She nods, grateful for his real sympathy for her invented woes.

Though he looks too young to drink alcohol himself, let alone serve it, I ask him, "Do you do Old-fashioneds?"

"Um, no, we don't." He looks at Bella. Her eyes are still red but she's recomposing. "But I know how to make them. I could make you one and charge you for a daiquiri?"

I look at Bella.

"Two Old-fashioneds, please," she says.

Our third Old-fashioneds arrive and I take a sup. "Gosh, that is still horrible!"

"I know," Bella says, wincing. "I never understood how he drank them. I think he liked to order them because they sound sophisticated."

"Bella," I whisper.

"Yes, Eddie?" she whispers back.

"I'm a bit drunk."

"Me too!" she says, and for some reason, we both find this hilarious.

The door gives way unexpectedly and we stumble into the island-themed bar with its stunning view of the ring road, and the look that crosses the barman's face is one of calculation: the risk that we will cause a ruckus versus the presumably low takings of the completely deserted bar.

He motions for us to come in as though we are clambering into a treehouse in secret.

We get to the bar and I am relieved to have something against which to lean. My knee did not care for the uphill walk to get here.

"What'll it be?" the barman asks, fastening the top button on his Hawaiian print shirt that looks like it was originally part of a Halloween costume.

"Two Old-fashioneds," Bella orders as my phone rings and Marjie asks me if I'm okay and if I plan to return to my place of work at any point.

As I turn away to answer the call, I hear the barman ask Bella, "Is that your grandad?"

"Don't be so ageist!" I hear her scandalized response and then something, something, ". . . he's my friend."

Friend.

So we *are* friends. *That's truly lovely*, I think through my Old-fashioned haze.

Marjie seems to find it hilarious that I'm a touch tipsy in the middle of the day. She tells me to take the rest of the day off, and when she asks me who I am having my impromptu bar crawl with, I decide to use Bella's word. "A friend," I tell Marjie. "A new one."

"Well, good for you, Eddie," Marjie says. "Go out and have some fun. If you need a lift home later, let me know."

When I return to the bar, I give the barman a smile and say, "Do you know, I think I'm too old to be her grandad. Wouldn't I have to be her *great*-granddad?" He looks embarrassed. "No, no," I say, waving a hand at him, "I'm not offended, and—fantastic shirt, by the way—if her mother is in her forties, I'd have had to have had her when I was nearly fifty. So I'm probably great-grandfather age. Maybe even older."

"Mick Jagger just had another child and he's in his seventies," the barman says helpfully.

"That's very helpful," I tell him and make my wobbly way over to the table Bella has secured for us by the window, where we can watch the cars on the ring road whizz by.

"I've not been this drunk in years," I tell Bella as I sit down on a squishy cube that wasn't designed with the stability of a nonagenarian in mind. I had forgotten how silly and fun it is to be drunk. "I can't even feel my teeth."

We clink our glasses together.

"To Jake," she says.

"To Jake."

"I miss him," she says, and just as I think she might cry, she takes a huge swig of her Old-fashioned and says, "Tell me, then, Eddie. Who was *your* first kiss?"

On no. Not this.

"I, er—" I look around the bar for some sort of distraction. "What do you think of the barman's shirt? It's growing on me."

But she is not so easily dissuaded. "Tell me. Go on. I can keep a secret."

My stomach twists. "I can't tell you about my first kiss. It's not possible."

"Are you respecting his or her privacy?"

"No, no, nothing like that."

"Then are you embarrassed about who it was?"

"I am embarrassed."

"How bad can it really have been? A girl at my school kissed a guy who turned out to be her second cousin."

"What? No. I just— It's not the time."

"It *is* the time"

"And it's not the place."

"It is most definitely the playze."

"Playze?"

"Plays. Plaize. Pla-eee-ssss." She laughs.

"It's none of those things, either."

"*Ed-die*," she whines. "Why won't you tell me about your first kiss?"

"I can't tell you," I say, raising my glass and toasting to her, "because it hasn't happened yet."

Pigeons

————

September 20, 1965

He arrives to return the key.

"Birdie," he says, tipping an imaginary hat.

"I'm a pigeon today," she says, "I have decided."

"Pigeons are my favorite animal." He places the master key on her desk and even this act, of coming closer to her, the clean smell of his aftershave, feels oddly thrilling.

"You're just saying that," she tests.

"On the contrary," Eddie says, warming to the task of defending pigeons to her. "They never give up! You see a pigeon hobbling around on a gnarled-up claw, or flapping about on a featherless wing, and they never once complain. Sometimes they just have a stump and yet, on they go. Still walking. Even when it would be easier to fly."

Bridie goes to the kettle and turns it on, upturns the slightly nicer mugs she brought from home this morning, just in case he came back for another cup. And Eddie takes a seat.

While she pours and stirs, Eddie, smiling at the collection of photographs on the windowsill, points to the photograph of Bridie and Alistair in Paris and says, "That is an excellent hat," and she has to turn around and study his face to check that he isn't mocking her.

"I love a good hat," he explains, and he helps himself to a biscuit.

Beginnings

———◆———

"This is brilliant," Bella says, throwing down her bag and squishing beside me on the bench, receiving a furious look from the woman with whom I had been sitting in pleasant silence—her eating her chicken-and-mayo sandwich and me eating a Scotch egg. Now that Bella has squeezed between the two of us, thighs all a-smooshed, the woman tuts and rises, giving both of us a look.

"I don't think *she* thinks it's brilliant," I say.

"No, you," Bella says. "I couldn't stop thinking about it last night when I went back to work. One of the biggest moments of your life is still ahead of you."

"It is?"

"Your first kiss is something you never forget." She pauses. "Well, most people. Some girl in the year below me had her first kiss at a party where she got so drunk, she was taken to A&E to get her stomach pumped."

"Crikey."

"She was fine." Bella waves a hand. "We've all been there."

"I haven't."

"That's exactly my point!" she says. "You have one of the biggest things in life still to do. It's so exciting!"

I have never seen her like this.

"It is?"

"I can help you," she says, and then, appearing to want to hedge how enthusiastic she is to help me, she adds, "You know, if you want."

And I recall what Bhav said when she dropped off the bags of jewelry for me to search through. *So exciting to be searching for something. It gives us purpose, don't you think?*

"Maybe . . ." I begin to say.

A pigeon flaps down from the tree above us and lands at my feet. We look at it for a moment. It looks back at us with its dark eyes.

"I often think," I tell her, "that if it were going to happen, it would have happened by now. Perhaps my first kiss was just not meant to be."

Bella and the bird exchange a glance. And she shakes her head.

"It's not too late, Eddie Winston."

Reflections

———◆———

A sturdy boat of a woman sails into the shop. She browses the women's jackets for a moment and then docks at the till.

From inside the tote bag over her shoulder, she heaves an oval vanity mirror onto the table, set in wood and painted cream. It's a little dusty, but otherwise in perfect condition.

"Here you are," she says, sternly, as though I have insisted that she surrender the mirror to me and she is still cross about it.

"Thank you," I tell her, and I get out the donations form and ask about Gift Aid tax exemptions, which I still don't fully understand, but I don't think anybody does.

"I'm not filling in a form!" she scoffs. "It's just a mirror, take it or leave it." And then she weighs anchor and steams towards the door.

And I am left looking into her mirror.

What has this mirror reflected back to the woman over the years and how has that reflection changed? I wonder. And what is it lately, that this highly polished glass showed, or did not show, to the woman that she felt the need to banish it from her home forever? Did it whisper to her, *You are not what you once were.*

The mirror clearly learned its lesson because it stays quiet for me, showing me myself reversed, left to right, but otherwise exactly how I am. A little shorter than I used to be, still narrow. Lines around my eyes, around my mouth from smiling. I hope to make them deeper if I have the chance. What is left of my hair is swept into a side parting. When the wind blows, it wiggles and whispers, *Hey, look, Eddie can't admit that he's nearly bald.* I find, though, that a jolly hat will preserve my vanity. And if the mirror wishes to admonish me for my pride, it keeps that to itself.

I smile at the mirror, and the Eddie that it shows me smiles back.

Not a bad-looking chap, I suppose, given the state of things.

Perhaps there is hope for me yet.

The Jacket

Before I've even opened my packet of Twiglets, Bella sits down beside me on the bench.

"A customer just tried to spit at me," she says, sipping from a water bottle with shaking hands.

"Are you okay?"

"He missed and then fell over. My manager called the police. They sent a PCSO to take a statement. He was so drunk he couldn't stand."

"The officer?"

"The spitter. He called me an ugly bitch."

She swallows. "I hate this job. My manager is four years younger than me," she says, drawing in again. "He's basically a fetus. He invited me out for his twentieth at Snobs."

"Did you go?"

"Did I fuck. I'm not going to a children's birthday party."

"Do you want a Twiglet?" I ask. It seems a paltry offering in comparison with how Bella's day is going. She shakes her head, staring into the distance.

"It's turned to anger," she says quietly.

"What has?"

"The grief," she says. "It's all I feel now."

"That's understandable, dear."

"Is it?"

"Of course. It's easier to be angry than to be sad. My grandmother used to say that anger is the jacket that fear wears to keep from shaking."

"I—" She stops herself and says, "I'm glad I met you, Eddie."

"Me too."

She looks ever so sad.

"I haven't cried since Jake died," she says.

"You haven't?"

"No." She looks as though she has just confessed to a crime. "I don't know what's wrong with me."

"There's nothing wrong with you, Bella," I say. "Nothing wrong at all."

She sniffs and nods. But I haven't solved her problem. I wouldn't even know how.

I take a deep breath.

"All right, then, what's the first step?" I ask her. "How do we find her?"

"Who?"

"Whoever my first kiss will be."

Bella's eyes light up. "Really?" she asks.

"Really," I reply. "Let's do this."

I'm back in the charity shop, sorting through a sinister bin bag of Encarta '95 disks and naked troll dolls when my phone pings.

Welcome to Platinum Singles, Eddie! The Number One dating site for single people over 70!

Did you know that someone finds love with Platinum Singles every second fortnight?! Get ready to meet the love of the rest of your life . . .

Click here to view and update your profile.

Excited to see the profile Bella has set up for me, I click on the link. There at the top of my profile is the photo of me she took in the park, my packet of Twiglets rolled up and tucked out of sight, below are my statistics.

Name:	Eddie W.
Age:	90 **years young** [The "years young" is part of the website design and can't be deleted.]
City:	Birmingham
Romantic Status:	Single
Star Sign:	Aquarius [I'm not an Aquarius; I imagine Bella took a guess here.]

The bio, short and sweet, reads:

Hello, everyone, my name is Eddie. I work in the charity sector and I have a pet guinea pig. I would like to meet someone kind and intelligent who will make me laugh.

And there we have it—Eddie Winston is looking for love.

Now I am presented with a button.

Browse, it says to me. *Go on, Eddie. Start browsing.* But the word *browse* seems wrong. I don't mind browsing the crisp selection at the supermarket, but I don't feel comfortable browsing for people's hearts. But there they are, all the ladies and gentlemen who are looking for love. There's Gladys E., who is looking for someone who will share her love of gardening; there's Dennis P., who collects miniature alcohol bottles; there's Katherine G., who writes, "I'm not sure what I'm doing here, but I'd love to meet someone who loves the theatre as much as I do!" followed by a laughing face emoji.

I keep scrolling. So many people all smiling at me. So much hope, it's hard to look at. All these people picked the best photograph they had of themselves, probably spent a lot of time on their hair, thought carefully about what to write about the heart they have to offer. It is so fragile, the notion that there might be someone out there for everyone.

I close the tab. Perhaps later. Perhaps never. Marjie rattles through the bead curtain. "That's far too many troll dolls," she says, looking at them lying on the back-room carpet, their neon hair sticking up as though they've all been electrocuted.

"Monster Munch?" she asks me, opening a big bag and holding it out.

"I'll probably wash my hands first."

A Regular Appointment

October 1965

Bridie Bennett wakes every morning at seven and says a prayer for the day. She retrieves her locket from the mantel above the bedroom fireplace and fastens it around her neck. Using the time it takes to connect the clasp to think about her mother. She says a prayer for her too. Then she makes breakfast for herself and her husband. She waits for him to finish in the bathroom and does her best to hold her breath while she brushes her teeth and washes her face. Then she takes her hair from its plaits, and assesses whether the waves will be enough to subdue her hair. Then she walks with Alistair to the university. Sometimes he will run a lecture from start to finish in bullet point form for her to listen and nod along to. Sometimes she is listening, sometimes she is not. Then he will kiss her on the cheek and walk smartly upstairs to his office. The largest of the offices in the arts faculty building, after he kicked up a fuss about being put in the one with the noisy pipe and the head of department offered to swap. It has a wide window view of the green space in the center of campus, where he can watch the students come and go at the top of the hour, passing on their way to learn in the lecture theaters or unlearn what they just learned in the pub.

And Bridie? She makes her way along the dark ground floor corridor of this grand mahogany building to her office, which is jammed with all the filing cabinets the department could fit in. She spends her days as the department administrator creeping around the egos of the more distinguished professors and managing the needs of the students who come to her for help. From nine o'clock onwards, Bridie makes sure her hair is as unterrible as it can be. She makes sure the room smells of her perfume. She makes sure there are biscuits. You wouldn't know it to look at her. Ostensibly, she is filing documents and making phone calls and stamping forms and allocating room bookings, but as she does all that, she is waiting for him.

Now that he is teaching undergraduates, Eddie has a more frantic and frazzled disposition and does not appear every day. But he comes most days. And each day, she waits for him. Hoping there will be a knock at the door and his smile, often accompanied by some biscuits. And this person who has only ever been nice to her sits opposite Bridie and talks to her as if she is intelligent. Laughs with her like she is funny. Smiles at her like she is pretty. And how could she not look forward to seeing him? Not wonder which bow-tie-and-knitted-vest-over-shirt combination he is wearing today. Not hope that he will come back. And when he does, hope he will come again tomorrow.

Pineapples

———◆———

It's so warm today that Bella has tied her uniform fleece around her waist. Beneath it she's wearing a black blouse with pineapples printed on it. I can't remember the last time I had pineapple.

"Have you seen the app?" she asks, sitting beside me and giving me an excited elbow in the arm.

"Should I have?"

"Look!" She hands me her phone—it's stickier than I'd like it to be. "I haven't read it yet," she tells me.

Val H.'s message came in yesterday evening at 19:29.

My stomach fizzes with adrenaline. I read aloud for Bella's benefit.

Dear Eddie.

This is only my second attempt at writing to a
gentleman online. As such, I don't quite know the
protocol. Ought I to be fascinating? It seems so from
everything I've read on the internet about how to impress
people on dating sites. There isn't much that would
fascinate about me, save for a birthmark I have in the
shape of a rabbit. That is all. I am a retired accountant,
widowed for twenty years. I live beside the sea. I have a
Schnauzer named Trudie.

If any of that fascinated you, please do reply. It would protect
my ego, as the last chap didn't respond.

Warm regards,

Val

"Well, *she* sounds like a barrel of laughs," Bella says, closing
her eyes against the sun.

"It takes a lot of courage to write to a stranger with the implied
prospect of love," I suggest.

"Yeah, but still. A little razzle-dazzle never hurt anybody."

"Perhaps she's warmer in person. The regards were warm, after all."

"Were they bollocks."

"Would you reply?" I ask her.

"Me? No," she says. "But this isn't about me."

"It's about you a little. You're my wingman."

"Wingman?"

"Sorry, wingperson? Wingwoman?"

"I actually prefer wingman," she says. "But I think you've got
to follow your instincts on this one, Eddie."

Bella makes her way back to work and I nip into the Tesco Metro on
New Street to pick up some pineapple. A nice tangy treat for the afternoon. And as I walk back to the charity shop, I think about Val.
Living by the sea. Living *alone* by the sea, except for a Schnauzer
called Trudie. How sad she must be to have lost her husband. How
brave to contact a complete stranger.

The pineapple zinging across my tongue, I pull out my phone
and decide it's always good to make new friends.

Dear Val,

Eddie here. How are you? I'm new to online dating too. And
your ego may be put at ease, in that I found your message very

fascinating indeed. Particularly the rabbit-shaped birthmark.
I would ask you where it is, but that seems a little forward.
So instead I'll ask, how do you find living by the sea? Do
the seagulls keep you awake? There are plenty of seagulls in
Birmingham even though we couldn't be farther from the sea.
But chips are chips, I suppose.

My best,

Eddie

I return to the shop, chomping merrily on the pineapple cubes,
and find Marjie using two biros like a pair of chopsticks to extract
something from a donation box.

"I *mean*," she says, "who donates dirty Teenage Mutant Ninja
Turtles briefs?" She gingerly carries them using her biro chopsticks
towards the bead curtain. I hurry ahead and pull the beads apart so
that the pants don't touch the beads.

"I can't say I'm certain," I tell her as she makes her way into
the back room. I dash ahead and press the foot pedal on the big bin.

"These are far too large for a child," Marjie says, her head at
an angle in order to keep her nose sufficiently distanced from the
underwear. "These are *adult* underpants," she says. "Who in their
right mind wears Ninja Turtles underpants as an adult?" And with
that she lets them descend into the bin.

"What are you saying?" I ask. "Turtle ninjas?"

"The Teenage Mutant Ninja Turtles," Marjie says. "My boys
loved them."

"And what are they?"

"Well, they were adolescent turtles who were trained in the
martial arts. Really, it's all there in the name, Eddie. I can't help
you more than that already has."

"I must have missed the boat."

"It's not too late for me to fish them out of the bin if you're
curious," Marjie says, laughing.

As she heads off to the loo to wash her hands with the rose-scented soap that makes me feel a little queasy, I pull out my phone and google the Teenage Mutant Ninja Turtles. They look like a great bunch of lads. I would read on about their adventures, except I notice an icon in the top corner of my phone screen that I do not recognize and when I click on it, I see that Val has already replied.

Revolving

———◆———

October 1965

He's balancing Grice and Brown and Levinson and Plato on top of *Wind in the Willows,* and when he gets stuck in the manually operated revolving door, they all tumble about. Everybody in the half of the door that isn't stuck makes their way back into the library, grumbling that they can't get out.

"Sorry, folks!" she hears him shout as he frantically picks up the books. Once out of the library and into the crisp night, he lets out a big puff of air. She's smiling into her scarf.

"Do you need a hand?" she asks.

"Birdie," he says, looking relieved to see her.

"I'm heading back to the department anyway," she lies, holding out a hand to take something from him. She takes the top three books and slips them into her bag.

"You are too kind," he says. And for a brief moment it seems as though he might cry.

"Shall we?" she asks, and they make their way down the stairs and across the grass towards the English department in the steadily darkening night.

"So, Eddie," she asks, "what do you make of Birmingham so far?" They pass a pair of students flyering for a protest due to take place next week.

"Confounding," he says. "Lancaster feels like it became a city by accident. Birmingham is just so large."

"I like that though," Bridie says. "In a big enough city, you can disappear."

"But why would you want to disappear?" he asks her. From over the top of *Wind in the Willows*, he is looking at her.

Bridie doesn't know if it's because she revealed something she ought not to have, or because of the way his bright blue eyes are looking right into hers, that adrenaline rushes to her stomach. And she feels guilty that she is what he sees, that he's not looking at someone prettier.

He shouldn't have to waste those eyes on her.

two

◆

dear jake

today the therapist said that she would strongly encourage
me to write you another letter
    *"he hasn't replied to the first one yet," i said and this
really made me laugh. i couldn't stop. it seemed so silly and
hilarious, and every time i tried to get myself together and
stop laughing, the thought of me waiting by the door for
your reply would set me off again*
    the therapist didn't seem to think it was so funny
    maybe she thinks i'm going mad
    maybe i am going mad
    *but it is funny. it is also stupid to be writing you letters,
it's not like you can reply. and i'm not surprising myself
when i write things like, i really fucking miss you. i already
knew that*
    *she asked me about my "support network" and i told her
i have a group of best friends who are rallying around me.*
    *she can't be that good of a therapist because she believed
me. "that's fantastic," she said, "and how do you feel when
you're with them?" and i imagined what it would be like to
have friends and i told her that it made me feel safe. i hope
i can remember their imaginary names next week*
    she said it is good to have friends to support us
    *i should have told her that you were my only friend and
we've been having a hard time keeping in touch on account
of your recent death.*
    eddie is the only person i can stand to be around right now
    you'd like eddie. he's a kook. he's also, i think, only

*looking for his first kiss to distract me. but there's a little
something in there too. a little hope. he must have been
lonely for so long*

he hasn't told me yet

but i think he lost someone too and he never got over her

*that will be me in sixty-six years—still dreaming of this
boy i loved when i was young.*

*i got an email on wednesday from the oxford alumni
department asking me to fill in a questionnaire about my
post-graduation "destination." i wrote back, i work in a
sainsbury's metro and my boyfriend is dead*

*i wonder who will read it. i can't be the only oxford
graduate working for sainsbury's but the others are probably
working in marketing or corporate or legal.*

i had to click a box saying how much i was earning

there wasn't a box for how little i earn

*but i got a free book at work the other day when someone
left it on the self-serve till before they ran for their train, so
there's that to include in my portfolio. i couldn't see a box for
that either so in the "future plans" section, i wrote read the
book.*

i love you

bells

A Little Razzle-Dazzle Never Hurt Anybody

—————◆—————

Eddie.
   Eddie?
   Eddie. Psst. Ed-die!
   I look up.
   A little razzle-dazzle never hurt anybody, the shirt whispers from the men's clothing rail. *Come on, Eddie. You can't wear that beige cardigan for the rest of your life.*
   It creeps up on you, dressing like an old person. First you eschew the things that make you cold—the thin jumpers, the short-sleeved shirts—then it's comfort, and out go the shoes that pinch or don't support your arches, the smart trousers that are too tight, and then you don't want endless buttons because that's a lot of faff for your fingers and soon, before you know it, you're heading, hands outstretched like a zombie, for the sand-colored section of Marks & Spencer's Very Old Menswear Department for the quarter-zip camel jumper.
   Take a good long look in the mirror, Eddie, the shirt says. *You don't belong in camel-colored comfort. You belong in splendor.*
   From behind the till, I make my way to the rail and pull him out. Emerald green silk printed with cheetahs prowling up and down the sleeves and the chest. If nothing else, I'll be protected from predators.
   Marjie will absolutely kill me if she comes back from her trip to the Beef Buffet or wherever she is having lunch this afternoon

and finds me in the changing room trying on a piece of stock, the till and shop left abandoned. *Changing room* is a generous term for what is a curtained-off area in the far corner of the shop with a scratched mirror that never sold propped up against the wall. And it is Marjie's beefy wrath that propels me to move with haste, popping into the changing area and undoing the easy zip of my camel-colored jumper. Off come my gray shirt and bow tie and on slips the silky cheetah shirt. I'm halfway through buttoning up and I'm already certain I'm going to buy it. It is like nothing else I have ever owned. And while I have a certain penchant for hats and I do have my bow ties, I don't own anything this singularly . . . jungular.

Now that my torso looks so dazzling, my gray slacks no longer look right. Still wearing the shirt, I reemerge into the empty shop and stop to listen.

You know you're coming our way, old bean, they say. *You remember the day you pulled us from a donations bag and thought, "What a pair of trousers!" Let us not waste time by pretending you want anything else. No other trousers will do.*

They're right, of course.

I pick them up from the pile of folded men's trousers on display near the window. They are a deep burgundy velvet corduroy. The color of a good red wine.

I'm zipping them up when I hear the shop door open.

"I'll be with you in two ticks!" I call to the customer. I button and zip the red corduroy trousers. Admittedly, they look fantastic. But I'll need a belt.

Well, the customer won't mind that. Perhaps they can make a recommendation.

I pull back the curtain and Marjie is standing in the middle of the shop, looking amused.

"Oops" is all I can manage.

Forthright

———————◆———————

"That shirt is incredible," Bella says as I come to sit beside her on the bench. The silk shines in the sunlight, making the cheetahs look even more majestic. They are spectacular. I have never felt so emboldened by a piece of clothing.

"I thought I'd need to improve my wardrobe if I'm to go a-courting."

"Probably best not to call it 'a-courting.'"

She opens a multipack of crisps and offers me my selection. I go for salt and vinegar.

"I replied to Val," I tell her.

"Good for you," she says.

"We have exchanged seven messages now."

"Sounds promising," Bella says. "And what's she like?"

"What's she like? Gosh, I don't know. Forthright. I think that would be the word."

Bella spits out her crisp, laughing.

"What? Being forthright is a good quality," I say in Val's defense.

"In a first love?"

As Bella returns to her cheese-and-onion crisps and resumes crunching, I assess her question as though it is a spider that has just crawled into my view and I am determining if I ought to fear it or befriend it. If it can be captured or if I should let it scuttle free and see what sinister things it does next. What have I learned about Val? Val is eighty-seven, she likes cross-stitch and classical music, her dog is named Trudie, and she has one adult son. Though

I am gathering information about her and I have her photograph from her dating profile—cropped white hair, violet earrings that look handmade, sensible scarf, only the hint of a smile. I find it hard to assemble all these pieces into a person. Perhaps people enjoy this about internet dating, the jigsaw assembly of a stranger into someone you love. I wonder if on meeting her I might discover I assembled the pieces incorrectly. That I put her heart where her mind is, or the reverse.

It is hard to convey any of the important things through these messages with Val, I realize—things like charm or a sense of humor or a frisson of a spark. I am being very careful with myself, as I'm not sure how jokes come across in large font of the Platinum Singles chat box. The messages are long, with each of us being careful to answer all the questions we have been asked by the other. In my latest reply, I relayed to her that I have no siblings, that my favorite color is blue, and that I have worked in the charity shop for nearly twelve years.

I pull out my phone and navigate to the app. Though my most recent message hasn't been marked as "seen," I write another. **Beautiful day! Hope you are enjoying the sunshine, Eddie** and I put a kiss. I believe we must blame the cheetahs for this fit of digital chutzpah.

To this, Val replies instantly: **It is beautiful here too. Trudie is running on the beach as we speak!** And after this, she has put an *x* too. Gathering the butterflies in my stomach, I sit for a moment. I have received my first digital kiss. That must be progress.

Into the Mystic

"I'm a medium," the tiny old woman says. "An expert in metaphysical connection."

Of course, she's a medium. Look at me! her jacket cries, all purple swirly velvet and glimmery bits of gold. The silver tassels that hang down from the sleeves at her elbows call, *Only a mystic would dress this mystically, you fool!*

"I'm a palmist too," she continues.

"A pianist?" Marjie asks, and I'm quite sure she has misheard on purpose.

"I read people's palms," the tiny old woman explains with patience. "Our hands hold the keys to our future."

"Mine are just holding this mug," Marjie says, and I stifle a giggle. Marjie does not suffer whimsy gladly.

"Would you like a reading?" the medium asks as Marjie gives her the change for the star-printed scarf she has just purchased.

"Thank you, but no," Marjie says. "It's just not for me. No offense."

"None taken, dearie," the woman says. There's a cheekiness to the way she smiles at Marjie.

"How about you?" She turns to me. "Are you open to the idea of a wide and mystical universe?"

I glance at Marjie, who communicates "Get this lunatic out of our shop" with her eyes, but then I look at the clock. It is only ten past ten when it feels like it should be at least a quarter to four.

"Go on then." I hold out my hand.

The medium looks incredibly pleased and scurries over to me, dropping her shopping bag on the floor and taking my proffered left hand.

"What's your name?" she asks.

"Can't you guess it?" Marjie asks, taking a sup of her Foxo. The medium ignores this and looks up at me.

"Eddie."

"Eddie, well, let's see now." She strokes the tips of her fingers across my left palm. It is odd and ticklish having a stranger touch my hands. "I see a good long lifeline, but I suppose one might venture that that is obvious." She darts a look at Marjie, who says nothing but blows on her Foxo.

"Now here, this is interesting." The medium runs her fingertip along the pad of my hand by my pinky finger. "I don't see much of a marriage line."

"I'm not married," I agree. And she beams.

"Never married?"

"Never married," I supply.

"I thought so." She looks greatly pleased. Marjie says nothing about the absence of a ring on my fourth finger.

"And here," the medium continues, running her finger down the center of my hand, "your money line is a good length and the indentation is fair. You have never wanted for money, but you have never been rich."

I agree that this statement seems true.

Buoyed by her success, she looks more closely at my hand, peering as though all the destinies of my life are written in small print across my palm. "Now, your heart line is interesting," she says, looking closer still. "I haven't seen one like this before." She traces her finger across my palm from east to west. "This is your love line. It tells the story of your heart. It's very faint, yet here at the beginning we have a deepening of the line, I would put this somewhere around your twenties, but then it fades out to almost nothing right down here." It tickles as her index finger runs along the line. "Heeeeere," she says, swooping down to the edge of my hand, "right at the end, almost the *very* end, the line deepens again."

She pulls back and frowns at my hand for a moment. "So unusual," she says, mostly to herself.

"So, if I were on the lookout for love . . . " I trail off.

She looks me in the eye.

"Now would be the time," she says.

She closes my hand, bending my fingers into my palm as though she is closing a book. She puts both her hands over mine and squeezes tightly, as though to underline and underscore the point.

Marjie sneezes and the moment is broken. The medium lets go of my hand.

"Very interesting," I tell her. "What do I owe . . ." I reach into the pocket of my red corduroy trousers for my wallet. She waves me away. "No, no, dear," she says, "I'll just . . . take . . ." She scans the shelf behind me and sees a ceramic duck figurine that we think might be a salt shaker but we haven't got the pepper. "This," she says, and she slips it into the pocket of her purple swirly jacket.

"Oh, um, I   "

She's taking many, many tiny steps towards the door before I can object.

The door chimes ring out and she is gone, shuffling off down Corporation Street with a duck salt shaker in her pocket. I can't help smiling when I spot her shamble over to a young man waiting for the tram and touch him on the knee. He looks up with alarm and slides his headphones off so he can hear her presumably offering him a palm reading.

I take £5 out of my wallet and put it in the till. It is probably more than the duck would have made us, but I can feel Marjie's eyes on me. And my cheeks are somewhat aflame.

Marjie comes over and places our large pump bottle of hand sanitizer down on the till with a thud. Giving me a look while she does it.

And then she rattles through the bead curtain in search of lunch.

Alone in the shop, I compress the pump and spread the slimy alcohol smelling gel around my future-revealing hands.

Now would be the time.

I retrieve my phone and I write to Val. Inviting her on our, and my, very first date.

Kylie

"Are those new glasses?" Bella asks.

"They certainly are. I'm giving myself a makeover."

"They're very chic."

"Thank you. They were designed by Kylie Minogue."

"What?"

"I thought to myself, 'If anyone knows about style, it would be her.'"

"Fair enough."

"They were from the women's section. But I don't need to be bound by a reductive heteronormative gender binary when selecting eyewear."

"That's true. You don't."

"That's what the young man who helped me choose the glasses said."

"Well, good for you. They look great."

She offers me a chocolate chip cookie, but I decline. While she splits her time between eating the cookie and scrolling on her phone, I take a moment to appreciate Pigeon Park. It is really excellent today. On the far right, two men with long hair are playing with a diabolo, and there's a woman with a white dog sitting beside her on a bench and she's sharing her sausage roll with it.

Into this pleasant afternoon comes a waspish buzz in my pocket.

"Is it Val?" Bella asks, turning to me and dropping the cookie, retrieving the cookie, blowing on it, and putting the whole thing in her mouth

It is.

I open the app.

Val has written three words:

I'll be there! x

Brighton

———◆———

Bella's car is full of things. And not just the usual things you'd expect to find in a car, like food wrappers and discarded pay-and-display tickets. There's a yellow Care Bear in the footwell of the passenger seat, a moon-print throw over the back seat, on which are piled several notebooks and paperback library books and empty cigarette packets. There's a little wooden nodding-head turtle who has been Blue-Tacked to the dashboard. He's painted in bright green and purple and he agrees as I get into the car. There are McDonald's burger boxes stuffed into various door pockets. She's drawn eyes on some of them so that their openings transform into big dopey smiles. And as I close my door, I notice the succulent plant that's sitting in the cup holder.

"First things first," Bella says, turning on the engine and putting the car in gear. "I need breakfast."

It is very early in the morning to be commencing a road trip. I have agreed to meet Val at noon on Brighton Pier and we need at least three hours to get to Brighton and Bella said she wanted "wiggle room" to get lost or crash the car (which I hope was a joke). And so, it is seven o'clock as we pull out of the car park of my apartment. There's something about the light of an early summer morning that fills me with promise. Reminds me of childhood days that stretched out beyond my view. *There's so much this day could be,* the morning sky tells me. *Why don't you take a chance, Eddie?*

"How do you feel about a McDonald's drive-through?" she asks me.

"I don't believe I've ever driven through a McDonald's drive-through."

"How?" Bella asks. "I live on them. I know there's all the deforestation and capitalism and everything, but ugh. *Yum.*"

When Bella has finished the burger that she had to request specially from a team of burger concierges who seemed to know her and I've finished my Egg McMuffin, which was nothing like any muffin I've had before, or any kind of egg, for that matter, and we've been on the motorway for about an hour, Bella turns down the music and asks, "Are you nervous?"

"A little," I tell her. To tell the truth, my stomach has been doing little dips and fizzes all morning. I'm wearing my cheetah shirt for luck. A suitably fantastic garment for a potentially momentous day.

"Does she know that were you to share a kiss, it would be your first?" Bella asks.

"She does not. I don't think a no-nonsense woman like Val would put up with any such oddness."

"It's not odd. You've just, you know, not had your chance yet." She switches lanes to get around a coach full of children. One of them—an elf-faced girl in a pink anorak—waves at me. I wave back.

"You'll get your moment," Bella says as the car in front of us moves over to the left lane. "Maybe today, maybe not. But you'll have your first kiss. I'm going to make sure of it. Think of me as your lucky charm."

"Oh, I do, dear."

She looks pleased with this.

I watch the road ahead, the middle lane open and clear, the lines on the tarmac darting past us like Morse code dashes. Dot dot dot. *Anything could happen, Eddie,* the road whispers. Dash dash dash. *Have some faith.*

When nature calls, Bella pulls off at a motorway services.

"Shall we get Burger King?" she asks as we get out into the fresh morning air.

"It's nine o'clock!"

She shrugs as we walk towards the service station. "Driving makes me hungry."

With bladders empty and the burger monarch's finest wares working their way through our intestines, Bella and I return to the road.

She's playing Enya on her phone, which is connected by a bright red wire into her car's open-mouthed dashboard. "My primary school head teacher used to play this when we came into assembly," she says. "It makes me calm."

The morning sun is getting stronger now but the motorway is quiet. And as Bella continues to monopolize the middle lane, the rhythm of the drive sends me into a little sleep.

When I wake, we are at a roundabout and Bella's phone says that we are twelve minutes away from Brighton Pier. My stomach drops. I shouldn't have eaten that burger or that cursed comestible that was masquerading as a muffin.

Val. I am going to meet her. We are having a date. I wonder what she's doing now. Is she walking her dog? Is she putting on her lipstick? Is she thinking about me? What does she think of me? Have we, in our seventeen messages to each other, begun something that will become *something*?

We get completely lost on the way into Brighton, turning down endless residential streets as the clock inches nearer and nearer to twelve. Once we have found our way, we merge into a long queue of traffic. It is already 12:01. Val might think I have stood her up, and so Bella, visibly stressed, tells me, "You'll have to just hop out."

And hop I do.

I ask for directions to the pier from a man with a hat that I think is fantastic and I would very much like for myself—a tweed deerstalker with a red feather. He points and I feel a fool because the pier is behind me, standing proudly in the calm waters. The man heads off before I get the chance to ask him where he bought his hat.

We've agreed to meet outside the entrance to the arcade—on the benches where there's a sign for ice cream. Of course, I don't know where that is, but I have been repeating those instructions to myself so that I don't forget them.

I walk along the pier, past a woman walking a wonderfully fluffy dog, past a toddler in a yellow rain mac pointing at the sea and shouting to his mother. I am hurrying, a little out of breath. It would be terribly ungallant for me to stand her up. I will my bad knee to go faster. And then, on the bench in the center of the pier that is closest to the arcade, beneath the sign for ice cream, I see the crossed legs, the sensible shoes, and as I get closer, a purple rain jacket, the violet scarf, and the pink earrings belonging to Val.

My fingers feel sweaty and, as I imagine we are about to shake hands, I wipe them on my jacket. Val hasn't seen me yet, so I take a moment to breathe. On the railing beside me, a gigantic seagull regards me with a beady eye that seems to contain a certain amount of evil within it. But I tell myself perhaps he is trying to communicate some encouragement. *Go for it, Eddie. At your age, what have you got to lose?* And then he flaps his giant wings, which makes me jump, and he takes to the air.

Go for it, Eddie.

What have you got to lose? He does have a point.

I walk up to Val quickly so that I don't have time to consider, for example, whether I smell of Burger King or if my collar needs aligning or if I can think of anything dashing to say.

And I stand before her. Ready to be evaluated on the criteria for love.

"Val?" I ask. She looks up from her phone and appraises me. Face, outfit, posture. I wonder what conclusion she comes to.

She smiles, but if this is her fullest smile, it doesn't completely convince. I'm not sure how I fared on the appraisal if this is the smile she smiles after it.

"You must be Eddie." Her voice is lower than I imagined it and much more confident. She stands and holds out a hand. No going back. I shake her hand and I am unsurprised to find that her handshake is firm.

"I'm so sorry I'm late," I say.

"How was the drive?" she asks, neither forgiving nor condemning my lateness. She pulls her purple handbag onto her shoulder and slips her phone inside.

"Not too bad," I tell her.

"Shall we?" she asks, gesturing to the pier.

Despite the McDonald's and the Burger King, I realize that I'm hungry.

"Would you like an ice cream for the walk?" I ask her, pointing to the ice cream kiosk where the attendant is leaning on the counter and reading the paper. "I believe we mentioned that on the chat. My treat."

"Thank you," she says, "but no."

And I think that is the moment that I know.

We walk through the arcade, with its bright lights that buzz and dazzle, the claw machines with the merry music and plastic prizes. There are three little boys in matching neon orange sweatsuits running about. Val neatly sidesteps them and walks smartly, ever so slightly ahead of me, and leads us out to the open air again. The wind is whipping about and I wonder if the man with the wonderful hat is successfully holding on to it. If it flies off, it might become mine.

"Will this be your first online date?" I ask Val.

"It will. However, I went on a date several months ago with a man I met at the garden center."

"How was it?"

"Oh terrible, he was very dull."

I hope I'm not dull.

"Well, this will be my first," I tell her. And I don't elaborate on all the firsts that this could be. I try to smile at her, but she is looking out over the water.

We walk around the fairground at the end of the pier and we try to estimate the last time each of us was on a roller coaster. For me, it has to be at least fifty years. What have I been doing with all this time? For Val, she recalls going on a roller coaster with her son when he was fifteen or so and she hadn't known it was to go upside down and she vowed *never again*. Her son works in Australia now, she tells me. She expects him to be taller each time he visits, even though he's in his early forties. She got so used to him growing that she is not ready for him to stop.

She asks me if I have children and I tell her I have not.

I feel a pang of guilt about Pushkin, so I remind her I have a guinea pig. She tells me she doesn't like rodents. And I feel another pang of guilt. Pushkin is many things but a rodent he is not. At least, not in my eyes.

Speaking of rodents, I ask her if she would like to go on the Crazy Mouse roller coaster because it makes me sad to think that I may never go on a roller coaster again.

Val tells me her neck wouldn't be able to take it and wonders whether rides such as that have an upper age limit, anyway.

We read the limitations on the sign at the entryway to the queue for the Crazy Mouse and find that it does not.

I ask her again if maybe she'd like to just risk it and she declines.

We turn course now, back down the pier, and I struggle to think of anything to say. Fortunately, Val asks about my job.

"I don't know how I'd feel about sorting through other people's knickers," she says with a laugh.

I sense she wouldn't enjoy hearing my anecdote about the Teenage Mutant Ninja Turtles briefs, so I ask her about her work and she reminds me that she was an accountant for nearly fifty years.

"And did you enjoy it?"

"Not really," she says. "The people were fine, but the work was dull."

Fifty years spent at a job she didn't like. I could happily work another fifty years at the charity shop and never have the same day twice.

"Well," Val says. And then neither of us says anything.

"Do you have any plans for the rest of the day?" I ask.

"My sister will call at six."

"That's nice."

"It's her turn," Val says, as though it can't be nice because she is simply adhering to their prearranged schedule. I wonder what Val expected of this date. Because I expected sharing an ice cream and laughing and so far, we have done neither. I try to think of a joke I could make, but I am feeling quite flat.

"And you?" she asks. "Do you have any plans for the rest of the day?"

"Just the drive home," I tell her. "I imagine I'll sleep for a lot of it."

"Yes." She smiles and there's a little release.

"Did you ever think," I ask her as we make our way back through the arcade to where we met, "that you would live this long?"

She looks at a large seagull that descends from the sky and flaps onto the roof of the shelter that runs down the center of the pier. "I don't suppose I ever thought about it. Why? Did you?"

"Not at all. I would never have imagined myself living to ninety."

"And yet, here you are," she says.

"Here I am."

When we reach the bench where we began, Val offers me her hand again and tells me it was nice to meet me. I wonder if it was. And then she pulls her jacket tighter around herself and thanks me for driving all this way and heads off in the direction of land.

And I watch her go.

I turn back towards the arcade, and spot the ice cream kiosk window. We were going to have an ice cream on the pier, so that is what I intend to do.

Holding my 99 ice cream in my hand (with two Flake chocolate bars in it because when the man said I looked like I'd had a hard morning and I told him that I'd been on a first date and she'd already left, he added the second Flake and an extra squeeze of raspberry sauce), I walk down the pier towards Brighton.

Off I go, with seagulls screaming at one another in the sky and two of them on the pier before me fighting over something beige in a takeout burger box.

I find Bella seated at a sticky booth in a 1950s diner that is so vivid and in no way how I remember the 1950s. I wonder if other people remember the fifties like this—milkshakes and juke-boxes and color simply because they have been told so many times, over and over, that this is what the 1950s were like. What will the themed diners of the 2020s be? I wonder. Hand sanitizer and face masks and toilet rolls stockpiled into towers probably.

Bella is also eating an ice cream. A Knickerbocker Glory sundae from a tall glass with an extra-long-handled spoon so she can get to the bottom.

When I sit down opposite her in the booth, she gives me a confused look. And then checks her phone. "Thirty-seven minutes?"

"It felt like longer."

"Do you want a burger?" she asks.

After her third burger of the day, Bella asks if we can stretch our legs before the drive back.

So we walk along the pier again and, I must say, it is much nicer being here with Bella. I believe we are truly friends now. I don't know what someone like her is doing being friends with someone like me, but I am not about to question it, in case she changes her mind.

Bella insists that we get a handful of change and play on the penny falls and the slot machines. Her mother loves them, she says. She will keep the money she started with in one pocket and the money she wins in the other, and once the playing is over, she likes to calculate what she won and what she lost.

I feel as though that's what I am doing now.

I pop the coins in and it is hypnotic. Eventually, my little gathering of coins shifts a group of three or four pennies and a plastic thing on a key ring and they clatter into the winners' trough.

"Jackpot!" Bella says, coming over with her empty tub and no pennies to show for it because she gambled away her winnings too. "What did you get?" she asks, and I hold up the plastic figurine.

"Ooh, Bananaman!" she says.

"Do you want him?"

"I couldn't possibly."

"Please, he's yours," I tell her, and she takes him, looking genuinely pleased.

"Now, what does Bananaman do?" I ask. "Apart from increase your potassium?"

"No idea," she says. "But he's going to look great hanging from my rearview mirror."

We walk to the very end of the pier where the Crazy Mouse roller coaster stands tall against the gray sky. The last opportunity for fun before France.

"Oh, we *have* to go on that," Bella says.

Convincing the ride operator that I will not die on the Crazy Mouse takes some time. I offer to telephone my doctor. Bella promises that if I *do* die, she will help the ride operator to drag my body off the ride and throw it into the sea and then they will call the authorities and say that I fell off the pier while clutching my chest. It is at this point that I think he decides the ninety seconds of uncertainty while I ride will be worth curtailing this conversation, which has already gone on for about ten minutes. There is nobody behind us in the queue and he collects our £10 and offers his arm for me to hold on to while I climb into the ride car, which is not, as I was anticipating, shaped like a mouse. Bella squeezes in beside me. "Woo!" she shouts.

"I haven't been on a roller coaster for fifty years!" I tell him as he lowers the safety bar and looks at me like he wishes I hadn't said that.

And then we are off!

We ascend the lift hill, *clunk clunk clunk. Are you sure about this, Eddie?* it asks. It is very loud and it feels as though the thing is working very hard to get us to the top, but the view to the right is incredible, just the wide-open sea. Up we clunk and I feel my bones rattle. I remember what Val said about her neck not being able to take it.

We reach the top and I am expecting a big dip. But instead, we ride straight towards Brighton and then twist at what I can only think of as breakneck speed to face the sea and then we repeat and then comes the first dip. Bella whoops and I clutch the safety bar as hard as I possibly can.

We are rolling faster now, gathering pace, turning and dipping, and Bella is still *woo-hoo*-ing and then there is only spinning, it is ocean and pier, ocean and pier, and I think they can't possibly spin us more, we're going to spin right off this track, and I'm definitely going to vomit. But still, we spin and I grip Bella's hand and I close my eyes, only to discover that having my eyes closed makes the spinning even worse, so I open them again and I can't even work out where I am.

On and on we spin into the end of the track and the brakes go on with a clang and a sudden jolt and I feel a twinge in my neck and we are no longer spinning.

"Eddie? You still alive?" Bella asks.

"Just about!"

It takes the help of the roller coaster operator and Bella both pulling to heave me out of the coaster car. And the platform appears to be spinning as much as the Crazy Mouse and suddenly it is too funny either that I just did that or that I survived it (or both) and I am bent double, wheezing.

"Is he having a heart attack?" the roller coaster operator demands.

"He's laughing," Bella says in a tone that conveys that the man is an idiot, and I can hear the smile in her voice, though I can't quite see her because I am bent over. And while the world spins a little faster than usual, I realize how close laughing, *really* hysterically laughing, is to crying.

But I laugh anyway.

Part Two

Communion

The shop is so quiet today that I am treating myself to sorting through a box of donated items from the comfort of the tartan stool behind the till (£25.99, stain on the seat). Out of the box I pull hats and jumpers and books (both thumbed and unthumbed), a glasses case with no glasses inside, several blank greetings cards, and a ball of wool. All quite unremarkable. I pile everything up by the till, ready to be sorted for stock day. Until there, in the bottom corner of the box, wrapped in tissue paper as though he is precious and not a terrible monstrosity, is Master Piggy.

"Bah!" I can't not let out a yelp. The bowl of the teapot is his awful pig body, little trotters clasped together across his tummy. Spout sticking off to the side in white. He's wearing a green bolo tie, white shirt, and green dungarees. His eyelashes are exaggerated in an attempt to make him pretty but it isn't working. He's horrible. The label says he was made and glazed in Staffordshire but I'm not sure if he wasn't actually made and glazed in the fiery pits of hell.

"Oh, he's so sweet," Marjie says, coming over and making him walk across the counter. "Oink oink oink!"

"Stop it, Marjie, he's horrible!"

Marjie picks him up and holds him towards me. "But, Eddie, I want to be your fwieeeend!" She shakes him as though he's speaking. I've backed away from the till and am standing behind a rail of men's T-shirts for protection.

"Don't," I beseech. "You'll anger whatever demons created him!"

"I won't hurt you, I looove you, Eddie!" she says in a high-pitched piggy voice and wiggles him in the air and that's when his horrible pig head wobbles off and shatters into a hundred porcine pieces on the floor.

"Jesus!" Marjie says, staring, aghast, at his decapitated teapot body.

"Let's hope someone donates some holy water."

It's not quite lunchtime when Bella's face appears in the shop window; her upturned nose pressed against the glass makes her look like an imp. When she sees me, she grins. Then she returns to appraising what the mannequin in the window is wearing—a purple tunic dress over bootleg jeans and a black mock crocodile belt around the waist "to cinch it in," Marjie said as we wrestled the mannequin into what Marjie hoped might be a fashionable outfit. The mannequin is wearing knee-high boots in brown and a pair of black sunglasses where her eyes would be if she had eyes.

Bella comes in. "Lunch?"

"I'd be delighted."

"What do you fancy?"

"Anything but bacon."

Marjie rattles through the bead curtain, brushing the crumbs of her own lunch from her chest.

"Well, hello!" she says, dusting her hands and holding one out for Bella to shake. "You must be Bella."

Bella shakes Marjie's hand and I notice her noticing the shredded fabric that makes up Marjie's calf-length skirt today, the green pen she has hung about her neck, secured with green ribbon.

"Tell me, Bella," Marjie says, "you're young . . ."

"I'm not *that* young . . ." Bella starts to say.

"Well, you're younger than us!" Marjie laughs.

"Okay . . ."

"Right. Tell me, honestly, what do you think of the mannequin's outfit in the window today?" Marjie asks.

"Honestly?"

"Honestly. Eddie and I have no idea about fashion."

I take undisclosed umbrage at this. My style is becoming electric. My cheetah shirt, my red cords, my new glasses courtesy of Ms. Minogue. I am evolving. I don't disagree with Marjie, though. I will let my style speak for itself.

"I won't hurt your feelings?" Bella asks.

"Not in the slightest," Marjie says. Bella looks from Marjie to me and I nod.

"Change everything," Bella says.

Marjie laughs. "Then that's just what we'll do."

As Bella and I exit the shop, we take one last peek at the mannequin, now wearing a pair of light-washed men's jeans, a white T-shirt advertising the Széchenyi Baths, a pair of white trainers, and a pink silky bomber jacket draped over her shoulders. Onwards we walk. Bella is smiling and Corporation Street is shining. The sun is bright and promising summer. *I have it in me*, she is saying. *Just you wait. One morning you'll wake up and boom! You'll have forgotten about winter. I'll touch all the dark corners. I'll bring you days, but doubled. I'll bring gardens and parks, drinks with crackling ice. I'll bring that feeling of possibility. Of hope. Just you wait, Eddie.*

We turn onto New Street. "Free coffee and a Qur'an!" a young man shouts from a long table offering the Qur'an in many different languages. A few feet down, the man with the sandy dog, by which I mean the dog made of sand and not a sandy-colored dog, is dusting his masterpiece and yet, you never see that dog half done. Beyond them, a young woman is leaning into a microphone in front of an open guitar case, singing about delirious love. Farther down, a young man in a suit that doesn't quite fit him is handing out leaflets.

"Here." The young man gives Bella a glossy A5 sheet that says "Christ Is Risen."

"Oh, I'm okay, thank you," she says, trying to hand it back.

"Please," he says. "You'll be the first today."

"I'll take it." I tell him, rescuing the flyer from Bella and turning the image of Jesus over in my palm. "Oh. He's had a trim," I observe.

"Yes," the young man says. "Research has shown that at the time Jesus lived, it would be unlikely for him to have the long hair and beard we all grew up seeing him with."

"And what do you think of his new look?" I ask.

"I'm getting used to it." He smiles.

We head up the hill towards Pigeon Park and as we reach the cathedral gardens, Bella grabs my arm.

"Look!" she says, pointing at the Mister Whippy van that has just pulled up outside the railings of the park and is playing "You Are My Sunshine" with all its love and melancholy notes pinging around the square.

Office workers in expensive suits are transformed into children, jumping up from their benches and emerging from buildings to join the queue, discussing whether they will have an ice lolly or a 99 ice cream, whether they will get sprinkles or a Flake or some bubblegum sauce.

We join them, of course. Ice cream for lunch, what would my mother say?

"Raspberry sauce?" the ice cream man asks before he hands me my rather generous 99.

"No, thank you," I reply and confide in Bella as we head for our usual bench that raspberry sauce will now always remind me of Val, not that I liked it all that much to begin with.

Our bench is currently filled with three besuited men in their mid-fifties happily licking a Twister, a Fab, and a Nobbly Bobbly.

So we sit in the grass among the dead to enjoy our iced treats.

"It's mad, isn't it?" Bella says as the Christian leaflet of Jesus with his short back and sides slips out of my pocket. "That people still believe."

"You'd be surprised what people believe," I tell her as I nibble the edge of my cone.

"Are you religious, Eddie?" Bella asks me. "Do you believe in anything?"

"Those are really two different questions," I tell her. "I have never been particularly religious, but I believe in plenty."

Bella smiles like this makes perfect sense. "This is delicious, by the way," she says, taking spoon to the bubblegum sauce and sprinkles on the top of her 99.

"I agree. We may have to replace Noodle Day entirely, B."

"B?" she asks.

"Doesn't anyone call you B?"

"Jake used to call me Bells," she says. "But he was the only one."

"I like that," I say.

"I did too," she says.

There is a pause.

"Eddie," she says eventually, through a mouthful of ice cream.

"Yes, Bella?"

"You won't give up, will you?"

"Give up?"

"On looking for love. After Val, I thought you might not want to . . ." She trails off.

A couple walks past us, across the grass, sent by Pigeon Park to remind me of what might be. They are both silver-haired and wearing matching outfits of navy slacks and a cream jumper, not hand in hand but close enough to touch.

"I won't give up," I promise.

Lord Braithwaite of Carmarthen

The fancy blue eggcup is going to look entirely out of place among the chipped bowls, the corporate mugs, and the wonky salad spinners of the kitchenware shelf.

Let me tell you something, the eggcup says. *I do not belong here, in this . . . this . . . jumble sale for peasants. I was important, once.*

Sorry, old boy, I think as I place a price sticker for £1 on his bottom.

One pound?! he demands. *One English pound? I am worth hundreds. There were ten of us, my brothers and I. Matching comrades in arms, serving breakfast to great men and their wives. Oh, the eggs I have held. And whom I have held them for, let me tell you! Ho ho! Does Lord Braithwaite of Carmarthen mean anything to you?*

It doesn't, sadly. But I decide to rescue him from the misery of his fate. I bring him with me back to the till and empty our plastic container of paper clips into him. He looks rather grand as a paper clip holder.

"Ooh, that looks good," Marjie says, coming in from the back room with her Foxo mug fox dancing in her hand. "Very fancy." She blows at the top of her Foxo and the brown liquid ripples. She takes an extraordinarily loud slurp.

"I was thinking of bringing out some of the summer stock, now it's May," she says as she rounds the till to sit behind me on the tartan bar stool. "Sunglasses, hats, and so on. It's going to be summer before we know it. We can put the winter coats back into storage? . . . Eddie?"

"What? Oh. Yes. Good idea."

"Are you all right?"

"It's summer. Already. Crikey."

"The years fly, don't they?" she says with a sigh.

I wonder if they do. Like birds, forever flapping away from us, off to sunnier climes.

How

"So, Eddie," Bella says. "Can I ask?"

"You can ask me anything. I'm an open book."

"How is it that a charming young gentleman such as yourself has never had his first kiss?"

"It's a long story."

"Did you ever come close?"

"Close?"

"To kissing someone."

"Well . . ."

Escapement

———————◆———————

"I'm *incredibly* drunk."

Eddie leans against the doorway of Bridie's office, cheeks flushed, hat askew, bow tie pointing north and south.

He's resting the weight of his whole body against the doorframe as though he wouldn't be able to support himself without the help of the wall.

Bridie tries to suppress her smile. She extends her leg under her desk and pushes the chair opposite her towards him. With the door open, the sounds of the party down the corridor in the common room are louder; someone is playing an accordion along with the record player. There would be clinking of glasses, but they are drinking out of the common room's communal mugs. And they're chipped enough already, so toasts are off the table.

Pushing himself off the doorframe and making his way over to the chair, Eddie looks like a puppet whose strings have been cut, all loose and ungoverned. Whatever thing is usually controlling him has left him to decide his own movements. And they are wobbly ones. He flops down into the chair opposite her.

"I'm so drunk, I've forgotten what we're celebrating," Eddie says, resting his elbow on his thigh and then his head on his hand in a balancing act that looks precarious, but which also makes him look as though he is incredibly interested in whatever Bridie will say next.

"We had a lot of wine left over from the October conference," Bridie says. "And if we don't use it, we won't get any new wine for the Christmas party."

"Isn't academia a scam!" he says.

"I've always thought so."

"I imagined it differently," he says.

"The party?"

"Being here."

Even his smile is wonky tonight, as though the wine has sent every part of him off on an angle, like a house falling down a cliff. Crumbling into the sea.

"So why aren't you at the party?" he says, a heavy hand flailing in the general direction of the common room where a roar of cheers suggests that the dartboard has been brought out. "Why are you here, in your office?" He gestures messily to the Eiffel Tower mug Bridie has been drinking her wine from. And the wine bottle she took from the common room at the start of the party.

She turns her locket from back to front on its shining chain and she does not give an answer.

Beside the wine bottle is an empty mug covered in quotes by Edgar Allan Poe. Eddie reaches for it and begins to fill it. "This wine is a lovely color," he says. "Like a duck's beak." When he has finished pouring, he swirls the wine in the mug and sniffs. "Excellent bouquet."

"Oh yes," Bridie agrees, nose over her own mug. "Hair lacquer and lemon."

"That's exactly it." Eddie takes a big swig. "Warm," he says, swallowing. "Lovely stuff."

It is only on speaking to Eddie now that Bridie realizes that she too is slightly tipsy.

"Birdie, I was wondering," he says, and she hopes he will not ask again why she is alone, why she can't bear to be around her

husband when he is merry and showing off and soaking in the ad-
oration of the lower-level academics who see him as their ticket
to rise. The right coauthored paper, the right name drop at the
right interview and Alistair Bennett can help them become the
next Alistair Bennett. She cannot bear to see Alistair's eyes shiny,
cheeks flushed with self-importance. And she cannot bear to be
asked again the ages of her children, for she has none, but the men
in the department presume that she must have *at least* two or three
by now, especially given the doughiness of her physique, which is
always inexpertly hidden behind long cardigans and mismatched
scarves. She cannot bear to be asked about her schooling by the
few females in the department who don't know what else to ask her,
stumped as they are to be presented with a woman with no discern-
ible ambition.

"Yes?" Bridie asks Eddie. Ready for it all.

"Can I have a biscuit?" he asks. "I think I might be sick if I
don't eat something."

She slides over her tin and pops the lid off for him.

He takes a jam-center biscuit and puts the whole thing in his
mouth; it makes his cheek bulge like a greedy parrot's. She starts
laughing and he starts laughing. And because he's laughing so
much, he can't chew the biscuit and has to slide the saliva-covered
thing out of his mouth.

There is another roar of laughter and cheers from down the corridor. He pops the slimy biscuit onto the table. "Come on," Bridie
says, standing and taking her navy wool coat from the back of her
chair and throwing it to him.

It is November now, but he isn't wearing anything over his short-
sleeved shirt and bow tie.

"Where are we going?" he asks as they make their way out
of the English department and into the stinging November night.
Campus is empty. The lights are off in the library that looms large
to their right, looking haunted in the darkness.

"I think you need some air," Bridie says.

"And why am I wearing your coat?" he asks, linking his arm through hers, slightly drowned in navy wool.

"It's freezing," she says.

"Then you should wear it," he says, the words slurring together. "I can't let you shiver while I wear your coat."

"I'm fine," Bridie says, "I've got my fat to keep me warm."

Eddie stops still and turns to face her, looking at her like a dog hearing a language it doesn't understand.

Bridie can't take the intensity of his gaze, so she turns and begins walking towards the clock tower that rises above them. There is a moment of quiet, and then she hears his footsteps behind her. It really is freezing; she folds her arms across herself. Her thin cardigan is doing little to keep her warm and her fingers are starting to feel rigid with the cold.

When they reach the base of Old Joe, Eddie has caught her up.

"Some people say," she says to him, aware that he is close by her side, "that if you walk underneath Old Joe before your exams, you'll have bad luck."

"That's not too rich for my blood," Eddie says, and they walk towards the arches.

Hope is a dangerous thing in the hands of the lonely. Hope certainly shouldn't be left in Bridie's hands, she realizes, as she and Eddie find themselves alone in the dark archway beneath the old clock tower, where nobody could see them, even if they were looking. Though nobody is looking for Bridie or Eddie tonight.

She fails to suppress a shiver and he takes off the coat he has borrowed and drapes it with such care around her shoulders that she could cry, just from the kindness of it. In the half darkness, she is aware that they are far too close to each other. She can feel the warmth of him.

"Bridie," he asks. Why is this sweet man so gentle? He is careful with her, as though she is something precious.

"Yes, Eddie."

"Why did you have that mug there?"

"The mug?" She's stalling.

"The Edgar Allan Poe mug."

She's caught. It is too cold and she is too tipsy for the lie. And so she simply says, "Because I hoped you'd come looking for me."

"Ah," he says, "'The Raven.'" And then he smiles. "It is always the birds with you." Then he takes a step back, as though he has realized how close they are to each other. As though *he* is the one who is married. As though it is his responsibility, and not hers, to make sure that she does not break her vow.

Bells

———◆———

"I can't understand why people get married in churches," Bella says, taking a bite of her banana. On the corner of Pigeon Park, the bride is just getting out of a big black car, hampered by her voluminous skirt. A bridesmaid in navy silk wiggles around from the back and hands the bride a jacket made of the same ivory fabric as the dress, which is far too angular across the décolletage.

"It just doesn't make sense," Bella continues through her mouthful of banana. "You're in your nicest dress, on the happiest day of your life, and you're hosting the thing in a garden of bodies and old bones."

"We have lunch in a graveyard," I observe.

"That's because we're edgy and cool," she says, taking another bite of her banana. "And also, because it's in between where we work. But a wedding is supposed to be about happiness and hope. And I don't find a graveyard particularly hopeful."

The man dressed in a cheap suit who has been loitering not far from our bench throws his cigarette onto the ground, pulls a DSLR camera from his backpack, and makes his way over to the bridal party.

"I suppose a church is traditional?" I suggest, though I must admit I am not particularly committed to this idea.

"Think of all the boxes of bones down there," Bella says, gesturing across the park, where the graves bear names of people for whom nobody brings flowers anymore.

"I'd rather not." I pull on the unyielding plastic container of my Mexican chicken wrap.

A stocky man in a gray morning suit emerges from the bridal car, balancing a gray top hat atop his head. Bella snorts a laugh through mushed banana. "A top hat? And who is he, the Monopoly man?"

As the Monopoly man links his arm with the bride's, her tiara catching the late morning sun, the photographer takes photos of them from a kneeling position. Those won't be flattering at all. Next, there are a series of photographs of the bride standing alone beside the above-ground tombs, which must contain only dust by now.

"Do you think you had to pay extra for a grave with a front-row view of the church?" Bella asks. "You know, in the old days."

"I would imagine so."

"It must be nice to be able to watch the comings and goings," she says. "People arriving and leaving for the Sunday services, the pigeons and all that."

In Bella's mind, what the gravestone sees, the dead soul sees as well. I find that idea quite fun.

As the bridal party makes its way towards the front doors of the cathedral, the photographer jogs ahead, catching them walking from all different angles as though they are models at Fashion Week. They pass us on our bench, sweeping past with a smell of hairspray and perfume and anticipation.

I wonder if we will be in any of these photographs—Bella and I, she in her Sainsbury's uniform and me in my red cords, Bella eating a banana and me trying to open a discounted Mexican chicken wrap. Hung up on this young woman's wall and consulted during times of marital trial. Will she ever notice us, or will she be preoccupied with her hair, her veil, her bouquet? Will she have concluded, as I have, that the bridal jacket was a sartorial mistake? Will she see anything other than a young bride filled with anticipation? A woman about to marry the wrong man? Will she return to the image often for a reminder of their perfect day with the living among the dead?

I pull as hard as I can on the plastic container that prevents me from reaching my lunch and then the thing bursts open and the top half of the "Mexican chicken wrap in a flour tortilla" flies across both Bella and me and lands on the ground.

I'm up in a flash. I pick it up and blow hard, dusting off the bit of the tortilla that was touching the ground. "Three-second rule," Bella declares. I don't know what this means, but by Jove, you'd best believe I'm going to eat it anyway.

I take a tentative bite. It's none the worse for being on the ground.

"Do you want to get married?" Bella asks me as I chew.

"I think it's a little late for that."

"*You are not too old and it's not too late*," she says, and then she hangs the now-empty banana skin by its stalk and gathers its unzipped pajamas into her palm.

It is a nice day for a wedding. The grass that rises up around the gravestones ripples in the soft breeze. I chew on my wrap and Bella looks with unfocused eyes at the gravestone closest to us that marks where some unremembered person rests.

"I didn't go to the funeral."

"Jake's funeral?"

"There was nothing they could tell me about Jake that I didn't already know. So I drove to our spot, listened to the last playlist he made me, put on his favorite hoodie, and smoked one of the cigarettes he used to keep in my car."

"Do you regret not going?"

"Never. It makes no difference to the dead person. A funeral is all for the eyes of the living."

After saying these wise words, Bella fishes a bag of chocolate buttons from her fleece pocket and tips about half the pack into her mouth. "So, you don't think you'd get married *now*," she says. "But did you ever meet anyone you wanted to marry?"

"There is one person I would have liked to have married, yes."

"And why didn't you?"

"Because she was already married to somebody else."

From inside the church, the notes of the organ catch on the breeze and bring "All Things Bright and Beautiful" to my ears and a pigeon flaps down from somewhere to peck at the bit of ground where my wrap fell. I give the pigeon a nod.

"She sends me birds from time to time."

Bella tips the remainder of the bag of chocolate buttons into her mouth. "I've been looking out for a sign from Jake."

"What do you think he might send?"

"That's the thing. I don't know. We didn't have one song that was 'our song.' We didn't have an animal or a poem or anything. How would I know?"

"You'll know," I tell her. "He'll make sure of it. Keep looking. Keep listening, it will come."

She swallows her chocolate buttons. "We used to talk about getting married sometimes," she says. "We wanted to go to a chapel in Vegas and I was going to wear a short black dress and a leather jacket with our initials on the back, in a white arrow-shot heart. And then we'd send our parents a Polaroid photograph of us in front of the Las Vegas sign with our rings held up. And then we'd go to the casinos and gamble so we could make use of all the free drinks."

"That sounds like a lot of fun."

"I wish we could have done it," Bella says in a small voice, and I put my arm around her and she rests her head on my shoulder.

We sit like that for a while, as inside the church, the bride and groom transform from ordinary people into a husband and a wife and somewhere faraway, Jake lies sleeping, having taken Bella's dreams with him when he went.

"We should go," Bella says, sitting back up. "My break ended twenty minutes ago."

As we stand and brush the crumbs from ourselves, the doors to the church open and the bride and groom tumble out, on a wave of excitement and love, confetti skittering around the side of the church towards us. And I wonder what that feels like. What their kiss at the top of the aisle felt like and if it was different from all the other kisses they've ever kissed. Because that kiss was sealing a union, a promise, a hope of forever.

Watching the bride and groom with an unreadable expression as more people follow them out of the church and throw confetti and fuss over the bride's dress and take photographs on their phones, Bella says, "I'm glad I got to love him."

And she then asks, "Do you know what I mean?"

And I do. I really do.

Resurrection

———◆———

Eddie appears in her doorway just as before. They drink tea and he brings biscuits to replenish her supply, having pilfered, in his own words, at least half of them since he arrived in Birmingham. Neither of them mentions the party, Edgar Allan Poe, or ravens.

It is easy to pretend, she thinks. And yet something has shifted. They are two poker players who accidentally turned their hands up on the table when they didn't immediately part upon finding themselves far too close together.

three

---

what will it be, then?

what are you sending me and when is it coming?

eddie greets every bird he sees like an old friend. it's weird. but it's his sign. i wouldn't mind looking weird if you sent me a sign.

he has only told me bits and pieces about his lost love. birdie he calls her, though that can't be her real name.

i wonder where she is now. i wonder where she flew.

"still no reply!" i said to the therapist when i arrived for therapy this morning and then i got the giggles again. she just raised her eyebrows and started writing

i don't see how she can think that's not funny.

it is definitely very funny.

as i laughed, i remembered what eddie said on the drive back from brighton. in between his naps, he said that laughing hysterically is very close to crying

and he's right

it's funny though.

i dreamed of you last night and it was horrible. i hate dreaming of you, which makes me sound like a bitch, but i just can't bear to wake up and remind myself that you're dead. i don't like the feeling of time moving on because it's taking me further and further away from you, to a time when i forget your laugh or what it was like to hug you tightly and bury my face in your hoodie and breathe in your mum's detergent. but i also want time to hurry up, to skip ahead to when my brain has categorized you as "dead." when my subconscious doesn't look for you in a room or

*my hands don't get out my phone to message you when
something funny happens.*

*the therapist wears a lot of neutrals. beiges and creams
and whites. i wonder if she's trying to look as plain as possible
so that you forget she's there, so that you talk on and on
endlessly about your pain, spilling your guts, while she sucks
it all up and devours it. a neutral-hued pain dragon.*

*she said i must have so many questions for you
but i really only have one
was it selfish of me to ask you to stay?*

A Letter Arrives

———————◆———————

"No guinea pigs!" Marjie singsongs as always as she heads out of the door. She's off to the dentist, probably for some sort of beef-related intervention. It can't be good for her molars to have all that chewy bovine in her diet. The door has only just closed when it arrives. A small square envelope addressed to:

Captain E. Winston, 24 Corporation Street, Birmingham, B17 9NS

Eddie,

May I begin by thanking you.
It has been so long since I last saw my little sister's beautiful name on an envelope that, for a moment, I completely forgot that she is dead.
A subtler woman might use a euphemism such as "she passed away" or "she has gone on to be with Jesus," but I like to face life (or death, I suppose) head-on and that is the truth of it, I'm afraid. My sister Elsie ("Else" to her friends) died in 2016.
But oh, how wonderful it was to receive your letter. For a moment, I thought she might just come running down the stairs, seventeen years old, all bruised knees and skinny elbows, and scoop it up from the doormat and then run back

up to her bedroom with it so that my parents wouldn't see.
That is what she did when the first letters from Mr. William
McGlew began arriving at our home.

"Are you in love with the postman, Else?" I asked her
one night when our parents were at a church dance.

She looked up from her book. "The postman?!"

Our postman was eighty-five if he was a day. Bony hands.
Birdlike neck. Absurd hat. Little shorts all winter long.

Elsie thought for a brief moment. I could see her
weighing up whether I would be a worthy confidante and
eventually, she placed her book down, wings spread on the
quilt so she wouldn't lose her place, and went to the top
drawer of her dresser. And out she pulled a stash of letters
and envelopes.

"His name is Will," she said.

She told me they'd met in Sunday school. She told me
they'd had a date on the pier. Told me they had kissed.
And because I'm obstinate and competitive and had yet to
be kissed myself, I made the mistake of teasing her about
it. And she never took me into her confidence again. Not
when, after several years of her loving him, William McGlew
seemed to have broken her heart. Not when she appeared to
recover. Not when she married, not when she divorced. Not
when she fell in love with a gardener she met during one of
her longer stays in hospital. I never got the chance to know
the secrets of her heart again.

But that's me, I'm afraid: brash. And that was Elsie:
unforgiving.

And so, we come to your fair Mr. William McGlew. I
would imagine his heart also suffered, as this unkind sister
did, from Elsie's reluctance to forgive. And whatever it was
that parted them kept them parted.

We drifted apart, Elsie and I. I lost myself in my writing,
relocated to London for the noise and the ritz and the

*glamour. I dove (fairly half-heartedly, I can admit, ha ha!)
into motherhood of my only son. And I often wonder, if I
had sat quietly (which is rarely my wont) in her bedroom
back in 1953 and listened rather than teased, perhaps she
would have told me about him. Perhaps we would have
stayed sisters rather than drifting into acquaintances and
then into nothing.*

    I will always wonder about Mr. William McGlew.

    *I was too late on the day she died. My flight to Glasgow
was delayed and when I got to the hospital, they said she'd
already passed. If my life were one of my novels, I would
have made it. Said my final things to her. But instead, I was
met with an empty corridor and a stranger in the bay where
she had been. I hoped that if Elsie's soul was still lingering
near, perhaps she would hear the words of her repentant older
sister who wished to clear the air and send her, lovingly, on
her way. But in my desperation not to cry, all my words got
swallowed up, so as I made my way down the corridor, all I
managed to whisper was, "Sweet dreams, Elsie."*

    *After she passed, I gave almost everything to charity,
with the exception of the art that she made during her time
in hospital and her photograph albums. And as I flicked
through faces familiar and unfamiliar, there was William,
in monochrome, smiling on what looks to be Margate Pier
some time in 1956. And because I cannot bear to read her
childhood diary, in case she has written angry words about
me, I have had to make my peace with not knowing more
than that for the rest of my life. Until, that is, the incredibly
expensive postal redirect I have for incoming mail to our
childhood house brought to my home in Corfu the words of a
kind gentleman with a piece of the puzzle of Elsie's heart.*

    *So may I end with a beginning. An invitation. I do not
wish to entrust William's precious epistles to airmail. I
enclose my address and an invitation for a week of sun at*

my home. I shall pay for all expenses, flights, sun cream, you name it. I have plenty of bedrooms. Bring a friend! My house will be your home. Do say you'll come and we can meet face-to-face.

It is so very rare that one gets to meet a pirate.

Emmeline Woods x

Hearts and Stripes

———◆———

Bella is wearing a striped black-and-white T-shirt and a pair of red heart-shaped sunglasses. Beside her, on the bench, a woman with a fast-panting dog is scrolling through her phone. Bella looks like she ought to be strolling in Paris rather than gently shooing an overly eager pigeon from her bag. But here she is.

"Those sunglasses are fantastic," I tell her. "Are they new?"

She takes them off and inspects them as though surprised to find that they are on her face at all. "They're from Topshop, I want to say 2015?"

"Well, they are sublime."

"Thank you," she says. As she moves up on the bench to make space for me, the fast-panting dog jumps down and pants about my ankles.

His owner smiles. "He won't bite."

I give the little thing a fuss on the head and its tail wags faster.

His owner stands and says, "Paul, come on." And he follows at her heels as she heads in the direction of the city.

Bella is watching Paul trot away when I place the letter across her lap.

She picks up Emmeline's words and says, "If I'm not your plus-one for this, I will never forgive you."

The Note

———◆———

March 1966

A note is slipped under her door.

your husband is sleeping with one of his students

There is no capital letter at the beginning, no full stop at the end. The handwriting is squiggly, in fine black ink. The tail of the *y* flicks sharply to the left.

In a way, it is kind. Whoever wrote this note wants Bridie to know that her husband is not faithful, to end the humiliation. But Bridie knows. She knew about the first one, six months into his post at Birmingham; she knew about the next one too, their next-door-but-one neighbor; she knew about another, who was an old friend from his school days. There may have been more in between. And what makes Bridie feel so worthless is not that her husband is unfaithful to her, nor that it is not the first time, it is that she feels nothing at all. It is as though she has jumped into a swimming pool with all her clothes on, her heaviest wool coat, her jumpers, hats, and scarves, wrapped and wound around her. All of it weighing her down, and she has sunk to the bottom of the pool. And there she is on the cracked, tiled floor; she cannot get lower.

She takes a single deep breath and goes upstairs to Alistair's mahogany office.

She walks in without knocking, and he turns, surprised, and then frowns at her for the disrespect she is showing him by barging in uninvited.

Bridie places the note down on the desk, and he glances at it, skimming. Then he stops and picks it up. Looks closer, turns it, as though it has more secrets to reveal.

"How old is she?" Bridie asks.

He looks at Bridie, and perhaps he sees the steel she feels within her. "What?"

"Is she a teenager?"

"Every student here is an adult and capable of making their own choices."

"How old is she?"

"You think this is true?" He tries out an incredulous, jovial laugh, to see if he can convince her. To see if he can convince himself. And he can't. He slides the paper back towards her. "It's just a joke, a student prank," he says.

"I have a meeting in ten minutes. I just want to make sure she's an adult." Bridie looks at her watch, and Alistair seems surprised to see no emotion in her.

He starts to speak. "I—"

Bridie interrupts. "I just want to make sure she's not a child."

"There are no children here."

"You know what I mean. I want to make sure she's in charge of her faculties. A woman. A postgrad at least, not a homesick eighteen-year-old who thinks you hung the moon."

Alistair arches an eyebrow. She has bested him. Beaten him at his own game because she knows and there is no scene, no drama, not a tear. For so long, he has treated her like she does not matter, like their marriage does not matter, and she has begun to believe it to be true. He seems disappointed by this. That he cannot trick her into believing it is a joke, that she will not cry or beg or communicate how important he is to her by showing her devastation at his infidelity.

"She's twenty-three," he replies.

"Fantastic." Bridie lets the heavy mahogany door thud behind her.

Pushkin's Opinion

———◆———

"We can't go to Corfu," I say, more for Pushkin to agree with me than to get his actual opinion. He carries on crunching his lettuce leaf. "I can't just leave work, we can't stay with someone I've never met. And who would look after you, small friend?"

Pushkin continues chewing, his cheeks moving frantically.

"I haven't flown in decades," I say, though it is a feeble reason for declining adventure.

Pushkin keeps chewing, leaving me to come to my own conclusions. I open the Platinum Singles app. I sent a lady named Phoebe what I thought was a charming message several days ago. Now the chat box says "read" but she hasn't replied. I sigh and click on the browse button once more. We have some things to tend to here that I can't just leave.

I pull out my notepad and I write to Emmeline. I thank her for the invitation, but I tell her that I can't be such an imposition. I will ensure the carrier of her selection gets the letters to her in perfect condition. She has my word as a pirate, of that she can be assured.

The List

———◆———

Bridie Bennett is compiling the list of lecturers and students who will be attending the twelfth annual Literature and Linguistics Association conference in Cagliari. She sees his name, written on the sign-up sheet in small block capitals: EDDIE WINSTON.

She is embarrassed for herself at how her stomach flies upon seeing it.

Alistair often asks her if she wants to come to the summer conferences. They are always in sunnier climes so that the academic staff can pretend that they are on holiday in between papers and plenaries. Whenever he invites her, Alistair often adds, "Of course you won't understand any of it," just to underline how much he doesn't really want her to come. There is a lot of drinking at these things. And there are a lot of secretaries and young female academics in attendance. She has no desire to be his millstone.

While Alistair is away, Bridie will declutter the house, organize her half of the wardrobe, attend Wednesday and Sunday Mass and keep herself busy. And at night, with a book balanced on her lap, she will eat. Biscuits usually, one after the other, not even enjoying them, just working like a machine placing one into her mouth over and over until the packet is empty and she is so ashamed that she wraps it in a loo roll and stuffs it to the bottom of the bin. Then she will buy another packet the next day, from a different shop, so that the shopkeeper will not know this is her second packet of bourbons in as many days. And all the while, she will urge herself not to think about what exactly Alistair is doing at that very moment. Who is being touched by him. Who is laughing at his jokes. Who is smelling his consuming, expensive aftershave.

But this time is different.

She takes out her pen and beneath Eddie's name, she writes as neatly as she can, "Bridie B."

May

It is unseasonably hot for May.

I undo the top button of my shirt and loosen my bow tie, which, today, has apples on it. Seemed a healthy start to the week. I lean back against the bench, which is not particularly comfortable, the way it digs into my back. But I stay here for a moment nonetheless. I can pretend I'm on a deck chair on the beach.

But thinking of the beach reminds me of Brighton, which reminds me of Val, which reminds me that time is a-ticking. And Phoebe still hasn't replied.

Out of the corner of my eye, I spot Bella as she ambles across the grass, walking between the headstones, which have the occasional irreverent can of Foster's or a McDonald's wrapper discarded beside them. Bella's walk always seems to imply that her right leg is a little heavier than her left. Her hair is all crinkly today, like she pressed it between a sandwich grill, with the dark brown roots contrasting with the candy floss pink.

When she gets to the bench, she says, "Can we go for a walk? I need to find somewhere with air con."

I don't need asking twice. It has been hot and humid all day and the shop doesn't have air-conditioning, unless you count the bright orange desktop fan covered in stickers of footballers from the 2014 World Cup that limply spits out warm air from the back of the shop. Which I don't.

"Up we go," I say, more to my knee than to Bella.

She loops her arm through mine and we walk for a moment like two good friends. "Nope, sorry," she says. "Can't do it, it's too hot for physical contact."

I enjoyed walking along like coconspirators, but I agree. The sun is burning down on the back of my neck and I wish I had had the foresight to purchase a pair of sunglasses from the bucket of eyewear that lives beside the board games. Bella is wearing her red heart-shaped sunglasses again and I continue to secretly covet them.

We walk down Colmore Row. I love this part of the city, the Regency buildings rising up above us with their shiny signs on the door depicting which lawyers or media recruitment agencies now work where once men in fancy wigs and women in big dresses lived their elaborate lives. The office workers who are streaming in the opposite direction are clearly not ready for this hot day either. The men have their ties pulled down, shirts open, jackets slung over shoulders. The women, in their polyester dresses, look sweltering, their hair up in an attempt to cool off.

A man in a shiny blue suit is walking towards Bella and me, staring down at his phone. He has long sandy hair and well-manicured brunette stubble that makes him look like he's a surfing instructor who's on his way to court. It becomes a game of chicken. Bella does not move out of his way, and he continues typing on his phone, not noticing us. They are on a direct collision path. I can bear the tension no longer when he flicks his eyes up and stops. He doesn't look too pleased, brow furrowed like he was just interrupted from deep concentration. Bella walks around him. "Enjoy your ham and cheese," she says to him. I wonder if this is a modern euphemism for "go f— yourself" I have not heard before, but something registers and his face transforms into a cracking smile. As we continue walking, he's still turned around, smiling at Bella, and if she has noticed, she doesn't let on and she keeps on walking.

"That's Ham and Cheese," she says. "He comes in every morning at eight-fifty to buy his lunch. Always has the same thing. Ham and cheese sandwich, salt and vinegar Discos, and an orange and mango smoothie."

"He's got a nice smile," I suggest tentatively.

"Does he?" she asks.

"Doesn't he?"

"Can't say that I've noticed," Bella says, and I wonder if I detect a hint of a lie, but when I look at those heart-shaped sunglasses, I can only see myself reflected back in them.

Secrets

He is a prurient man. That is truly the best that can be said about him. Perhaps these words will not be written in his obituary or uttered at his funeral, but that is really the only remarkable quality about this priest, Bridie thinks as she hears the chair creak on the other side.

It's a charade, this grille that divides the holy from the lay. She can see straight through it, if she really wants to. And God is on both sides, listening. So what is its purpose? The priest has arranged his chair so that he cannot be seen, has his back right up against the confessional door. Perhaps it is the illusion of isolation that is important to prompt the secrets of her soul. As a child, she would ask her mother, "If God saw me sin, why does He want to hear about it a second time?"

The chair creaks. "You were saying?" Father Owen prompts. Bridie reaches out a gloved finger and touches the grille that divides them. The wire that has filtered the secrets of the sinners to the ears of the blessed for hundreds of years. The residue of six hundred years of transgressions caught up in it like fish in a net. What secrets had those first few confessors? Were they like hers? she wonders. Has the tapestry of all that *is* now come about from the fallout of the very sins whispered in these cloister walls?

The priest coughs.

What was she saying? She can hardly remember.

"I . . ."

It has never been difficult for Bridie to believe. She feels lucky in that way. "She has a rich imagination," her school teacher told her mother, and if the other children didn't seem to devour every second of literature and drama and creative writing like she did, she didn't notice. Her mother thought *rich imagination* was a euphemism for *badly behaved* and asked Bridie to please try harder to be good. But it was never difficult for Bridie, sitting in the cold pews of Saint Michael's in East Acton, to imagine the stained glass of Adam and Eve to move, to twitch slightly, for Eve to crane her neck to look at the sky, for the snake to slither farther around the tree, for Angel Gabriel's wings to unfurl even wider, their silk feathers making sounds like boots on snow. For Jesus, hanging tortured up on the huge crucifix above the altar, to twist, the nail in his side piercing his appendix, and look down on the church congregation of 1953, at his disciples, gathered in clothing he might not have recognized, in a cold country he had never seen, singing hymns in a language he never spoke, and smile that something of what he said must have got through.

She truly thought she was being ministered to by Saint Paul himself during a night spent with a fever following a particularly bad case of bronchitis. And when she woke, she wondered if perhaps it was possible that he really *had* knelt beside her bed, all green like a statue made of jade, and, palms touching in prayer, stared out across her bed as though looking at something very far away. He was too low down, as though he wasn't kneeling on the floor but kneeling some way beneath it, his knees floating just above the living-room ceiling. She spent the next day looking for signs that she might be blessed.

Now, Bridie wishes it were a little harder to believe. That it was easier to see the cracks, the flaws in the logic, the omissions and the errors that Alistair was always talking about during their first years together until he abandoned his mission to have her "see sense." If she didn't know God like she knows Him, she could run to Eddie. Or she could run backwards, go all the way back to the day that she waited outside her own wedding for Saint Expeditus to give her a sign and have him turn to her, raise his foot up off the swearing crow, and tell her to wait.

The problem with having such a rich imagination, however, is that it enables Bridie to imagine hell. On a school trip to a cathedral, she once saw a huge painting of sinners in hell being spiked and burned and tortured, but it wasn't the spiking or burning or torturing that she stared at, but their faces of agony. Bridie did not fear the spiking or burning. She feared the eternal anguish.

"I . . ." She stops.

The priest sighs. *Get on with it*, she presumes he is thinking. *Get to the good bit.* "You were saying" —he adds a "my child" here in an attempt to soften his otherwise fractious tone—"that you fear you are developing romantic feelings for a person who is not your husband."

Said out loud, read back to her like that, it sounds awful. But not untrue.

This person, she wants to say, isn't just some average person. Some random man. He is light. He is unusual. He is hers, she is quite sure of it, just come to her too late.

"I won't act on it," she says quickly and wonders if Father Owen recognizes her voice from Sundays at Mass. She comes alone to Mass because Alistair, who was raised by lapsed Methodists, has declared it all "spooky" and "unfounded." Could she sit on the opposite side of the confessional booth and identify the voices of the other congregants with any accuracy? Probably. Father Owen most likely knows exactly who she is.

"That you have brought your feelings to confession suggests that you fear you *might* act upon them without God's guidance," Father Owen says.

"No, I—"

Eddie's closeness to her under the clock tower, for the briefest of moments, a steadying, the way he looked at her, shoulders draped in her coat, how her stomach flew on seeing his name on the list for the Sardinia conference. It comes to her quickly, but she says, "I don't believe I will."

"Hm," the priest replies. He does not believe her.

"I don't believe I will," she says again, "but that is why I am here."

"I don't follow."

"Because I already regret it. I know I will regret it for the rest of my life."

"We never regret obeying God's law," Father Owen says, and she wonders if perhaps he has that embroidered on a tea towel in the parochial house.

"Is it a sin for me to love him?" she asks. "Simply to love him from afar?"

"The commandment is quite clear: 'Thou shalt not covet.'"

"But what if I do not covet? What if I only love? And never act upon my feelings?"

The priest is quiet for a moment, thinking. He does not know.

"If you love him, you must also covet him."

"What if I can teach myself not to?"

"Only God can teach. And He has taught us that it is a sin to break the holy vow, the sacrament of marriage."

To be counseled on love by an unmarried virgin is one of God's more amusing tricks, Bridie thinks.

They stop there when there's a knock at the door by some impatient sinner. Bridie is given ten Our Fathers, ten Hail Marys, and told to read all of Genesis chapter 11, as penance. When she does, she can't find anything in it that relates to marriage or love or finding yourself married to the wrong person. It is interminably boring to read, so perhaps that was the point of the penance. It tells of how God scattered the people across the earth and had them speak in different tongues as an additional challenge. So perhaps that is the message, that God scattered Eddie and Bridie across the earth and wanted to watch them come back to each other. Or perhaps she is looking for meaning where there is none and, as she has often suspected, Father Owen selects the chapters and verses he doles out as penance entirely at random off the top of his head.

Just before she exits the confessional, Father Owen asks, "What does this young man say about your feelings?"

"He seemed to want to prevent anything happening," she tells him.

"He sounds like a good man," Father Owen says.

And Bridie will always wonder if Father Owen told her that Eddie sounded like a good man to encourage her to follow his example, or because he was trying to encourage her to indulge, so that he might hear, next week, what happened when she did. Because this priest is, more than anything, and above all else, a prurient man.

Islands

———◆———

Bella told me that Thoreau said we ought to beware all enterprises that require new clothes, but as I stand in the River Island changing room bedecked in my new green jeans and the black striped shirt that the saleschild recommended, I conclude that the thing we *really* ought to beware of is people who try to dissuade us from evolving our look.

"How's it going?" the saleschild calls through the curtain. He can't be more than twelve. He seems amused by me, keen to break the monotony of his day of labor with some styling advice.

"Excellent," I call through the curtain. "I'll take the lot!"

I emerge into the frantic Saturday crowd in the Bullring shopping center with my River Island bags crinkling in my hand and as I am swept by the tide of people towards the jeweler's, I feel as though anything might be possible.

I pull out my phone. Ethel123 has not replied to my message and neither has Olive_8. Phoebe is online now, but she hasn't written back. Nobody has sent me any "roses" and nobody has matched with me based on the photograph section.

Suddenly, fewer things seem possible.

Perhaps my photograph isn't flattering. Perhaps my messages were dull. Perhaps I am too old to be looking for love. Perhaps I will disappoint Bella and prove for us both that some things just aren't meant to be.

The swirling crowd feels momentarily overwhelming.

I need some new words in my head besides my own. To the book-shop!

I step on the crammed escalator. Just beneath me, a group of young ladies in headscarves is squeezing together to take a selfie. Their laughter lifts me. The young couple behind me speaks in gentle Italian to each other. *All is not lost, Eddie*, these happy people whisper.

Yes, Eddie, you've got to keep going, the escalator agrees, *and not least because if you don't keep moving, you'll fall off the end.*

I'm browsing on the top floor of the bookshop at the photography and travel books. This wasn't where I intended to be, but the lift stopped here and I got out. I've found a heavy, glossy photographic book of the Greek islands. I'm turning past the foreword in search of Corfu when a hand presses firmly on my arm. There is a ring on every finger in gold and silver.

"Would you mind if I took your photo?" she asks.

"Me?"

It is only us two on this quiet floor of the bookshop.

A fancy-looking camera is hanging around her neck suspended by a floral camera strap, her gray hair is pulled back in a pink velvet scrunchie. She's wearing a pair of black corduroy dunga-rees over a white blouse. She can't be younger than sixty, but Bella would definitely wear that entire outfit, no questions asked. I won-der if I could pull off dungarees . . .

"Grace Toppin." She extends her hand. "I'm doing a street style series on the people of Birmingham," she says.

"Street style?" I ask.

"Yes, you know, people of the city who have unique style, good fashion sense, people who stand out for one reason or another. It started as a mini portfolio I was submitting for the Black Artists of Birmingham award, but then I won that"—she smiles—"so I decided to keep going."

"I have street style?" I ask.

She pulls a face like she wants me to stop being ridiculous. I look down at myself. I'm wearing my tropical floral bird shirt that I found in the women's section of the charity shop and a pair of dark jeans. "I have been evolving my look lately," I say more to myself than to Grace. She laughs. It is a very good laugh.

"So . . ."

"Eddie," I tell her. "Eddie Winston."

"So, Eddie," she says. "May I take your picture?"

"You certainly may. Do you want me to pretend to continue browsing?"

"No, thank you," she says as she raises the camera from her chest and turns it on without looking at the buttons. "All I need from you is for you to stand exactly as you are and look straight into my lens."

"What should I do with the book?" I ask.

"Just as you are," she says again, and her surety is oddly comforting. I let the book hang loose in my left hand and I align myself, square my shoulders, and look at her camera.

"Perfect, Eddie, hold it," she says, and I hear the clicks. A run of them, one two three four five. *You're a model, Eddie,* they tell me.

"Putting the flash on now," she says. "And just as you were, blink a few times and then look back at me." There's something so calming about being directed. I do my best to do as I'm told and while the flash temporarily blinds me, I wonder what it must be that she is seeing through the lens.

The lift bell rings to announce its arrival on the top floor and a young man in the bookshop uniform emerges from the lift and hovers nervously, clearly wanting to tell Grace that she can't commandeer the travel section of the bookshop for an impromptu photoshoot but equally loath to interrupt her.

Grace keeps photographing, crouching down to get a better angle, seeming entirely unaware of his presence. I can see the anguish on his face out of the corner of my eye. In the end, he sneezes.

"Jesus Christ!" Grace jumps and that somehow scares the young man, who lets out a squeak.

I burst out laughing. Seeing this, Grace quickly pulls the camera back up to her eye. I hear a final click and Grace is beaming. "That's the one," she says, getting to her feet with little trouble. "Not a doubt in my mind,"

"You haven't even seen it yet."

"Sometimes you just know," she says. Grace turns the camera off and smiles at me. "Right then, what's your poison, Eddie?"

We settle into comfy seats in the corner of the bookshop café. Through the window we can see down to the crossroads where New Street meets the High Street and, just beyond, where the huge bronze bull sits guarding the entrance to the Bullring shopping center. It's almost mathematical how the people move among one another, managing to never collide.

The waitress places a pot of tea between us and a slice of carrot cake for Grace and a Victoria sponge for me.

Grace is looking at the display on her camera again. "It's *so* good, Eddie," she says. "I can't stop looking at it. There's a portrait competition coming up in Oxford—I think this will be my submission." She turns the camera around and there I am, standing in the center of the shelves listing "Travel" and "Adventure" and I've got my head tilted back, eyes scrunched up with laughter. The colors are richer than they are in real life. My floral shirt looks bright and punchy. I look . . . Well, I look stylish.

"I'm honored," I tell her. And as she is still beaming at the photograph, I pour tea into each of our teacups. "Would you mind, actually," I ask, "if I got a copy?"

"Of course!" she says.

"My online dating profile isn't the roaring success I hoped it would be," I explain as I add milk and take a sup of my tea. "I've been wondering if my profile photo isn't doing all that it could for me."

"Online dating?" Grace asks. "You're looking for love?"

"For my sins. It's not going very well, though. I don't know how the young people do it. The ratio of rejection to success is so . . . dispiriting."

"May I have a look?" she asks, stirring the contents of a paper packet of sugar into her tea.

I navigate to my dating profile and hand my phone over to her.

"You're not ninety?!" she says, looking at me as though I've claimed to be a unicorn.

I shrug.

"Ninety!" she says. "You look very good for it, Eddie," she says. She scrolls down my profile. "I don't think there's anything wrong with the picture, although mine is of course better. I think it's your wording that's the problem," she says.

"You do?"

"It's far too sparse—it needs some color," she says. "Hobbies, interests, books, television—give them a little more, Eddie, and I'm sure someone will bite."

"Someone did bite."

"Oh?" She scoops some icing from her cake onto her finger.

"Val," I tell her. "We had a somewhat disheartening date and it made me wonder, perhaps there just isn't a fish out there for everyone."

"Don't say that," she says. "God, that is delicious." She scoops more icing onto her finger. "I just got divorced and I want to pretend that there is a soulmate out there for me, just waiting. Someone . . . surprising, someone fun. Someone"—she glances up at me—"who wouldn't hesitate to let a stranger photograph them in a bookshop."

Grace's business card has gold foil writing on a photograph of a navy sky.

GRACE TOPPIN–PHOTOGRAPHER, *BA, MFA, AOP, BIPP*
STREET, WEDDINGS, FAMILY, COMMERCIAL (*SI PECUNIA SUFFICIAT*)
INFO@GRACETOPPIN.COM

Si pecunia sufficiat. I google its meaning: *If the money is sufficient.* I chuckle as I tuck the card into my pocket and make my mathematical way through the crowds, thinking of her.

Ham and Cheese Says Good Morning

———◆———

We are sharing pre-work coffee and doughnuts from the Canadian shop on the corner when Ham and Cheese appears.

"Morning," he says, passing by our bench with a smile. It is a devilishly handsome smile. His suit is expertly pressed, sandy blond hair in a bun at the back of his head.

"Ham and Cheese," Bella replies, giving him a salute.

"Good morning, Mr. Cheese," I call. He looks thrilled with this as he heads off in the direction of whatever swanky office he works in, readjusting the bag over his shoulder.

We watch him go.

And then I peep at Bella to see if she is as pleased by seeing Ham and Cheese as I think she might be.

Ham and Cheese, Part One

———◆———

Crispin Edmund Julian Wilkerson III has had everything handed to him. The best school, the best after-school fencing club, the best university, which he sleepwalked into, because how could he not get top grades with a class size of twelve and a weekend French tutor with the biggest boobs he'd ever seen in real life? The best graduate internships with his dad's friends in their plush London-based companies, with their fridges full of free Diet Coke and top-quality pastries. But this job, *lead copywriter* at the Little Fly agency, he got on his own. Applied in secret, interviewed while his father was skiing in Val d'Isère, and he got it. By himself. Mostly because he made Rav, the company director, snort water out of his nose during the interview from laughing.

When his father found out, once he had recovered from the shock of his son wanting to work in "Birmingham, of all places," and not "in Town," and with some unknown creative director who "went to a polytechnic" and not with his father's hunting buddy Wifty Jenkins over at Jenkins and Harrow Ltd., he insisted he gift his son a wardrobe of the best tailored suits made bespoke on Savile Row. If his son was going to be in *Birmingham*, he could at least look nice.

And you would think that all those things, all that privilege and private education, would make Ham and Cheese an unbearable dickhead. But Chris (he added the *h* at university so people would presume his name was Christopher) is just a good egg. At least, that's what the barman at his terrible local pub would say after Chris paid for the pub's stray cat to have surgery when it was hit by a taxi. The friends he stayed in touch with from uni weren't the legacies and the exhaustingly ambitious middle-class children, they were the ones who worked in the library coffee shop and would hang out with him when he was up late studying because there weren't any big-breasted French tutors to help him out and he was finding he actually had to put effort into learning at university. His football-club friends would say that he's a terrible goalie, a top laugh, and always shares his cigarettes. His theater friends would say he's a fast improviser who "yes-ands" with affection but can't do accents to save his life. His flatmate, Terrence, has no complaints, given that Chris always empties the dishwasher, hoovers once a week, comes to every ballet Terrence has ever costumed, made rainbow jelly shots for Pride, and didn't mind when Terrence's boyfriend threw up rainbow vomit all over their cream living room carpet, almost definitely losing them their deposit.

The thing about Chris is he just likes people. The weirder the better. People who have a little jaunt to them, who don't do things the way they should. After a lifetime of pin-sharp ironed uniforms and matching Mercedes cars at school pickup, all he craves is difference. It's why he got into a creative industry—because that's where all the best weirdos are. He was supposed to go into steel or law or finance, something impossibly boring, but the thought of all those dull men conversing at the weekend about the cricket and the strength of the euro made Chris want to pull his hair out. And his hair is glorious. He started growing it when he moved to Birmingham and now he has enough to scoop into a pretty generous bun. His father isn't keen. But his father has also been bald for forty years, so Chris suspects his opinion is tinged with envy.

Chris's obsessive-compulsive disorder doesn't run his life like it used to. His therapist has said he's doing really well. His rituals used to prevent him from leaving the house before they were complete. Now, he has got it down to one. And nobody apart from the girl who works in Sainsbury's seems to have noticed. It was his second day of working at Little Fly and Chris came in on the train to the misleadingly named Snow Hill (there are no hills and very little snow come winter) and ran to Sainsbury's to grab lunch. He was pitching for the following year's Christmas adverts for a candle company, and he got it. Brought in over three million pounds for the agency and was swiftly taken out for shots by the whole team. The next day, he nipped back into Sainsbury's again, bought some other combination of lunch things, and ballsed up his computer, spilled coffee on his colleague's dress, and got locked in the toilets. Clearly there was something about the combination of ham and cheese and salt and vinegar and orange and mango that was just lucky for him. Or, rather, *not unlucky*. It is primarily about the prevention of bad things. The girl in Sainsbury's has started smiling every time he comes to the till with his specific combination. Perhaps she thinks it's just a quirk, a foible. Perhaps she sees his OCD for what it is. But still, she smiles at him. She spoke to him on the street the other day, told him to enjoy his ham and cheese. He was midway through reading an email about an ex-client who was suing the agency and there she was, brightening his day.

He's seen her eating lunch in Pigeon Park with the incredibly old man who wears bow ties and has recently been evolving his look and is now a bit of a style icon. A senior fashionista. Chris thought the old man was her grandad at first, but now he is not sure. Sainsbury's Girl dresses like it's 2005 and the emo style never went out of fashion. It looks terrible under her uniform. A commitment to the cause that Chris appreciates. This morning, he has nipped to the big Tesco for Rav's birthday cake and there they are, Sainsbury's Girl and the old man, sitting on a bench together in the sunshine.

Just seeing her makes him smile.

Candy Floss

———◆———

July 1966

He lost his tail at the fairground. That's what she tells herself. Bridie likes to imagine that rather than some terrible accident with a car or a lorry or the sharpened teeth of a dog. She likes to imagine he took himself to the fairground and sat down on an old wooden roller coaster and got up once the ride was over and forgot his tail, so excited was he to eat some candy floss. Off he went (she imagines him walking on his hind legs like a fluffy human) and had some candy floss and never missed his tail. Not once. Got on the Ferris wheel and looked at the sky, checking for birds.

At the RSPCA when she first saw him, the vet said, "He's feeling very sorry for himself. His tail was degloved." And she promptly tried to forget the image that the word *degloved* conjured. He was incredibly fluffy. A Ragdoll, his tag said, but he looked small and scared and alone, peering at her from the corner of the cage, and Bridie just knew.

He didn't have a name. So Bridie named him the first time he hopped up onto the sofa beside her and made biscuits on her thigh, claiming her for his own. "Ferris," she said. "How about that?" And his low, deep purr let her know that he was pleased with the name. Or at least did not care to challenge it.

Ferris walks in the lyrical way of cats along the hallway to greet her at the front door as she arrives home from confession.

"Hello, gorgeous boy," she says. "Sorry I'm late, I had lots to confess." She puts her hand down and he bunts his forehead against it, hoping she will scratch the balding patches in front of his otherwise floofy ears. She stops talking and he looks up.

Go on, he seems to say, *I can listen* and *bunt*.

"I can't stop thinking about him," she says.

Ferris is a better confessor than Father Owen ever will be.

Her penance is scritches between his eyes.

four

the therapist keeps telling me it's okay to cry. it was our fourth session today and i think she's disappointed that i haven't cried yet. if i told her i haven't cried once in all the time you've been dead, i think she'd start writing furiously like she does whenever there's a delicious juicy moment for her to nibble on. i'm trying not to give her anything else. i want to make it as hard as possible.

    i don't know why i hate her
    it's not her fault that she can't help me
    but i think i resent her for trying
    for the very suggestion that i might be okay without you
    for thinking that nodding while holding an expensive pen and wearing a taupe suit dress would do anything to make me better. i can't be better without you. i won't let myself.

    if i let myself even consider the fragment of the thought that ham and cheese is kind of cute, then i can't have loved you very much, can i? and i doubt all the things in the world, but i don't doubt that i love you

    after therapy, i called in sick to work and i sat on a bench in pigeon park waiting for eddie.

    he shuffles about the world with all this sunniness. despite all those years of longing, of being alone. i think he's on to something with this photographer. the way she captured him, laughing, guard down. although eddie always has his guard down. he moves around the world as if he's just happy to be here. you would like eddie. i think this all the time.

    i offered him the sandwiches i stole from sainsbury's

*yesterday and he went for the ploughman's. a wise choice
since the other one was prawn. i thought better of eating a
warm prawn sandwich, so i ate my stolen satsuma instead.*

*"how did you end up at the charity shop?" i asked him.
i've been wondering this for a while.*

*"i was looking for something," he said, eyes on the
pigeon that flapped down for the crust of his ploughman's,
"and i kept coming back to see if it was ever donated. marjie
and i got talking and eventually she offered me the position"*

"and you don't mind working at ninety?"

*"retirement didn't sit well for me. it's not for the lonely,"
he said*

"you're lonely?"

*"i was then. i'm not now. i met marjie. i met pushkin. i
met you"*

*the pigeon he'd leaned down to offer his sandwich to took
the entire crust from between his fingers and then ran like hell*

and this made eddie laugh

i love it when eddie laughs

it's so sunshiny

*i don't know why some handsome older woman hasn't
snapped him up. i googled grace after eddie showed me
the photo she took of him and i can just imagine eddie
and grace in matching dungarees living on a riverboat
somewhere, painting things and adopting stray animals and
being happy.*

*since i'd called off work, i went for a walk. i didn't
have a plan, but i made my way to the jewellery quarter.
i walked past a postbox. and i stopped. i thought about
posting the letters I have written to you. this one too.
addressed to "jake, somewhere hopefully in heaven." i
wonder what they do with all the letters addressed to places
that don't exist. if i worked in the sorting office, i would*

have to read them all, take them home with me like eddie
does with this eddie shelf
   but I didn't post them and i kept on walking.
   and i wondered if i will ever be able to cry for you.
   please write back
   (and i'm laughing again)

bells

The Magpie

———◆———

The magpie wiggly-walks along the top of the roof.

"Oh, so you're a magpie today, are you?" I ask.

There is something about magpies—I cannot remember if they are good luck or bad. But I'll take it as good luck that she's thinking of me. The magpie stands for a moment at the edge of the corrugated roof of the block of flats opposite mine before taking to the air.

Pushkin is supping at his water bottle, lots of tiny nibbles and sups. The water bottle makes a pleasing bubbly noise.

"Do you ever get lonely?" I ask him, coming over to his cage.

He carries on supping. Not a fan of talking about his feelings is Pushkin. Which is ironic, given his namesake.

I sit on the dining table and peer in at him.

I put a finger between the bars of the cage. "Hey, buddy," I say, and I stroke the back of his magnificently long hair. He allows it. Lets out a few little squeaks.

"You've got such a fine bouffant," I tell him. "Shame to waste it on human eyes."

Whether he agrees or not, Pushkin does not let me know. Continues his fast breathing and then shuffles over to his food bowl for a nibble.

"Perhaps we ought to find you a friend," I say, more to myself than to him. I take the last sup of my tea and, as it is ten minutes to nine, I collect my hat and keys. Those dead men's shoes won't sell themselves.

The lift doors open and there's Thitima and Daniel, both flushed in the face. She's wearing a tracksuit, he's in shorts and a T-shirt and has an armband on that holds his smartphone.

"Hi, Eddie!" Daniel says, still short of breath.

"Hello, you two," I say, and smile. "Been jogging?"

"Personal best for both of us," he says. "We do a mile along the canal and back before work."

The lift doors close and we begin descending.

"Oh," Daniel and Thitima say in unison, and they look at the illuminated buttons, or lack thereof. "We forgot to press five." He laughs and presses it now.

They are just fizzing with happiness.

"Do either of you two know," I ask, "where one might procure a female guinea pig?"

Badgers

———◆———

Guinea pig sought to be a companion for a lonely ginger Peruvian named Pushkin. Caring owner, lifetime commitment, incredible hair.

It feels nice to have a friend doing this online dating thing with me. Though Pushkin is looking for love on findapet.org, the process is much the same, upload your photograph and write your particulars and wait for a match.

He hasn't had any matches yet, but then neither have I. I'm dusting the ceramics shelf with Marjie's absurd rainbow feather duster when I spot a badger staring back at me. He's wearing his gold spectacles low, looking at me from over the top of the news-paper he's reading. He must have only just woken up because he's wearing his nightcap still (when did people stop wearing hats to bed? I wonder; I love nothing more than a hat opportunity). Beneath Mr. Badger's breakfast table, which is laid extravagantly with eggs and butter and a teapot and milk jug, two child badgers are playing on the floor with a toy car, a teddy bear, and a frightening-looking jack-in-the-box. Whoever Leonardo, the artist inscribed on the gold plaque, was, he must have been a few badgers extra to a picnic, if you know what I mean. The price tag on the bottom is £16.

"Did the badgers just come in?" I ask Marjie, holding the stripy fellows up.

Marjie looks up from a donated *Prima* magazine from 2021 and puts her glasses on the end of her nose (and in doing so looks temporarily like father badger). "Hm? Oh, yes, the badgers. Came in yesterday."

I say, "They're fantastic," at the exact moment that Marjie says, "They're quite creepy." And we take a moment to consider the other's perspective.

"Sixteen pounds, though?" I ask.

"I googled them. Those badgers go for sixty-five new."

"Yeeshk."

Marjie laughs and holds her old *Prima* magazine far away from her face so she can continue to read. My phone lets out a merry ping. Hope swells in my stomach. But it is not a reply from Betty_313 or Freda.J or usernamemadge on Platinum Singles. It is an email from info@gracetoppin.com.

> Eddie! I'm photographing the Winterbourne gardens the Saturday after next if you fancy joining me. 10am. Wear something fun.

"Shit," Bella says, scrolling down to the bottom of the email and then back to the top.

"So," I ask her, "do you think it's a date? It could be another photography session."

"It *could* be another photography session," she agrees.

"But it could be a date?" I ask with a tiny sparkler of hope igniting in my chest.

"It *could* be a date," Bella confirms. "I think you're going to have to ask her."

"You can't *ask* someone if it's a date!"

"Can't you?" she asks.

"No, it would ruin the magic," I tell her. "I mean, I don't have any real-world experience, of course, but my instincts tell me that I oughtn't ask her."

"Well then, we'll have to consider it a photography session but hope for more."

"That's wise," I conclude, and she taps her forehead as though to show me where her wisdom originates.

"But what shall I wear?"

Ashes

August 1966

Bridie descends the stairs of the plane.

She holds tightly to the handrail, her green dress whipping about her in the humid air, and feels that she has just emerged into a blustery kiln. The heat rises up from the tarmac as the passengers cross from the back of the plane into the airport terminal.

When there wasn't enough space on the morning flight from London to Milan and then from Milan to Cagliari for all of the staff attending the conference, Bridie volunteered to fly alone and it has been illuminating. She did not know she was capable of doing this. She has flown only once before in her life, with Alistair for their holiday in Paris, and she didn't enjoy the trip. She's only traveled alone by train a handful of times, fearful of all the mistakes she'll make, worried that she'll read the timetable incorrectly and find herself on an express service to Scotland.

And while the feeling of rising up into the air, of leaving her life in England behind was thrilling, it was doing it alone that made her feel free.

And now, here she is, in a hot and new place, looking with squinted eyes at the mountains in the distance. And she did it. She, Bridie, all by herself.

Eddie, Alistair, and the rest of the department staff arrived at midday and will already be checked into their lodgings at the hotel

near the University of Cagliari buildings. The hotelier told her on
a crackly phone line when she made the booking that it is only a
short bus ride from the university to the beach. And that is where
she will go when Alistair delivers the opening plenary. She will not
be among his adoring audience. She will be soaking her feet in the
cool water of the Mediterranean Sea. A little act of defiance he will
probably not notice because, as always, he is not looking.

The airport is hotter inside than outside and with the addition
of the cigarette smoke, it feels claustrophobic and inescapable. Her
light green dress was the wrong selection, her sweat is pooling in
dark patches under her arms and beneath her breasts where the
underwire of her bra digs into her flesh. She lifts her locket from
her neck for a moment, to allow herself to breathe.

"Traveling alone?" the woman ahead of her in the queue asks.
She looks to be about seventy, perhaps older.

"My husband is already here." Bridie smiles.

The older woman smiles. "I'm taking mine too," she says, and
she pats her emerald green handbag. When Bridie's face betrays her
confusion, the older woman opens the mouth of her bag and inside is
a wooden box with a name written in shining silver.

"Gosh. I'm sorry," Bridie says.

The woman shakes her head. "It was his time."

The woman strokes the outer part of her bag, as though her
husband can still feel the tenderness. Seeing this lady showing
kindness to her husband even now that he is dust does something
to Bridie's heart. "Till death do us part and all that," the woman
says. "He had a great sense of humor. He'd have thought it was very
funny to be my hand luggage."

Bridie isn't sure what to say because a lump has formed in
her throat. This is what a wife should do. This is what marriage is.
God placed this woman in the queue beside her as a reminder of
what she promised Alistair. And supreme above that, of what she
promised to God.

And then, as if God is underlining His point, as she carries her suitcase out to the front of the airport in search of a taxi, there is Eddie, not her husband, sitting in a hard airport chair and writing in a notebook. As she approaches, Eddie spots her and smiles. "Birdie," he says.

She must look confused that he is sitting there. "I didn't think you should have to make your way to the hotel alone, so I offered to wait."

"You waited?" she asks.

"I waited."

"I've just been having this lovely sandwich"—he raises a paper bag of crumbs—"and waiting for you to arrive."

Windows

———◆———

Bella is in the shop window, arranging the faceless mannequin into a black beret, tilted jauntily to the side, but because the mannequin's bald head is so plasticky, the thing keeps sliding off.

A stern-faced woman is at the till to pay for a First Holy Communion greeting card.

"Balls!" Bella says loudly from inside the shop's bay window.

The woman gives me a look. It wasn't me who said it, but she's glaring at me like it was. I give her a conciliatory smile, but she continues to glare.

"Jesus!" Bella shouts as the beret slides off again.

"Could have been worse," I say warmly to the stern woman, as I scan her card. "She might have said—"

"FUCK!" The mannequin tips over and crashes into the display of board games and tchotchkes behind it with a cacophony of breaking things.

Once the window is reorganized and the mannequin's beret is taped onto her head, we go out onto the street to appreciate Bella's work. It is stunning. Our usually bland mannequin is wearing a black-and-white-striped midi skirt, a black blouse, and the beret, with a black bag hanging from her shoulder. She has a black neckerchief tied around her long, gray, alien neck.

"You've got such a good eye for style," Marjie says, and Bella waves her comment away. "I would have thought it was too much black, but it is *so* chic."

"One can never wear too much black," Bella replies.

"Is that Coco Chanel?" Marjie asks.

"What? No. Just a rule I live by."

"What do you think, Eddie?" Marjie asks, clearly enjoying building Bella up and cueing me in to say something nice. But I do not need to be cued; the monochromatic mannequin looks very stylish indeed.

"She is exquisite," I reply. "Madame Spider."

Marjie gives me a "you're so silly, Eddie" look while Bella grins.

A man about to enter the shop pauses when he sees the three of us staring up at the window.

"Er," he says, "am I all right to go in?"

"Right with you," I tell him and follow in behind. As we head into the shop, I overhear Marjie saying to Bella, "Would you mind giving me a hand with an outfit for next weekend? I'm going . . ."

My interest is piqued but the shop door closes on their conversation and I am engaged in assisting the man to find a T-shirt to wear to his boarding school reunion that "implies wealth." Good thing I bought my cheetah shirt before he came in.

Books

———◆———

I am extraordinarily excited about my lunch this afternoon. Sensationally excited. Sausages with mash and gravy from the pub on the corner—they found a polystyrene box for me to take it outside because the sunshine was too glorious to miss. Bella has a platter of sushi that she found in the discount section. Should one eat discounted supermarket sushi? I asked. She seemed to think so.

"Eddie," Bella says through a mouthful of her sushi.

"Yes?" I ask through my own mouthful of gravy mash, which is proving just as delicious as I'd hoped.

"What did you do before you retired?"

"Hm." I swallow. "Before the charity shop, I worked in academia."

"So you're Professor Eddie Winston?"

"Oh no, I was never good enough to be made a professor."

"Doctor then?"

"I did get my PhD, yes."

"This is so cool! What was your field? Have you written any books?"

"Linguistics. And just the one."

"Fuck. Off!" Bella says.

"Oh, it was only an academic book." I wave my hand at her. "It's probably out of print now."

"What was it about?"

"It was an analysis of some of the most famous romantic scenes from literature."

"Was it any good?"

"I'm probably not the best judge of that," I tell her. "I don't even have a copy. I think it had a pink cover. Reminded me of an ice cream sundae."

"Dr. Eddie Winson," she says. "Do you miss it?"

I think about this. "Not really. I enjoyed teaching my students, but the charity shop is much more fun."

A few days later, as I am sitting in Pigeon Park attempting to open a particularly tricky packet of nuts, something is placed on my knees. I recognize the dusty strawberries-and-cream cover with its abstract rectangles in the color of ice cream sprinkles at once. And in a black box near the top: "The Language of Love: Stylistic Analyses of Romance in Fiction. E. Winston."

"You were right," she says. "It's out of print but there are plenty of secondhand copies online."

"I never thought I'd see this again," I say, turning the page, and on the inside cover is the name "Gemma Neville, Cartmel College 1994," and then beneath her name in much more certain ink is "Ruby V. UCLAN, 1999," and beneath hers is "K." and something that looks like "McKinley from 2004, Warwick." All these people held my book in their hands. How wonderful.

"I haven't started it yet," Bella says.

"Oh, you don't have to read it," I tell her, given that I have no idea what is inside. I remember being very proud of the last line on the first page. I believe there's a pretty juicy analysis of a scene from *Othello*, but other than that, it's all crumbled into unimportance in my memory.

"I know I don't *have* to," she tells me, taking the book back and flicking through the oranging pages. I can see some passages are underlined, some are highlighted. A few paragraphs have little asterisks in biro drawn beside them. What a compliment that anyone thought my writing worth annotating. "But I'm going to anyway," she says. "You wrote a fucking book, Eddie. You should be really proud."

"Oh, I don't know."

"Stop that," she says. "Don't be bashful. Own it."

"And how would I do that?"

She thinks about this. "At the very least, tell Marjie. Get a copy for your flat. Read some excerpts to Pushkin."

"Oh, I doubt he'd have much patience for the humanities."

"Eddie, he's a poet!"

Keys

———◆———

The typewriter is a sea green. Or sea foam, I can't decide. The dust cover was in such poor condition, I was not expecting the typewriter to emerge from it in perfect condition.

The keys have yellowed with time, but when I put a piece of printer paper in, it types out a friendly greeting.

Hello, Eddie Winston

I wonder what words this typewriter has typed, love letters or court orders or song lyrics. I wish it could tell me, but now that we have greeted each other, it has fallen silent. My phone, however, has not. It buzzes in my pocket to tell me that Grace has sent me an email with a photograph attached. You're famous, Eddie Winston! she writes. And there I am, laughing, on the wall of an art gallery in Oxford, lit by an overhead spotlight.

You're the best one! x

Bella is searching through the rails to find me an outfit for Saturday.

"Let me see." She takes my phone from my outstretched hand and stares at the email intently. "You know, I think Saturday *might* be a date," she says.

"Do you really think?"

"I *do* think," Bella says, picking up a purple shirt, holding it vaguely near me and then thinking better of it and returning it to the rail. "I think she likes you."

"Oh." My face feels hot.

"It's good to be nervous." Bella turns and begins flicking through a rail of lightweight men's jumpers.

"Is it?"

"It means it matters." She pulls out a navy cable knit and tucks it over her arm for me to try.

"Suddenly, it seems so huge," I tell her. My mouth is dry. "Looking for love. What am I doing?"

"It's not as big as it seems," Bella says.

"It isn't?"

"Love is really just two people who can't keep away from each other."

Alora Winston

August 1966
Cagliari

Eddie is holding a map and turning it and his head at a ninety-degree angle. From her spot at the café table, she can't hide her smile. He peers closer at the map and then turns it upside down, confounded. He has reached a crossroads: The road straight ahead of him would take him to the harbor, to boats bobbing, to the morning sun dancing on the water. The road to the right would take him towards the town—the market, the bright fruits, the noise. The road behind him would take him back from whence he came. And the road to the left would take him to Bridie.

Come this way, she wills. *This way.* If he gets a little closer, she can call out his name. To do it now, she would have to bellow, and the other café patrons would turn, would look at her, would hear the excitement in her voice. They would be embarrassed for her, just as she is embarrassed for herself at how happy she is to see him.

Eddie takes a step towards the souvenir shop on the corner of the crossroads and the seller comes out and says something, but Bridie is too far away to hear. Eddie shows him the map and the man turns it to what must be the correct way up and Bridie is certain that Eddie is laughing. She holds her breath as the shopkeeper studies the map, then he places a hand on Eddie's shoulder and points to exactly where she is sitting. As though he knows.

And though, at first, Eddie is looking down the narrow alley-way, perhaps thinking of his destination, it is not long before he sees her. And he illuminates. Shaking the shopkeeper's hand, he picks a postcard from the closest rack and purchases it by way of thanks.

Then he takes off his hat and makes his way toward Bridie. She places her book back inside her bag.

Under the generous parasol above the table, the sun relents and Eddie sits down opposite her and sighs with relief. Bridie takes off her sunglasses and wipes away the sweat that has gathered on the bridge of her nose, hoping Eddie doesn't see.

"I ought to be in a paper on metonymy and synecdoche," Eddie says, glancing at his watch, "but I got lost." A man walks a bounding dog along the little side street where they sit and Eddie beams at it. "This is turning out to be much more fun, though."

The waitress—tall, tanned, and beautiful—comes and hands Eddie a menu. "Grazie," he says.

"Ah, English?" she asks. Even her voice is sweet.

"Guilty as charged," Eddie replies, raising up his hands as though the waitress is holding a gun.

"Then you must want tea?" she says, smiling, shielding the sun from her eyes. The black apron tied around her waist shows just how tiny she is. Bridie feels like a barge beside her.

"Far too hot for tea," Eddie says. He asks for an orange juice and Bridie orders another lemonade. When the waitress returns, she places their drinks and a small bowl of salted crisps between them. As she bends down, her name badge falls off and clatters across the patio. Eddie is out of his seat in an instant and picks it up.

"Alora," Eddie reads in quiet wonder under his breath as he passes it back to her.

Once she is gone—disappearing inside the shady doorway of the café—he says it again. "Alora."

Bridie watches Eddie staring into the middle distance. "Eddie?" she asks.

"I've never heard a prettier name," he says. "Alora. If I have a daughter, that is what I shall call her."

"Alora Winston," Bridie says, and she smiles. She can picture the name written in large, messy pencil on the front of an exercise book, she can hear it called on Prize Day at school, hear it ringing out across a ballet class. And she can picture too the little girl holding the hand of Eddie and the young woman who wins Eddie's heart. Alora's mother. She'll have long red hair. Pretty eyes. They'll live in a sweet house with ivy on the outside, a middle name for their first and only daughter. Alora Ivy. They'll have knitted throws on their mismatched sofas, books all yellowing on shelves in every corner. They'll retire to the sea, and Eddie and his red-haired bride will look out on the water with their aging eyes but they'll always see each other as they did when they first met.

And perhaps Eddie will remember Bridie, who by then will be just a lost acquaintance, and feel gratitude that she let him be free to find this love, to have the adventure of a lifetime. And Bridie will look the Father in the eye when he reads her her last rites and takes her final confession, because she was true to her word, honest to the promise made all shaky on a gray afternoon in 1954. She will have done what's right. That's all that she can have done. And Eddie will be happy. And Bridie will have been good.

God grant her the strength to release him.

A Second Letter Arrives

This letter too is addressed to "Captain E. Winston."

Eddie,

Thank you kindly for your reply and, if you'll permit me, what utter nonsense! Your visit will be no imposition at all. And I do insist you visit, you know. I have plenty of air miles but not another living person in the world who has letters written for my darling Elsie. And I simply must have them.

Now that I've convinced you, let us chat awhile.

Do you enjoy working in the charity shop? I do love a good rummage. The few charity shops we have on Corfu are not the same—they don't have the treasure hunt, jumble sale feeling of the ones I used to frequent in England. Many years ago, I bought a clutch bag in a charity shop in Ealing for an extravagant publishing gala. And when I opened it up on the night, I noticed a stain of what looked like soy sauce on the inside. I love making up stories for the things I buy secondhand, so I decided the clutch bag belonged to a violinist who had ended a showstopping performance at the Royal Albert Hall with a visit to one of those sushi restaurants where the food slides about on a conveyor belt. It made me like the bag all the more. Stories are my currency, you see, but I write under a pen name that requires at least two glasses of fizz for me to reveal.

Please do say that you'll stay. Tell me who you'd like as a guest and I'll make it so. Two guests if you wish. Bring the guinea pig!

Yours persuasively,

Emmeline x

Transparencies

———◆———

August 1966

"To conclude, the finding we have about gestural metaphor," the young woman says, slipping a new acetate onto the overhead projector, "is that the 'source domain' can exist in the gesture, while the 'target domain' exists in the speech."

Eddie is up next. He's going to present his doctoral thesis. If she came just for Eddie, it would be suspicious, so Bridie has been sitting in conference room B all morning, the only room with windows that do not open. There will be tentacles for the buffet lunch again, set out in the blazing sun. The thought turns her stomach.

There's a glamorous professor sitting in the row in front of Bridie, fanning herself with one of those hand-painted wooden fans that are sold in all the little tourist shops, and the movement of fanning herself is making all the dainty gold bracelets she is wearing clink against her gold wristwatch. She looks so cool and composed. Whereas Bridie can feel the back of her thighs sticking to the chair. Her locket is slimy with the sweat from her collarbone as she absentmindedly twists it forwards and back. Bridie resolves she will go to the shops this evening, when the night has cooled from the ovenous temperatures of the day, and she will become this glamorous woman. Of course, Bridie can never be her, but it is fun to imagine that she might emerge from a boutique dressed in black and suddenly chic, gold trinkets at her wrist. She will buy a fan, at the very least.

There's a ripple of applause and Bridie realizes the nervous young woman has finished her paper and joins in clapping. There's a shuffle of people on the dais and the chair says, "Next up we have Eddie Winston, doctoral candidate from the University of Birmingham." Delegates start standing up, leaving the room to attend a talk in one of the other parallel sessions. Bridie finds that she is holding her breath for Eddie, hoping people will stay. "Papers are being distributed," the chair adds, and stacks of paper make their way from the front, passed from academic to academic as though the delegates are children in primary school once again.

Once the majority of people in the room has left, a scattering of people enter, here just to see Eddie. She hopes it makes him feel proud. If you're not against a big name at a conference, it is all about the title and Eddie's is a good one, "Sealed with a Kiss: Fictional Representations of Love."

And then there he is, bow tie askew and making him look like a young man dressed up as his own grandfather. His face is a straight line of concentration as he turns on the overhead projector and the first sheet is illuminated on the wall. It says, simply and in his own handwriting, "Eddie Winston." The room looks up at this. "There's more," he says, and there's a ripple of laughter. And with that, Eddie Winston smiles his lopsided smile and says, "This paper is going to examine the literature of the kiss . . ."

He's made the audience laugh more in his fifteen minutes than the entire lineup has all morning. He's at ease in front of people. They're at ease with him. He is going to make a fantastic lecturer when he passes his PhD, she is sure of it. Much more approachable, less cocky than Alistair. More vulnerable too, she thinks, and as if the universe can hear her, a question is raised that is asked by kindly academics of novice speakers, "What inspired you to do this research?"

Eddie was expecting this one. "In my teenage years, I began researching kisses because I had not yet had my own first kiss," he says. "I wanted to know what Shakespeare and Brontë and Austen had to say about the matter, so that I might be better prepared."

It is an unflappably honest answer.

There's a pause and then a hand is raised and a brusque man who is someone important from somewhere far away asks, "And we assume that you are no longer in need of guidance?"

"*Well*," Eddie says, and there's another ripple of laughter as the chair claps his hands and says, "And let's call it a day there. I believe a delicious lunch is being prepared out in the courtyard. Let us once again thank Mr. Winston and all of today's speakers." Everyone rushes to collect their things and get down to lunch before there are only tentacles left. And Eddie catches sight of the overhead projector and realizes that he never changed the transparencies, so throughout his presentation he's had his own name projected beside him like the headliner of a West End show. He laughs, folding himself over. And that's the thing about Eddie Winston.

Gardens

———————◆———————

The bus winds its way through the grayer parts of the city. I sit with my knees neatly together, hands clasped. *Do not be nervous, Eddie*, the bus bell dings. And yet, my hands are determined to have a little quiver. The sun is doing her thing, lighting the office buildings and the expressway with all the possibilities of morning conveyed in her light. *It will not be like the date with Val*, I promise myself. Only the sun herself knows if it will be better or worse, but I know it will not be the same.

Stepping through the gift shop and out into Winterbourne is like walking into the Secret Garden, and I am Mary Lennox. It barely seems possible that I am only minutes from the city center. The bus and its squeaky brakes, its smell of body odor and diesel, suddenly seems so far away.

It is so green. I take a deep breath.

"It's beautiful in the mornings, isn't it?" Grace says, appearing beside me holding a takeout coffee cup.

The gardens are spread out before us, the grass carpeting down the hill towards a tree-lined walk where the branches stretch up to the sky. It is beautiful. And yet, it is Grace I am looking at now. Beneath her denim dungarees she is wearing a pink silk shirt beset with flowers and insects. Her hair is held in a neat bun at the back of her neck by a pink silk flower and every finger has a different ornate ring. Bella would absolutely adore this outfit. Madame Butterfly.

"You look very dashing," Grace says.

"The invitation said to wear something special."

"And you did." She reaches out and touches the sleeve of my silky shirt. "Are those leopards?"

"Cheetahs."

"What's the difference?"

"Cheetahs are slinkier."

Grace has a wheezing, joyous laugh and by eliciting it, I feel as though I've done something wonderful. From the top pocket of her dungarees, she pulls out an orange inhaler that is shaped like a seashell, blows out, clicks it, and breathes in.

"Are you all right?" I ask her.

She holds her breath but nods and smiles, placing her hand on the sleeve of my slinky, silky shirt again. And for a moment, I can think of nothing else besides her warm fingers on my arm.

After Grace breathes out and declares herself "all better," she asks me if I would like to walk with her among the gardens.

And there can be no other answer.

As we walk along the winding paths, dipping beneath the trees, in and out of shade, spotting industrious bumblebees paying visits to the flowers, we talk. We talk about everything: living in the city, bookshops and bumblebees, where squirrels go in the winter, getting older, staying young. She tells me about her ex-husband; I tell her about Marjie and the shop. She asks about my time at the university and I discover she guest-lectures on photography in Leicester. I tell her about Pushkin; she tells me her asthma prevents anything other than pet fish, though she does like the name Pushkin. As we make our second loop of the gardens, we reach the pond, with its huge lily pads and its arched wooden bridge. I remark to Grace how the surroundings look almost Jurassic. I can imagine that dinosaurs would drink here to cool off on a hot day.

"I've never been convinced," Grace says as we cross the bridge and stop at its apex, to look at the reflections of the trees in the water.

"Convinced?" I ask.

"First, they said dinosaurs were big, scaly beasts, and now they want us to believe they had feathers and were basically giant chickens. They need to make their minds up before they convince me."

"So you don't believe in dinosaurs?"

"I do not."

"And all the bones that they keep finding?"

"Someone somewhere is having a very big laugh."

I can't help laughing myself and Grace joins in, leaning over on the rail of the bridge and pulling out her seashell inhaler so she can breathe again.

We wander onwards. Watching as the day warms and people enter the gardens, families with children, students with heavy textbooks, older couples, just like us, who make a beeline straight for the tearoom. And I wonder as we wander why Grace's camera has not left the bag that is slung across her with its floral strap.

"This garden is beautiful," she says, "but it's people for me."

"People?"

"I have tried. Often. To photograph trees, flowers, beaches, parks, you name it. I can't do it. What I photograph has to have a soul."

"Trees have souls, in their own way," I say, looking up at the whispering branches above us.

"Do you think?"

"Eggcups too on occasion."

Grace gives me a look that tells me that she can't be sure if I am being serious or not.

"This shirt," I say. "Don't you think it has a soul?"

"It does when you wear it," she says.

I treat us both to a cup of tea and we sit on a bench at the edge of the terrace overlooking the gardens.

"Oh, look at them."

Set up on a bench beside a tree are two students, each with

a textbook open on their laps. They are holding hands but keep having to let go whenever one of them needs to turn a page. Grace studies them, eyes squinted, and I wonder if she is sizing them up for how they would look in a photograph. I wonder if she sees everything through a lens, imagining how she might preserve the moment. Portrait or landscape, color or black-and-white?

"And it all begins," she says, "with just one moment where something tips, from friendship into something else."

"You know," I tell her, "I've never known how somebody turns from a friend to a sweetheart."

"You haven't?" Grace asks.

"I've been trying to work out whether this is a date since you invited me on it."

"You have?" She smiles at me that same smile from the first day we met that seems to communicate how silly I'm being. "Eddie," she says, touching my knee, "I don't put my lucky flower in my hair for just anybody."

"Really?"

"You surprise me, though, Eddie," she says, leaving her hand there on my knee, my heart galloping. "You're a spark," she says. "I'd have thought you'd have swept a person or two off their feet in your time."

I shake my head.

"I've never been too lucky with moments," I tell her.

"Well, that's the thing," she says. "It does have to be the *right* moment."

I turn to her and realize just how she is looking at me. Her eyes are so twinkly.

My horse heart gallops faster. *This is it, Eddie, here we go!* it whinnies.

Grace puts down her tea and places her other hand on my hand, purposeful. Sure. Her hands are soft and warm. And I can hardly breathe.

Here we go, Eddie.

And then . . .

Between us comes a sound, a round sound, booming and large.

Ding

Ding

Ding

The chimes of the clocktower. Old Joe. He's half a mile away at the center of the university campus, and yet out he rings. Even here, among the flowers.

And I am no longer in the Winterbourne Gardens but standing beneath Old Joe's arches with Bridie, wearing a borrowed coat and looking into her eyes, the two of us standing far too close to each other. And the longing to be back there, to see her again, is physical. Right on the borderline between joy and pain.

I must have lingered too long. Because Grace's smile, almost imperceptibly, changes. And the grip of her hand on mine loosens.

I would give anything to be back there with Bridie. To have my chance again. To sweep her off her feet. I want to claw at the face of time, just to be back there with her.

"Are you okay, Eddie?" Grace asks.

I swallow. Just at this moment, I can't speak.

Grace takes her hand from my knee and picks up her tea. She is studying me.

"Old Joe," she says as she sups. "Is he a friend of yours?"

"Something like that," I tell her, and I find that I might very well be on the verge of tears.

The moment has passed. I don't know where it went, that moment of possibility, who it will find, who will fall into a kiss because of it, but off it went, passing between us and out into the blue sky. Grace smiles. She felt the moment pass too, I'm sure of it.

"Thank you," I tell her. "For a lovely day."

"You're very welcome, Eddie," she replies.

And I know we will not meet again.

five

———

the therapist shook my hand at the end of session six this
morning. "i wish i could see you more," she said, "but
unfortunately, there are lots of people waiting." it sounded
like she wanted me to feel guilty for all the other people
waiting, that i had taken up their space. i wanted to tell her
several things before i left, like that beige doesn't really suit
her, that she has more of a true winter color palette—she'd
look better in blacks and whites. i wanted to tell her that
paying to park in sparkbrook every other week was costing
my first hour's pay at work, i wanted to tell her i still hadn't
cried, so she had failed, but i also wanted to thank her
for trying. because she did try. she tried her best to fix me.
and she only had three hours to do it in. so i decided to
honor her efforts and as penance for not gifting her even a
single salty tear, i will finish the six letters that she asked
me to write to you. i didn't pay her anything, after all. i
didn't even like her that much. but i do feel like i owe her
something. so here is number five. and just know that i
think it's really rude that you still haven't replied to any of
them yet.

dear jake,

i don't think that eddie knows that marjie is in love
with him
    it's blindingly obvious to me
    maybe this is why he has never been kissed—
because he can't see the love right in front of him. it's

the way she smiled when i saw them dancing through
the shop window, it's the way she listens when he talks
    i went into the shop to help her dress the
mannequin in the window for birmingham pride when
eddie was on his date with grace
    "you love him, don't you?" i asked as we pulled on
the rainbow sequin leggings.
    "yes," she said quickly, immediately, seeming
relieved to have been able to tell someone. "but i'm
working on it"
    "you're going to tell him?" i asked
    "oh god, no," marjie said
    "then what are you going to do?" I asked her
    "i'm going to get over him," she said. "i'm online
dating"
    "are you sure?" i asked
    "if it was going to happen, it would have
happened. i got my hair cut a few months ago. i'm
ready to move on," she said
    "good for you," i told her
    "i don't think he's noticed," she said, and then a
look of concern clouded her face. "hold on, has he?"
she asked
    "oh, he's completely oblivious"
    she laughed. "i thought so. i prefer it that way,"
she said. "i won't make a fool of myself"
    "and you never thought about telling him?" i
asked
    "god no," she said. "it's been twelve years. if he
was even considering thinking of me in a romantic
way, it would have happened by now. i can't bear the
thought of being let down gently"
    we went out to the front of the shop to look at
her, our rainbow-clad mannequin—jazzy pants, i

think i will name her. over her pastel tie-dye t-shirt she's wearing a pair of butterfly wings that marjie found in the children's toy section and a pair of very convincing fake Ray Bans. if only there was some way to get paid for dressing the shop window mannequin for the rest of my life

"you are such a talent," marjie said. she says lots of nice things like that to try to make me feel good about myself. you can tell she's a mum. and a good one too

we went back inside and marjie flicked the kettle on

"how is online dating going?" i asked her

"pretty well," she said with a little smile

"oh yeah?" i spotted the mouse trap board game in the corner of the game section. the sticker said it's missing its boot piece, but how important can that be?

"you fancy a drink?" marjie asked

"i'll take anything," i called back, "except that beef thing"

she laughed. "peppermint okay?"

she rattled through the curtains with a tray with our mugs and a plate of biscuits on. i think it had been a slow saturday

"so the online dating?" i asked her

"i met someone actually," she said. "we're going on a . . . we are meeting in person next week." and she opened her phone and after a lot of swiping, showed me a photograph of a true silver fox

"fuck me," i said, "he's handsome. very vulpine"

"i know," marjie said worriedly. "i hope it's not one of those scams where i turn up and they steal my debit card"

i scrolled through the photos

he looks pretty real. there are a lot of photos of

him in smart winter coats in nice locations, one in a christmas jumper, one with a golden retriever, and one of him holding what looks like a beef pie. he might just be her soulmate

"i can be your wingman if you want," i told her. "i'll go with you to wherever the date is and if he turns up, i'll leave, and if he doesn't turn up, or if it's a bunch of thieves stacked on top of one another in a trench coat, we can tell them to get fucked and go and get cocktails"

"you're a star," she said

and i liked that but then i told her we had to talk about something other than men because this conversation would not have passed the bechdel test, and once i'd finished explaining the bechdel test to her, we concluded that discussing the bechdel test would probably allow us to pass the bechdel test

i don't know why i told you all of that

but it was a nice day, you know?

all things considered

today has been okay

bells x

Sala Settecentesca

The conference dinner is a grand thing. Or, rather, it is a piss-up masquerading as a grand thing. Somewhere midway through the night, Alistair has completely lost the run of himself. The bottle and a half of wine he drank during the dinner and speeches can't have helped. But now he stands on the dance floor while the jazz band plays, with his warm hands on the hips of a twenty-five-year-old research assistant from Sheffield, whispering in her ear. Bridie is watching, wordless, remembering what it feels like to have her husband's warm breath on her. Then, as though her imagination has manifested the experience, she feels someone's warm breath on her neck.

"You don't have to watch this." It is Eddie's voice in her ear, his hand lightly on her inner arm.

She looks at him and the kindness and pity that she sees there breaks whatever thing was keeping her from crying and she feels her face crumple.

"Come on," Eddie says, reaching out his hand to her. "Let's get you out of here." He leads her through the clusters of people, past the mostly abandoned dinner tables bearing forgotten cheesecakes and spilled red wine, and through a side door into the night.

Out in the fresh air, Bridie hears her own sobs and is surprised. She feels so distant from them. Perhaps the wine is kicking in, at last.

Eddie hands her the lilac handkerchief from his top pocket. It matches his bow tie.

She presses it over her face, so that he can't see her crying.

"I'm so sorry," she says, regaining some control over herself. She presses his handkerchief into her face. "I don't know why I'm crying," she says, resurfacing. "It's not like I didn't know."

A look that is almost guilt passes across Eddie's face. Or perhaps it is concern. Perhaps it's pity again. She feels pitiful, certainly.

"You knew?" he asks.

"Oh, for years."

Eddie turns. Beyond the path dotted with lights, the sea is somewhere. She wonders if he can hear it. She cannot, but perhaps Eddie can.

"Why do you put up with it?" Eddie asks, his back still to her, and it could sound like an accusation but from Eddie it is gentle. Like a request for the center piece of a puzzle that makes no sense without it.

He turns. She holds up her left hand to show him her ring, the gold dulled now from many years of never taking it to be polished. "Until death do us part," she says. But really, she ought to be holding up the gilded evidence of another man more important to her than her husband, Christ. It is Him, it is God, it is every priest who ever taught Sunday school or led Mass. It is her long-dead father and her very Catholic grandfather before him. It is all the men who have told her what to do with her life. And all she has to do is be faithful to the first man who chose her, no matter what that man might do.

The side door opens and two hysterically laughing men tumble out, one holding a bottle of champagne. Eddie turns and the two men make their way between Eddie and Bridie and down in the direction of the town.

Bridie runs her fingers under her eyes and they return to her covered in mascara.

"I can't go back in."

"I wouldn't ask you to," Eddie says. Then something like his normal affable expression reappears. "You know, Birdie," he says, "I missed Alistair's opening plenary because of the tentacles from the arrival luncheon."

"I missed it too," she says, though she does not say that she missed it because she took the bus to the beach and put her feet in the ice-cold sea, in a single, unnoticed act of defiance. She treated herself to an ice cream covered in strawberries and little bits of biscuit. And she watched the people play in the water and she didn't think.

"Ah," Eddie says. "The thing is, Alistair's plenary was held in the Sala Settecentesca and I have been absolutely dying to see that room. My guidebook says it is full of rare and beautiful books."

"Then I was a fool to miss it," she says.

Eddie takes a step towards her and whispers, though they are completely alone, "Shall we take a peek?"

Bridie Bennett and Eddie Winston ascend the steps along the old town walls. The heat of the day has not left yet, and the night is muggy with it. Bridie finds that she is a little wobbly as she lifts the hem of her red gown so that she doesn't trip over it. Was it two glasses of wine she had or three? Her legs are shaky and not from the effort of climbing the steps, but from the knowing that wherever they are going, she and Eddie are going alone.

Upwards they go and they walk along the quiet streets, among beautiful old buildings and doors sitting quietly in the night.

"Here we are," Eddie whispers as they arrive at a marble arched doorway. The door must sense good intention because it opens to let them through. As though they are invited in.

They creep inside, onto beautiful marble floors in black and white.

"Sala Settecentesca," Eddie says, reading a sign. "That's the one." The building is in half-darkness and they ascend a set of stairs.

She follows Eddie, noticing now how his shoulders look in his dinner suit.

When they reach the door marked "Sala Settecentesca." Eddie turns and looks at Bridie. Those eyes. She wants to look away but never stop looking.

"This feels a little clandestine, doesn't it?" he asks, and she doesn't know whether he means their sneaking into this old building when it is meant to be closed or the two of them being alone.

They pause for a moment more at the doorway. And Eddie reaches for the handle.

It is like a church. Full of quiet awe.

The ceiling rises high above them and along the walls, two stories high, on ornate cream bookshelves are hundreds and hundreds of books, every one of them wrapped in cream and white.

The room is cool and quiet, an oasis from the heat of the day. Wooden chairs are laid out in neat rows such that Bridie is surprised to see that at the top of the room there is not an altar, but a gilded globe that looks incredibly old and a grand piano. Music. And travel. Appropriate things to worship, she supposes.

"Well, my goodness," Eddie says, and he undoes his shirt collar and his bow tie and looks up.

He approaches a row of ivory books, their skins delicate and already damaged. He holds out his hand, fingers almost at the spines, but beneath is a sign in gold instructing: NON TOCCARE, PER FAVORE. Please do not touch.

"I won't," he says, as though the sign might be able to hear him.

As they walk around in the silence of the library with all these waiting words, letting the cool calm their synapses, Bridie and Eddie end up together, facing each other, right in the center of the aisle.

Bridie feels, all of a sudden, entirely sober. She looks up at Eddie; he is so close. He has a little fleck of something on his left iris; she has never been close enough to notice before. She is so busy wondering whether that speck is brown or green that she almost misses that he is looking at her in the same way as every man who has ever kissed her.

It is now, the thudding pulse in her ears tells her. He is going to kiss her. She can feel the heat coming from his chest. And she wants nothing more from the earth in this moment.

Only, Eddie deviates. He closes his eyes, he exhales, and he presses his forehead against Bridie's. The contact sends electricity through her. Her face so close to his. She feels his breath on her cheek. The faint smell of alcohol and something sweet. Her heart is beating so hard she is quite sure he will be able to hear it. Just this, their foreheads in contact, feels more intimate than any kiss. And then he pulls back. And he smiles at her, this young man she wants so badly, standing in front of all these beautiful books written in a language she can't read.

Eddie's hand finds hers.

"I won't," he whispers. "But gosh, how I want to."

He gives her hand a squeeze and takes a step backwards and then he walks away from all the words.

Part Three

Rain

———◆———

It is absolutely tipping it down. People scuttle past the shop holding their hoods over their faces, umbrellas turning inside out. Every so often a very wet person comes in and pretends to browse while glancing out of the window to see if the rain has abated. And when it hasn't, back out they go into the downpour. We sell three umbrellas in the morning and then the gloom of the rain must get around because by lunchtime it is quiet.

A ping on my phone is from Bella: **Tomorrow?**

Tomorrow, I reply. We are not ducks.

Our lunches are not scheduled or agreed upon in advance. To talk about it might be to break the very magic of my happening to have lunch in the park when she happens to turn up.

Marjie is at the doctor's for her arthritic wrist, poor thing, so I rattle through the bead curtain in search of lunch. Marjie stocks the kitchen cupboard, and the mini fridge, so I select a packet of Monster Munch and hope the unfortunate monsters' severed claws will hold me over until the rain stops.

Wiping my Flamin' Hot fingers on my trousers, I turn to the box that came in yesterday. It used to contain bananas, but now it contains the last earthly possessions of a lady named Gloria. Her grandson was checking his watch when he dropped off the box. "I've got a meeting, sorry," he said when I asked him if he would fill in the Gift Aid tax relief form. He did give me her name. Granny Gee, he knew her as, but Gloria Sweeney was her real name. "She was a widow for almost as long as she was married," he told me. "Grandad Jim was lost to the sea in 1989."

And with that, Gloria's grandson scuttled off in his squeaky-smart shoes.

Granny Gee's perfume was sweet and soft. As soon as I open the box, I can smell it. And inside, a cashmere jumper in a color that is neither pink nor cream, but somewhere in between. Then scarf after scarf, all silk and printed with different patterns. Driving gloves in black leather. A set of books on gardening. A jewelry box that's empty (based on her donations, I would imagine that Granny Gee's jewelry was too nice for her grandson to give away for free). Lucky Granny Gee, to have such nice things, I think as I pull out a buttery soft purple jumper. I hope her parting from this earth was soft too.

I'm placing the *RHS Complete Guide to Growing Roses* in the nonfiction section of the bookshelves when four black-and-white photographs slip out. And there she is. Granny Gee. Or, back then, simply "Gloria," as someone has written on the back of one of them. She's astride a moped, hair in a silk scarf, and with a smile that seems to betray that she is having a riotously good time.

Next, I find her in a blur at the Trevi Fountain, a patterned dress wasping in at her waist, sunglasses hiding her eyes, though she seems to be looking up at the photographer rather than the camera lens. Then she's on a beach, turning the camera on herself and a man with beautiful eyes who is kissing her bare shoulder. Then there they are again. Gloria and this young man whose eyes, though the print is black and white, appear to be a clear green or blue against dark lashes, seated at a café table on a square, the photograph taken from up high, I imagine by a waiter. And on the back of these photographs, Gloria has written his name, Vincenzo, and drawn a small heart. This gentleman is certainly not Grandad Jim, then.

And that is it. The entirety of Gloria and Vincenzo's love story. Perhaps she kept the photographs hidden from her husband so she could take them out and look at him, at those eyes, from time to time. The book about roses wasn't chosen by accident.

I carousel through the photographs again as though they might give up some more information this second time around. And they do. I notice that on the fourth finger of her left hand, Gloria is wearing her wedding ring. But Vincenzo's hand is unwed.

And I smile because I know that pain, just a little.

And, of course, I place the photographs in the lapel pocket of my jacket. I will keep these lovers safe. And when I take them out, I shall think of them and their Italian summer romance and wonder if she ever tried to find Vincenzo when Grandad Jim was lost to the sea.

And perhaps it is the misery of English rain that is still battering against the window. Perhaps it is the photographs of Gloria's unforgotten love. Perhaps it is my regret at the abandoned almost-kiss with Grace. Or the feeling that time is running out. But I pull out a pad of paper from behind the till. And I write:

Dear Emmeline,

I'm in!

Water

August 1966
Saint Thomas Catholic Church, Edgbaston

It has been a dull day at God's house.

Father Owen has had very little to do. The cleaner did not stop to talk, just muttered something in her indistinguishable accent and took her caddy of furniture polish and dusters and headed elsewhere. Perhaps home. Perhaps to another church. Perhaps she cleans all the chapels and churches in town? The thought is an alarming one. Father Owen resolves to ask her where she goes after cleaning the pews of Saint Thomas. It just won't do to share furniture polish with men of other *denominations*.

And then, nothing. Not a confession, not a prayer, not even a squeak from the family of mice that Father Owen is relatively certain live in the baseboard beside the baptismal font. He presumes they drink the water, make their insides holy. He wonders why he himself has not done this, for if baptismal water can bless without, perhaps it can bless within. Father Owen would like that; his stomach pain has become intolerable recently, especially at mealtimes. He'll eat even the simplest of things, an apple perhaps, some sausages with onion gravy, and then there they come, great waves of pain that send him rushing to what his grandmother euphemistically referred to as the "ladies' lounge."

He can't go to the doctor; his doctor has come to confession.

And how could Father Owen trust the voice that instructs him to remove his trousers and cough when that same voice has admitted to an affair with his receptionist, despite the wedding band the good doctor wears beneath the surgical gloves holding Father Owen's testicles. No, he can't go to the doctor.

The holy water arrives, distilled, in large bottles from a company in France. It used to be tap water that he held his hands over and blessed, but it was harder for Father Owen to believe that this liquid from Edgbaston's pipes could be anything divine. Filling a jug from the tap in the back room and then whispering an invocation to God to bless it didn't feel, well, *magical* enough. Now that he knows it is shipped from Lourdes, he can really believe. And if he believes, they will believe. That is what his favorite seminary teacher had said.

Father Owen walks over to the font. The baptismal water is rarely changed, has blessed the heads of countless babies, squealing and wriggling and mewling with little regard for the importance of the ordinance being bestowed on them. He dips a finger into the water lying still in the font. It is cool. In the heat of this summer day, that feels like a miracle. He presumes it is at the very least refreshing for the babies. Father Owen swirls his finger around in the water, making a figure eight. Eternity.

O Christ the Lord, from your pierced side, you gave us your sacraments as fountains of salvation.

Those are the words he must recite at baptisms, but he does not like them. *Pierced* puts him in mind of Jesus pricked in the side with a fork like a baked potato. It is a mental connection he cannot separate and it is undignified. He much prefers Isaiah 55: "Ho, every one that thirsteth, come ye to the waters." He makes his hand into a scoop and collects the cool, clear water on his palm and is raising the holy water to his mouth when there is a creak of the door. Quickly and self-consciously, he turns his palm over, and the water splashes back into the font. Father Owen wipes his hands on his trousers and turns. What the young man saw, if anything, he does not know. Father Owen realizes afterwards that it is because he is caught off guard that his first greeting to this young man is not as kind as it ought to be.

"Yes?"

"Oh, er, good morning," the young man replies, taking off his hat. He is tall, skinny, seems like he would topple over in a strong wind. He is wearing a bow tie that looks all wrong on one so youthful and he is clearly not a Catholic because he does not cross himself with the holy water at the door, does not genuflect in the aisle.

"How may I help you?" Father Owen asks, his hands still wet between the fingers.

"I'm wondering," the young man says, "if I could ask you some questions. About your faith?"

"Certainly," Father Owen says. "Please—" He gestures for this young man to sit on the front row pew and he drags over an altar boy's chair so he may sit opposite, his back to Christ's suffering on the altar.

"Father Owen Bishop." Father Owen extends his hand, and if the young man finds it amusing, as so many before him have, that this priest has the surname Bishop, he does not express it.

"Eddie Winston," the young man says.

"So?" Father Owen asks.

"You see, the thing is, I've been wanting to know—" The young man tumbles over his words, then pauses and looks at Father Owen. There's a fleck in this young man's blue eyes that looks like God picked up his green brush by mistake when he was coloring them in. Father Owen likes to think of God making people by the mixing of paints and colors because, if nothing else is evident from the world, God is an artist. Father Owen's own flesh is exactly the shade of his cup of tea when he puts a little too much milk in.

"What is heaven like?"

"Oh." Father Owen sits back in his chair. "Well, it'll be very nice," he says. "There'll be no pain, only peace, and . . . lots of light and of course we will be reunited with our loved ones."

"I see," the young man says, and he turns his hat over in his hands. Father Owen feels he may have undersold the afterlife.

"Heaven will be," he tries again, and casts around, "glorious and very . . ." He wants to say *heavenly* but that seems redundant. "Nice," he lands on again, his English teacher turning in his grave. "We'll all be very happy," he concludes, and while the *we* could refer to him and Eddie, it is meant to refer to Father Owen and his congregation, and Catholics the world over. But nobody else, of course.

The young man turns his hat over again, revealing a tired lining and something written just above the band. Father Owen wonders if there might be another convincing adjective he ought to have used but there is nothing so dull as talking about heaven.

"And," the young man says, "what is hell like?"

Father Owen's eyes light up. "Hell," he says, delighting in even saying the word, the feel of the *l* on his tongue as it meets the roof of his mouth.

When Father Owen was a little boy, a lonely child with no siblings to occupy his attention, his mother would send him out to play in their small backyard and he would crouch at the paving slabs and watch for ants, and when one came, he would pick it up and, one by one, pull its legs off. Then he would set it down and watch it struggle.

His father, a bookish man who drove a bus, told him that some people believe in reincarnation. Father Owen had asked his father who would be reincarnated as an ant and his father had replied somebody bad, probably. And so Owen had taken it upon himself to make sure that these bad souls had suffered. And it is the eight-year-old Owen who lives inside the priest now who delights in explaining to the young man the types of torture that will exist in hell, of how souls shall scream for mercy and regret their misspent lives on earth. Bones will break, eyelids will be ripped off, the screaming shall never cease. Around five minutes into Father Owen's description of hell, the young man is looking peaky

"Son," Father Owen says, having realized he has forgotten the young man's name, "are you quite all right?" Father Owen did not expect this fellow to have such a weak disposition.

"And adultery," the young man says. "The punishment for that is that you might go to hell?"

"There is no 'might' about it, my lad. Adulterers will burn in hell for eternity."

The young man nods, says, "I understand," in a hoarse voice, and then bends over and vomits into his hat.

Lucky

———◆———

Nobody is going to want this *Users' Guide to Microsoft Word 2007*. It's heavy enough to make a doorstop. How can there be this much to Word? Perhaps I don't know how to use it, after all.

It is the last item in a bag of donations from someone who was, I imagine, rather dull. There was a whole folder with clippings of news articles relating to a burst water main in Edgbaston in 1996, a set of VHS tapes on canals of the UK that totaled fifteen hours of content, and a book about the history of boules.

I pop a sticker for £1 on the guide and place it by the till, feeling very sorry for it.

"I'm just not sure about this one," Marjie calls from behind the dressing room curtain. "It feels a bit . . . much."

"There's no such thing as a bit *much*," Bella says as she riffles through the pile of clothing Marjie has brought from home.

"Sam seems quite casual in his profile picture," Marjie says. There's a lot of ruffling behind that curtain that would suggest that Marjie is putting on an incredibly difficult and complex ensemble.

She comes out from behind the curtain and she looks fantastic. Marjie's usual long skirt and baggy cardi and pen tied around her neck with a green ribbon are gone and she's wearing skinny jeans and a black top that flares out at the elbow and makes her look like a fantastic bat.

"Yes," Bella says, simply.

Marjie turns to face the changing room mirror, and adjusts the top, moves the waistband of her jeans up.

"I haven't worn jeans in about thirty years," she says. She tilts her head, observing and studying herself. I can see that she is pleased with what she sees, but she's not willing to admit it yet.

"What do you think?" She turns to Bella, looking for confirmation that what she sees in the mirror is good.

"Come on now, Marjie, I think we both know you look amazing," Bella says.

"This Sam is a very lucky man," I tell her. Marjie beams.

"Oh," Bella says, rooting around in her bag as she's about to head back to work. "I have something to donate." She pulls out a copy of a book in strawberries and cream colors.

"Thank you," Marjie says. And she inspects the book further, turning it over. "I don't think I've seen this one before." And then she laughs. "Oh look, Eddie, this author has the same name as you."

"Fancy that," I say, giving Bella a look.

"I might give it a read," Marjie says. Bella gives me a wink.

A Plane Ticket Arrives

A plane ticket arrives.

Mr. Eddie Winston will be sitting in seat 47F on a plane bound for Corfu and *Miss Isabella Williams* will be sitting in 47E beside him.

Emmeline has written on pink notepaper paper clipped to the tickets,

See you on August the 19th.
I'll be the one in the big hat. x

"I think she's the one," Bella says as I hand her the ticket in exchange for a packet of giant salt and vinegar Hula Hoops.

"*Emmeline?* Are you sure?"

"Are you not?"

"I quite honestly hadn't thought of it."

"Eddie!" Bella says, laughing.

"What?" I ask her, crunching on a hoop. "Should I have been thinking that?"

"I think you and Emmeline were destined to meet."

"We were?"

"The letters you found for Elsie? Her reply? It all seems like it aligned at the right time for you to fall madly in love with Emmeline."

"Gosh" is all I can say about that.

six

dear jake

when i used to dream of you, it was this frantic thing
  i was trying to reach you
  or you were trying to reach me
  bobbing around in the ocean, i could see you and then
not, pushing against the waves to find you
  searching for you in a crowded shop, thinking i saw you
and then finding it was just someone who looked like you
  being told that you would be at a party and then looking
everywhere and not finding you
  but last night i dreamt of you
  and it was calm
  and there you were
  we sat on a bench in a clearing between some trees and
looked at the stars
  and it was quiet
  we were together
  but there was no panic
  no desperation
  i was there
  you were there
  you weren't going anywhere
  we had all the time in the world
  to just be
  i could feel the warmth of your arm beside mine so
vividly it felt real
  it was peaceful.
  like you were coming by to say,

hi
don't forget me
let's for a moment
or for as long as your subconscious can generate me
be together
sit beside me, my old friend, there is so much to say

Congratulations

————◆————

November 1967

A deep and sad thought settles in Bridie's mind as the doctor begins congratulating her.

It is already too late.

"Twelve years of marriage, but you got there in the end," the doctor says, as though this is the result of perseverance and hope and not an accident of fate.

"Congratulations, Mrs. Bennett. A hearty well done." He shakes her by the hand. "You stuck at it. And now here we have this happy conclusion." He smiles a ruddy smile at her. "Fortitude!" he says, as though the word has just occurred to him. As though Bridie is relieved, not devastated. She twists her locket between her fingers, twirling it back and forth and wondering what is wrong with her heart.

He hands her pieces of paper and makes her a midwife appointment.

She feels so guilty for how she feels that she attends Thursday Prayers on her lunch break, forgetting she was meant to collect Alistair's books. So, she returns to the library in the evening, the bright lights of the humanities wing contrasting with the darkness of the night outside.

P.299.H66.C85 is the last book she is looking for. Why must it all be so obscure, this world? Even looking for books is a coded mission, could they not just be alphabetical? She gets onto her knees and is met with P.299.H66.C but there is no 85. She stands up, a rush of blood to her head. She rounds the corner of the shelves. She will have missed the train home now. She will have to walk. She keeps running her finger along the spines. The backs of all these authors, waiting to be tickled by a stranger into opening.

The gray metal stacks don't suit the room. With its old wooden floor and high ceiling, air heavy with all the knowledge that has risen up and then, finding the intricate lead windows closed, has had nowhere to ascend to so hangs about making the room feel dusty.

There it is. She pulls the book off the shelf.

And then there is a cough.

He is summertime, Eddie. Even now, in the coldest, most despairing months of winter. Wrapped up in a giant blue scarf so thick around his neck that he looks like a tiny turtle emerging from a sky-blue shell.

His face illuminates upon seeing her. And she feels guilty and protective of it. *This is mine*, her heart says. *I want it*, says her greed. And the longing, accompanied with the knowledge that he cannot be hers, is what makes the first tear fall.

There is to be strictly no talking in the humanities room. Eddie steps towards her and for a moment, her instincts dance against each other. He takes the books from her hands and tips his head as if to say "follow me." And she does, to the large tables in the center of the room. It is not a busy time. Night surrounds the library. Only one or two students are studying, books open, pens a-scribbling.

Bridie sits and sniffs, holding her index fingers beneath her eyes.

Eddie sits opposite and pulls a folded piece of paper and a pencil from his top pocket. He writes for a moment and then slides the paper over to Bridie. In the silence of the library, even the sound of the paper sliding across the table seems huge. Despite all evidence to the contrary, Eddie has written to ask her,

Are you all right?

Bridie has managed to stop the tears now. She sniffs hard, tries to steady herself. Eddie slides the pencil across the table. As she picks it up, she looks at him. His eyes. She drinks it in, how he looks at her. This longing, this warmth, this comfort. It is all the sweeter because she knows it will change. It has to change. And it does change as she writes in shaking hand the two words and slides the paper back to him,

I'm pregnant.

Somewhere in his busy schedule of conferences and meetings and extramarital affairs, Alistair found the time to take Bridie to dinner. To buy her the nice wine. To run his foot up the inside of her calf under the table. And her fury at his numerous infidelities, which had turned to tiredness, and had eventually become a gray numbness dissipated at his touch. There he was, his attention undivided; he worked hard to make her laugh, he stroked his moustache when ordering, which he only did when he was nervous. He refilled her glass, he listened when she spoke, he touched her hand across the table. They were out across the city somewhere, all the other women, waiting for him to return a phone call, waiting for his thoughts, his answer, his body, but she had him. She. Bridie. Who was two sizes too big for the dress she was wearing, which was making her breasts swell out the top of the neckline, and being so exposed had made her self-conscious when they arrived at the restaurant, but now that she was three glasses of wine in, it made her feel alluring.

He was hers again for an evening. There was nowhere else he wanted to be. There was no checking of his watch. There was no evident purpose to the meal: it was not her birthday nor their anniversary, nor Valentine's Day. It made her feel chosen. Special.

He smelled the same, as he lay on top of her. The expensive

aftershave and his smell. Alistair's. Not sweet or sour, just the smell of his skin.

If a child should come from a night, it was a good one.

The next morning, he stroked her hair, lying naked on his side, and he smiled when she opened her eyes. "I forgot to say last night," he said, "I've been offered a post in Vienna for the summer school."

And she tried to swallow. "How long?"

"Just six weeks. You'll have the house to yourself. That'll be nice."

"But—"

"Don't make me feel bad," he said, the tension making his jaw pulse. "It's a great opportunity. Professor Ghio is running it."

It was over. The attention, the warmth, the charm. Bridie rolled onto her side, gathered her dressing gown, and wrapped it tightly around herself.

"I need to start working on the plenary," he said, more to himself than to Bridie. She stood, slipped her slippers on, and, feeling heavy, went downstairs to make toast.

Greetings

———◆———

Emmeline wasn't exaggerating about the big hat.

It's huge.

WINSTON AND WILLIAMS, her sign reads in neon pink high-lighter. With a little drawing of a pirate beside it. She has very nice swirly, swoopy writing. Her nails peeping out in the front of the sign are incredibly long. Like those of a sloth, except they're painted in pink and each finger has a gemstone stuck on it. Her tan might be real, but it looks very fake, and her hair can't decide if it's bright blonde or white with a bit of yellow, but it's shining all the same.

"You came!" she says, dropping the sign to the floor and hugging a surprised Bella in a tight embrace and then pulling me in too. She smells incredible. Expensive. The kind of perfume that probably costs hundreds of pounds a bottle. We don't get anything that nice donated to the shop. It's mostly half-used Britney Spears perfumes.

I reach into my pocket to return Elsie's letters, but Emmeline puts her hand on my hand. "Oh, let's wait," she says. "We ought to do it with a little ceremony, don't you think?"

I duly return Mr. McGlew's words to my pocket.

Emmeline takes my suitcase for me. "We shall!" she says, even though nobody has said, "Shall we?" And Emmeline sets off at a swift pace ahead of us.

"Oh wait," Bella says, just before we reach the automatic doors through which we can see Emmeline making haste towards the car park. "I have a present for you." She tips her heavy shell suit-case onto the floor with a thud and opens it. Her clothes are all smooshed and mixed around but from within the chaos she pulls out her red love-heart-shaped sunglasses that I have been admiring for weeks and then pulls out another pair, exactly the same as hers, and places them in my palm. They are fantastic.

Walking through the airport doors out into the blinding sun-shine, wearing heart-shaped sunglasses with Bella by my side, is wholeheartedly the coolest I've ever felt. And probably will ever feel. We walk as though an incredibly funky soundtrack is playing, though there is never any music playing when you want there to be.

"Wow," Bella says as we pull up in front of Emmeline's house in her yellow VW Beetle ("I like other road users to see me," she'd said). And I agree. Emmeline's home is audacious. There's an infinity pool at the front and, behind that, a patio with an awning covered in purple wisteria that is being attended to by a group of diligent bumblebees. The house is two stories and made of old stone, and each window has its shutters flung wide open.

It is certainly an upgrade on our usual lunches in Pigeon Park, sitting beside Emmeline's glistening pool under a gigantic sun um-brella that must have been made by the same designer who created Emmeline's huge hat, the table laid out with Greek salad, breads, and meats.

"I wasn't sure what you'd like," Emmeline says, "so I got a little of everything. If you haven't had Greek salad before, you simply must." She offers me the pitcher of frozen margarita.

"This is amazing," Bella says, holding out her glass towards Emmeline's pitcher.

"You're of age, aren't you?" Emmeline asks her, frowning.

Bella laughs. "I'm twenty-four."

"It's your skin, dear. Makes you look like a newborn baby. You must cherish it."

Emmeline pours Bella a margarita right to the top and then settles into her chair. "To new friends." She raises her glass.

"New friends," we agree.

"Seriously though, this house," Bella says.

"I have been very blessed with my work," Emmeline replies. "When we bought this place, it was nothing like what you see now—no pool, no second floor. Once my husband had left me for his business partner, and my son, Mikey, went back to the UK for university, all I had was time, and I decided I wanted to live somewhere suitably fantastic."

"Well, it is certainly that," I agree.

"So now, I spend most of my days writing and have the occasional visit from Mikey and his fiancée. She's Swedish. The legs on her—you wouldn't believe."

"And what do you write?" Bella asks.

"It's mostly Mills and Boon."

Bella illuminates. "Anything we'd have read?"

"Oh, I doubt it. My most recent novel was about a countess who falls in love with a stable hand."

I nearly spit my margarita out. "I've read it!" I cry.

"No, you haven't," Emmeline says.

"*Saddle of Desire*!" I tell her. "It ends with the showdown between the stable hand and the lord of the manor in the hot tub!"

Bella pulls a face that seems to exclaim, *What?*

Emmeline laughs. "Well, then, Eddie, it seems that you and I were destined to meet."

Bella gives me a knowing look over the top of her heart-shaped sunglasses.

The Last Letter He Sent Her

We've come down to the water.

I'm a little tingly from the champagne. Emmeline has brought the bottle with us.

The waves are coming in, sparkling in the last of the light.

We arrange ourselves on the sand. I have none too much of an idea of how Emmeline would like the handover to take place, save that she said she wanted to do it with a little ceremony.

Bella is watching us both with a mixture of curiosity and amusement.

"Right," Emmeline says.

"Are you ready?" I ask her.

She nods. "I'm ready."

I take Mr. McGlew's letters from my pocket.

I pass them over to Emmeline.

Everybody is quiet, except for the ocean: she continues to whisper.

Emmeline opens the first envelope and pulls out the very first letter he didn't send.

She stares at it for a moment and when she blinks, two tears tumble from her eyes.

"Em?" Bella asks. "Are you okay?"

"Would you read them, dear?" Emmeline hands the envelopes to Bella, who looks alarmed at being given such a significant responsibility. "Please?" Emmeline adds, and so Bella clears her throat, opens the first letter, and reads. She has a beautiful reading voice. Clear and kind, as she reads the words William meant for Elsie. When she reaches the last letter he sent her, I advise Bella to look again inside the envelope and she finds the poem.

Bella reads, quietly now,

I would return to the forest
again and again with my axe,
never resting,
so that you might live forever.

A wave sweeps towards us and, for a moment, the whirl of the water is the only sound.

Emmeline is crying, wiping tears on the sleeve of her blouse. Bella replaces the letters into the envelopes and hands them back to her.

"I didn't love my sister well," Emmeline says, and she holds up a hand as though I am about to say something unfounded and conciliatory to her. "No," she says, "it's true, I didn't. But it is nice to know that she was loved like that by William. Even if she didn't know. There is no limit on love. I am glad to know she had more than even she knew."

"He really loved her," Bella agrees.

"These will be precious to me forever," Emmeline says, holding the crumpled envelopes to her chest. "Thank you, Eddie. Thank you both. Sincerely." Then she breathes in. "Right. Shall we get home and pop some fizz?" She gestures to the road where her yellow Beetle awaits us, and we ascend back into the heights, to raise a glass to William and Elsie, wherever they are now.

Fire

◆

Captain Thomas Wainright was a wrong 'un. A violent, dangerous, volatile man. Everybody knew it. Everybody feared him. And those who didn't quickly paid the price for their hubris. The men who survived being aboard his crew to the end of a voyage would shudder about their time on board the *Saint Marie* and swear to God and the bright blue sky, "Never again." And yet, Duchess Florentine's arrival in the port of Cabot Cove brought about a change in the dark soul of this man, such that by their third meeting, he swore to her that he could not continue to live without her as his wife and they shared an incredibly steamy kiss in the barrel store beneath the tavern. And by the time the Duchess, dressed in white lace and carrying a bouquet of tropical flowers, walks across the sanded beach to pledge the rest of her life to this rugged, chisel-jawed pirate, I find myself unable to breathe until the ring, a once-cursed emerald looted from the bottom of the ocean, is placed upon her finger.

I close the book and place it on the table beside my sun lounger. And I close my eyes against the sun, which is still dazzling even behind my love-heart sunglasses. The warmth surrounding me, the sun on my skin, and the sound of water lapping in the pool. I can't help but surrender to it.

"What did you think?" Emmeline asks, her flip-flops announcing her emergence from the kitchen with a jug of iced water.

"Hats off," I say, "and bravo. What a book!"

Bella, who has borrowed Emmeline's giant hat and is reading a book that she assures me is fiction but is at least a thousand pages and looks like a textbook, looks up. "Hats?" she asks.

Emmeline laughs. "Don't worry, it is yours for the weekend It suits you so well. You have that neck. Have you ever danced?"

"Only when drunk."

I hand the book back to Emmeline. "I love a romance, but this one truly had it all. Pirates, cursed jewelry, passion, a tarantula."

"You'll love what I'm working on now, then," Emmeline says, sitting on the sun lounger beside me.

"Tell me there's a sequel," I implore her.

"There might just be," she says with a wink. "Let's just say the soothsayer wasn't completely successful at removing the curse from that emerald . . ."

Beneath the huge hat, I can just see Bella's shoulders rising and falling with the giggles. It's how I imagine she might have laughed at the back of a maths lesson, or in a school assembly, when she wasn't supposed to be laughing. She is so light here.

When the sun has set and we've eaten pizza from Emmeline's outdoor oven and Bella and I have done the dishes (despite Emmeline's protestations), we gather in the darkness around the fire pit. Emmeline offers us marshmallows and sticks. "I've been dying to use this thing to toast marshmallows," she says, "but it seems a little sad to toast marshmallows by oneself."

Bella nods. "There are some things you just can't do on your own."

"It is hard to be by oneself," I agree. "Have you ever thought about getting a pet?"

"Oh no, I would forget to feed it. I was a bad enough mother to my son, and I have no intention to repeat the experience." Emmeline laughs loudly.

"Tell me," she asks once she has composed herself, "are either of you in any romantic entanglements at the moment?"

Bella fumbles with her phone to avoid the question.

"I am actually on the lookout for love at the moment," I tell her. "I was a bit of a late bloomer, you see, and—"

"I was a *very* late bloomer too!" Emmeline interjects excitedly.

"I can't imagine that," Bella says.

"Oh, I *was!*" Emmeline says, as though she is just mortified. "I was a little chrysalis and it took me many years to flap, flap, flap." She makes butterfly wings with her hands and raises them up as her butterfly takes to the night.

"I doubt you were as late as me," I tell her, taking a bite of molten marshmallow.

"Try me," she says. "I was *twenty-three* years old before I even had my first kiss." She says it as though the word *twenty-three* is music that must be sung, emphasis on each syllable.

"I'm ninety," I tell her.

And her expression changes as she comprehends my meaning and then says, "You win, then, Eddie. You also win the best anecdote at this table thus far."

"I haven't told an anecdote."

"No," Emmeline says, "but you are about to." Her eyes sparkle.

I look at Bella for support, but she tilts her head to one side curiously. "To be honest, Eddie," she says, "I am curious about Bridie."

"If you don't mind sharing," Emmeline says. She refills my wineglass with more sangria.

"Now, where would you like to begin?"

I begin at the beginning, of course. At the University of Birmingham in the autumn of 1965.

Three Rings

———◆———

The telephone in the hallway is ringing.

"Leave it," Alistair calls. "It's just my brother giving me three rings for his flight back from Portugal."

Except it does not end at the third ring. The telephone continues to four, five, six. Alistair is up and out of his armchair, newspaper dropped to his feet.

From the kitchen where she stands observing potatoes boiling alive, and eating the cheese intended for dinner because she simply cannot eat enough salty things right now, Bridie can hear, "Yes, no, of course, it's not an imposition at all, I'm glad you called. Yes, I do, that is . . . fantastic . . . Thank you. And the salary? Mm-hmm I see, well . . .." and then he must turn away from the hallway door because she can't hear the rest.

Eventually, just as the steam from the potatoes is beginning to make her face sweat, Alistair appears in the kitchen doorway looking flushed and elated. "I only went and fucking got it!"

He got it. What? The plenary paper? It can't be that—he wouldn't be so excited, and it seems even too big a reaction to relate to the edited volume he is proofing at the moment. It can't be. Oh God.

He swoops towards Bridie, presses his body against her, leaving a gap for the emerging bump, takes her hand in his and makes them dance, arms raising up and down like they are doing the tango. "Cambridge, here we come!" he sings at her, and when he lets go, he says, "You won't believe the salary, Bridie, it's absurd!"

And he disappears into the living room. She can hear clinking as he gets out the champagne glasses and one of the bottles of champagne he saves for when he is celebrating himself.

She manages to masquerade her tears as happy ones. The potatoes overboil and they do not eat them.

The Old Town

———◆———

The thrill of being somewhere else. Somewhere that is not my home or the charity shop or Pigeon Park, but somewhere completely new. It has enlivened my bones.

That is how I feel as we drive along the winding and steep Corfu roads. Emmeline's yellow Beetle has one of those scented things hanging from the rearview mirror that makes the whole car smell like bubble gum.

It is odd being driven by Emmeline, a person so fanciful and loud. She's very quiet when she's driving and I'm glad of it because the road twists and turns, taking dives down steep hillsides and then chugging back up again. The air con is blasting and it feels like we are pootling along in a little yellow fridge.

"I'm sorry I can't spend the day with you today," Emmeline says as we stop at a set of traffic lights. "My editor likes to go through his notes over Zoom and he is a fantastic editor but incredibly thorough. He says he has some issues with the lore around the squid king, so I think it will be a long one."

From my position in the middle of the back seat, I spot Bella pressing her lips together to try to stifle a smile. If she gets the giggles now, I will go too, so I am thankful when Emmeline asks her to fetch the road map from the glove box as three cars in succession beep their horns at Emmeline for lingering at the traffic lights.

She pulls up in what I am quite sure is not a parking bay and says, "Have fun, you two!" waving as she rejoins the flow of traffic to a chorus of beeping horns.

Bella and I walk the narrow alleyways of the old town, looking up at laundry that hangs between the balconies of apartments, wondering about the agreements that exist between the neighbors on opposite sides and how they reel the clothing in at the end of the day. We browse in touristy shops. We stop for a coffee, we fuss the mangy stray cats that come looking for crumbs. The heat is beating down on us and I am grateful for my hat or my remaining wisps of hair might have ignited.

We walk, gloriously directionless down endless narrow alleys and come across a tour group gathered outside a church, all shady and cool, listening to their tour guide who is holding a sky-blue umbrella and counting them, like a mother cat making sure she doesn't lose her kittens.

Bella and I stand just far away enough that it doesn't look like we are trying to steal the tour, but close enough that we can hear that this church is named after Saint Spyridon, the patron saint of Corfu. The bell tower is the tallest bell tower of the Ionian islands and is something something something. The microphone crackles. "Saint Spyridon is known as the Keeper of the City."

The tour guide tells her gathered kittens and Bella and me that the body of Saint Spyridon is held within the church and though he has been dead for over a thousand years, his body has not decayed.

"It is incorruptible," she says, which I suppose is a good quality for a saint.

"At night," she continues, "he wanders the world working wonders. And so the slippers he wears upon his feet become tired and used."

There are murmurs of amazement among the tourists. How fantastic they seem to find it that on any given night, wherever you might be, the dried-out corpse of Saint Spyridon might appear and perform a good deed for you. Like repairing your cracked phone screen or letting you into your house when you've locked yourself out.

"His body is stood upright twice a year so that his slippers might be changed," she says.

If the gathered tourists find the idea of refreshing the footwear of a thousand-year-old corpse as macabre as I do, they do not show it.

Someone in the crowd raises a hand and the tour guide gestures to him. How quickly we all become schoolchildren again when the conditions are right.

"The bells will ring again at"— she checks her watch—"one o'clock, but do not worry," she says with a wry smile, "though we move on, we will still hear them!" The group shuffles onwards down the narrow alleyway with their backpacks bumping into other passersby, taking photos on their phones as they go.

Bella and I go through the side door into the church. It is quiet and cool and so ornate.

The only sound is the shuffling feet of the other tourists, who, like us, are not looking at the saint's body in its baroque coffin, but instead looking up. The ceiling is a gallery, the pictures painted, gilded and beautiful.

Bella is craning her head, looking up at the artwork.

"The last time I was in a church," I whisper, "I threw up in my hat."

She pretends her snort of laughter was a sneeze.

"Bless you," I tell her.

We make our way out of the church and back into the alleyway. Opposite the church door is a shop selling icons of Saint Spyridon and other religious artifacts and lots of slippers with brightly colored pompoms on the toe. The alleyway is busier now, bustling with tourists milling in and out of the row of shops. We find ourselves in the middle of it all when we hear, clear as a bell above the hubbub: "Jake!"

Bella turns.

It is a woman's voice. She is not afraid; it is a songlike call as though she is playing hide-and-seek. Which I suppose Bella and Jake are playing now too.

"Jake!" she calls again.

The young woman is standing with an empty pushchair, smiling indulgently. "Jakey!" she shouts again.

A little blond-haired boy runs out of a souvenir shop. He's wearing dungaree shorts and sandals. He runs to his mother and jumps into the stroller.

"There you are, gorgeous boy," the woman says to her son as she clips him in, brushing the bright blond hair from his eyes.

His father follows behind, coming out of the shop with a pair of slippers with bright pink pom-poms on the toes and handing them to the woman with a kiss on the cheek.

Bella smiles at me, seeing that Jake has been found, but it is an incredibly sad smile.

And then, from the spire of the old church above us, a bell.

And then another.

And then another. It's a sharp clanging sound, like an alarm clock urging us to awaken. *Ding ding ding,* the high note clangs and the lower note booms.

The sound fills the alleyway—it is so loud that it hurts my ears. I check my watch: it is twenty past twelve.

The bells are not supposed to be ringing.

And yet, the bells ring.

High notes and low notes pealing and it sounds urgent, like they have something pressing to communicate. *Arise, arise! It is time!*

Bella is standing very still amid the hubbub of people and this urgent, clanging noise.

Here it is. Her sign.

"Bells," she says.

She looks at me.

And finally, finally, Bella is able to cry.

A Goodbye, of Sorts

April 1968
Edgbaston

She left the photographs in her office on purpose so that now that Alistair has completed his leaving lectures and leaving parties and leaving drinks and her job has quietly ended too, she has an excuse to return to the university and see Eddie one last time. Alistair doesn't grumble when she abandons their half-packed house to return to campus. Perhaps because she has started waddling now as she heaves herself and the baby within her from place to place, he even offers to drive her himself.

He's midway through cleaning out a box of old university papers from his undergraduate years and he's found himself unable to continue without reading each one and making comments on the marker's assessment. "Unfair," he has said several times, and "this is better than I remember it." It is as though he is an archivist in the story of his own life. He finds himself so fascinating. "This should have been a first," he says for one and places it in a separate pile. What he is planning to do with them, or what meanings the piles have, she doesn't know. The movers arrive in two days' time, but he will likely be in exactly the same position when she returns home.

Bridie tells him she'd like the walk. And walk she does, quickly, knowing that Eddie's lecture starts at eleven, so he will likely be arriving in the building at ten forty-five. If they are to bump into each other, she needs to be in the foyer before him. Her feet are so big now. Squished up against the bars of her sandals, spilling out like meat around the butcher's string.

Campus is oddly quiet. She is not wearing a watch, so she asks the time of Old Joe's face and she is not late.

But the arts faculty foyer is empty.

Eddie is not there. Nobody is. Then she remembers. It is reading week. And the students are all at home, doing anything but reading. And the lecturers are sleeping.

It is too late. She will not get to see him one last time.

She goes to twist her locket between her fingers, before remembering it is gone. Slipped silently from the bedroom mantelpiece where she lays it each night into one of the boxes of bric-a-brac they were donating to the Salvation Army, driven off in Alistair's car.

When Eddie saw her without it for the first time amid the hubbub and noise of Alistair's farewell drinks, he offered to accompany her to the Salvation Army shop to ask for it back. But Bridie told him she would not be searching for it.

And when he asked her why she wouldn't search for this thing that she loved so dearly, she told him, "Because looking and not finding it would be worse than not looking at all."

This feels true now.

Bridie makes her waddly way down the corridor and unlocks the dark mahogany door. Her office is empty now, all the files and folders moved into the assistants' room, as the four of them will be subsuming her role, as though what she did was so inconsequential it can be easily divided between four young girls straight out of secretarial college. Her kettle and mugs are gone, everything that would suggest she spent the past ten years working here is gone, except for the row of gray framed photographs on the windowsill. And, Bridie notices, with a little thrill, a small piece of paper on her desk.

When Spring, Nature's Beauty,
And the burning summer have passed,
And the fog, and the rain,
By the late fall are brought,
Men are wearied, men are grieved,
But birdie flies into distant lands,
Into warm climes, beyond the blue sea:
Flies away until the spring.

It is the goodbye he couldn't say. The writing energetic, the words not his own. Borrowed from Alexander Pushkin.

The handwriting is squiggly in fine black ink.

It is a love letter.

And it is a confession.

Bridie retrieves the note that was slipped beneath her door two years ago from the back of the framed photograph of her and Alistair smiling on the Seine. Her in that hat.

your husband is sleeping with one of his students

It is the *y* that is the real giveaway, the way its tail darts off to the left at an almost right angle.

Eddie.

He thought she did not know. That she ought to be warned. He was trying to save her. He was trying to free her. He was knowingly hurting her.

But she will not accept it. She refuses to believe that Eddie could be anything but good. She has to preserve him perfectly. So she tucks the poem into her pocket, to be examined on a better day.

seven

—◆—

thank you for the bells.
 eddie told me to listen and i've been listening
 you made sure i was listening
 thank you for that
 for letting me know that it's time.
 those bells
 the sound wasn't pretty or sweet
 it was more like a fire alarm
 "it's time, bells. wake up!"
 so, here we go . . .

 dear jake,

i've written you six letters
 this will be number seven. a bonus, you lucky
thing.
 this is the last one
 emmeline has procured me a bottle. it looks like it
used to contain some really expensive champagne
 but now it holds six letters written to you
 the therapist never told me where to send them, so
into the ocean they'll go. this one too.
 emmeline and eddie are down on the shore
already. she's just said something that's really made
him laugh. he's got his hand on her arm and he's
thrown his head back. even if she's not the one, i'm
glad we came.

do you remember what you said the night i left for oxford? you said that two things can be true. "you'll be far away and i'll still love you"

well, that is true now. except it's you who's far away

so two things are true: it is the end. and it is the beginning

i have to say goodbye and i'll never go anywhere without you

they're waiting for me by the water

afterwards emmeline is taking us for old-fashioneds in the old town.

and we will toast you on your way.

and i will listen out for bells, just in case.

i will listen out forever.

it's getting cold now. so only time left to say

i love you

bella and jake forever.

Timing

————◆————

I feel as though I am broiling.

Bella is snoozing in the sun, Emmeline's giant hat tipped over her face. The pool water is wiggling in the sunlight and inviting me for a dip.

My phone pings and I swipe on the burning hot screen to see that Marjie has sent a photograph of Pushkin nibbling on some carrot sticks. "Happy as a clam!" she has captioned. But that is not Marjie's striped wallpaper or yellow kitchen table. I do suspect that she and Pushkin might be sleeping over at Sam's house. Good for her.

Through the fog of heat, I am vaguely aware that the *tap-a-tap-a-tap* of Emmeline's speedy typing clacking from her office window has abated. Her flip-flops announce her as she emerges poolside in a glittering kaftan, huge sunglasses over her eyes. She notes Bella sleeping and smiles to herself. Then sweeps up to me in a wave of sweet perfume and asks, "Shall we take a walk, Mr. Winston?"

It's now or never, Eddie, the water whispers.

We walk along the path that leads away from the pool towards the landscaped gardens that are stepped along the side of the hill. We walk beneath a long trellis of plants that makes me feel as though I am back at the Winterbourne Gardens, enveloped in green. And finally, we reach an alcove of shady trees. From here, we can see everything, the sea sparkling below, the roofs of other houses, the crest of another island in the distance.

From here we can also see through the trellis tunnel and back to the pool, where Bella lies sleeping.

"It's a good thing you're doing, Eddie," Emmeline says.

"Oh, I'm not doing anything really."

"Aren't you?" Emmeline says. "That poor girl is so lost." She pauses. "I'm glad she has a friend like you."

"To tell you the truth, I can't understand why she wants to be friends with me."

Emmeline frowns at me. "Can't you? I think you two are very alike."

"I take that as a great compliment."

She thinks for a moment. "I imagine you and Bella are friends because you couldn't *not* be friends."

She's right, of course. And I realize that Bella's definition of love will have to be expanded to include friendship. Because friendship is just two people who can't keep away from each other.

"Really, she's the one helping me," I tell Emmeline. "She has so much hope for me."

"Hope?"

"That I'll find my first kiss."

"I must say, Eddie," Emmeline says, "I'm truly fascinated about that. Have you had any luck recently?"

"I don't think you'd call it luck."

Emmeline steps a little closer.

"I had an almost-kiss in the Winterbourne Gardens. And that is as close as I have come."

"Perhaps you're looking in the wrong place," Emmeline says, and I wonder if this might be a moment. Would Bella be screaming at me to look at her? And I do. And Emmeline is a handsome woman, there is no doubt about that. There's a feeling of electricity in my stomach.

"You know, Bella had me convinced you are the one," I tell her, feeling brave.

"Me?" Emmeline asks.

"Because a love letter brought us together."

Emmeline smiles softly.

"And because you're a hoot," I add.

"She thinks I'm a hoot?"

"Actually, I do. But Bella is equally besotted with you."

Emmeline laughs. "Oh, Eddie Winston, I would kiss you right now if I wasn't spoken for."

I take a breath in. For a moment, the closeness, the seclusion of this leafy corner of the garden, it felt like something. And I am a fool again.

Emmeline pulls out her phone. "Her name is Nancy," she says, showing me a photograph of herself, smiling, beside a woman with a jet-black straight-cut bob, whose beringed fingers are laced between Emmeline's.

"She's a very expensive headshot photographer. That's how we met—she was taking my photograph and I was driving her mad being unable to look seriously at her lens without laughing. Her studio is in London, so we don't get to be together as often as we'd like."

"But she makes you happy?"

"Oh, deliriously." She pauses. "My son asked me if I had a *preferred label*. They're like that, aren't they, the young ones? He wanted to know if I am bisexual or pansexual or demisexual, or what have you."

"And what did you say?"

"I told him that I am Nancy's. And that is all I care to be."

"I know that feeling well," I tell her.

"It's a bit hilarious, isn't it?" Emmeline says. "All these years writing romance novels about strapping, handsome men, all those years unhappily married to Mikey's dad. And I find my Nancy now, at my age!"

"Life is all about timing, in the end," I say.

"And your time is coming, Eddie Winston." She puts a hand on my shoulder. "You must keep looking."

"I wouldn't dream of doing anything else," I promise. "Someone very wise once told me that it's not too late."

Returning

————◆————

I feel a touch bereft as Emmeline's yellow Beetle pulls into a parking space at the airport car park. I do not feel at all ready to leave this place. But leave we must. There's a guinea pig I miss quite dearly and there's a kiss I have yet to find.

As we stand beneath the shiny screens of the airport, Emmeline, wearing her giant hat, hands me an envelope.

"Open it when you're in the air," she says, pressing it into my palm and giving my hands a squeeze.

Then she turns to Bella. "And you, you wonderful thing," she says, and then she removes, ceremoniously, the giant hat and places it into Bella's hands, as reverently as if she were handing over a newborn baby.

"You must keep it," Emmeline says, and Bella's eyes light up. "Oh, you must, I insist," Emmeline says, even though Bella hasn't protested. I get the feeling Emmeline was expecting a fight and even though Bella isn't putting up a fight, she's saying what she thought she would have to anyway. "It is yours."

Bella grins and puts the hat on, sweeping her pink fringe out of the way.

"Perfection," Emmeline says. "You wear it so much better than me." And then she briefly touches Bella's cheek. "Oh, that skin," she says.

And then it is time to say goodbye.

We thank her; she thanks us. We tell one another how much fun we've had. Bella subtly wipes a tear as Emmeline wraps her up in a big squeezy hug, the brim of the hat so large it covers them both like a parasol. I catch Bella's eye as they pull apart and she looks pleased that she's crying.

And then it is really time to say goodbye because we haven't been through security yet and they've already announced our gate.

Emmeline waves at us until the very last.

"Thank you, Eddie," Bella says as we look down on the sky, as though that is a normal thing for humans to be looking down on. God's view. As though the flight of this plane is not a miracle. As though it isn't insane that there is nothing below this plane but thousands of meters of sky.

"For what?" I ask.

She just smiles.

"Well, you're very welcome, dear." I clink my teeny plastic cup of water against hers.

I pull the envelope Emmeline gave me from my pocket. "Eddie" it says in swirly, looping writing on the front. It's a good job she doesn't handwrite her novels, it would take forever. First, I find two pieces of A4 paper folded into quarters. A return flight from BHX to CFU for Eddie Winston and Isabella Williams has been booked for late October. "A little autumn sun . . . ?" Emmeline has written at the bottom of the ticket with a drawing of a stick figure lady in a giant hat.

"What are you doing in October?" I ask Bella, and she peeps over my shoulder.

"I'm so in," Bella says. "I hope it's still warm enough to wear the hat."

And beneath our plane tickets is a slip of paper. It looks like it's been cut from a notebook. The paper is lined and delicate. The handwriting is so tiny that it is an exercise to decipher exactly what it says.

August 4, 1969

I wrote a letter for W.
 I didn't send it.
 I think about him all the time
 I will not forgive him for kissing H.
 I wrote a letter for Emmeline too.
 Didn't send that one either.
 I am an almost-person today. Everything I do, I almost do.
 I must pull myself together. I remembered this morning what Nanny used to say: Throw the window wide open, Elsie, and start again!

When we land, the pilot informs us over the loudspeaker that the local time is 12:42 and the air temperature in Birmingham is seventeen degrees Celsius. My phone illuminates and I smile at my screensaver, a photograph of Pushkin eating broccoli. And just above his floofy ginger ear, there's an envelope. A day of envelopes. From Marjie—mobile.

Eddie, it says,
Get here as fast as you can.
I think I've found it!

Inside Bridie Bennett's Heart

"Sit down, Eddie," Marjie says when I arrive at the charity shop, breathless, abandoning my suitcase at the door. I sit down on the tartan bar stool, heart hammering away.

"Now, I might be wrong," Marjie says, going to the door and flipping the shop sign to CLOSED.

"But I just had a feeling about this one," she says.

Marjie unzips her handbag and pulls out an emerald velvet jewelry box. She opens the lid and picks up the necklace by the chain, holding it up so that the heart dangles between us. And there it is. Even from this distance, I know.

There it is. After all this time.

"You found it," I say.

"Really?"

"That's it!" I leap up, knocking the barstool to the ground with the back of my knees. "You found it!" I hold out my hands. This is it.

Marjie places Bridie's shining golden heart in the center of my palm. And we are together again, we two things that belonged to Bridie Bennett.

I turn the locket over in my hands and stroke my finger across the letters *B.B.* that are inscribed on the back. "How?" I ask. "How on earth did you find it?"

Marjie looks just a touch embarrassed as she gabbles quickly, "There's a website, vintagelockets.com, and I sent them an email, oh, years ago now, just asking them to keep a lookout, and their buyer spotted it on eBay. So I messaged the seller and we agreed on a price and it arrived this morning. It came all the way from an antique shop in Plymouth."

"Plymouth?"

"I have no idea," she says. "Vintage Lockets was just one of, erm, many websites I'd contacted. A few said that secondhand stuff can really travel, especially jewelry." Her cheeks are a little rosy, now.

"You did all that for me?" I ask.

"I really wanted you to find it."

Marjie leaves me alone with Bridie Bennett's heart.

The last time I saw Bridie Bennett, she was eight months' pregnant; she didn't know what she was having because people didn't back then, but she was quite sure it was a boy. Dressed in a black floral dress that hung about her, standing in the corner of the arts faculty common room, watching as her husband gave a speech about his time at Birmingham. I found it hard to look Alistair in the eye in those days, so I was watching her. Truth be told, no matter who was speaking, I would have been looking at Bridie. She was softer now, from the pregnancy, her cheeks rounded, and her whole self just seemed more peaceful. She went to twist the locket from about her neck but her hand fell flat against her chest and a look of loss crossed her face. I had to fix it. But as we talked in quiet voices so as not to disrupt Alistair's commemoration of himself, she said to me, her gray-green eyes locked on mine, "Looking for it and not finding it would be worse than not looking at all."

And I have thought about that for nearly sixty years. And it seemed to me then and it seems to me now that quite the opposite was true.

And now, here it is, held tightly in my shaking palm, and though I am a little too afraid to look within, looking would be better than not looking.

The gold is tarnished but still bright, and the filigree pattern swirls around the front.

Sometimes I wonder if I imagined her, embellished her. Conjured her out of my loneliness. But no. She was real. And here is her heart.

I struggle to open the clasp, slipping the lock under my thumbnail. It takes a moment until finally, Bridie Bennett's heart swings open and lets me take a look at what's inside.

And there he is, smiling up at me, his handsome face, his green eyes, it makes perfect sense that this gentleman was inside Bridie Bennett's heart all along.

This dashing chap. How could it be anyone else?

"Hello," I say to him. Feeling the sting of disappointment that it might have been me inside. Oh, the arrogance to assume I had a claim to make.

"You can come out," I call to Marjie, and I hear a rustling of the bead curtain.

She comes over. "What was inside?" she asks, and I show her.

"Oh, he's so handsome," she says. "What's his name?"

"Ferris," I say fondly, stroking the photograph.

"Sweet," she says.

"He didn't have a tail," I tell her. "She used to say he lost it at the fairground. He was a lovely boy, would wind around your legs to say hello."

I pull gently on the heart-shaped photograph that has been enclaved in Bridie's golden heart for all this time, so that I can pass it to Marjie. Out it flicks and I pass it over to her, almost missing entirely the letters *E* and *W* that have been scratched into walls of her heart.

Oh, my Birdie.

After the Locket

———◆———

"Bella," I say as I sit beside her on the bench in the afternoon sun.

"Yes?" she says, as she turns very slowly, like she's a wise old owl who is about to dispense some sage advice.

"I've come to something of a conclusion," I tell her.

Her face changes. "No, Eddie, you can't give up. I won't allow it."

"It's not that I'm giving up," I tell her. "Really."

"Really?"

"It's not giving up if you're satisfied with your lot."

"Your lot?"

I take Bridie's locket from my inside jacket pocket and I hand it to her, the gold shining in the sun. "I've been searching for this almost as long as I've been looking for my first kiss," I tell her.

Bella takes the locket and turns it over in her hands. She opens the clasp and sees the photograph of Ferris. "Oh look at him!" she says. "What a floofy boy!"

"His name was Ferris," I tell her, and she looks at me, ever more intrigued.

"And how do you know that?" she asks.

"Lift the picture," I tell her, and, carefully, she does.

And there they are. Seeing them again sends a whole new thrill into my body.

E.W.

Bella turns to me.

"Is this Bridie's?" she asks. "You found it?"

I nod.

"So, you see," I tell her, "I can call off the search."

"You can?"

"If I'm in Bridie Bennett's heart, that's enough for me."

Ham and Cheese, Part Two

One week, she's reading a faded book on literary criticism that looks like the cover art was inspired by a melting strawberry ice cream, and the next week she's reading the *Users' Guide to Microsoft Word 2007*. It's an eclectic taste in literature to say the least.

Today as Ham and Cheese rushes past the till, she's reading the *Birmingham Post*, unfolded in front of her face like a grandfather reading by the fire.

It's 8:56, so he has to be quick if he's going to buy lunch and make it to the Monday morning meeting at nine.

Salt and vinegar Discos are on the lowest shelf of the crisp display; he grabs them and then the mango and orange smoothie. It's a tiny bottle, and probably his day's worth of sugar, but he's a smoker, so sugar is the least of his body's problems really.

Then off he goes to the sandwich fridge. He slides the glass door open, in anticipation of his ham and cheese on brown bread with mayo. There they are, lined up neatly and waiting for him. It is always a relief to see his favorite lucky sandwich, like an old friend assuring he will have a good day. Always exactly the same, inside and out.

Except that today, a yellow Post-it note is stuck to the ham and cheese sandwich in the front of the display.

FAO: HAM AND CHEESE, the Post-it note says.

And beneath that is her phone number and a smiley face.

He can't stop smiling for the rest of the day.

Next

———◆———

"*Eddie,*" Bella says, sounding like she is about to ask me for a favor.

"Yes, Bella?" I say indulgently, only too happy to oblige, of course.

"Now that you've stopped looking for your first kiss, we'll still be friends, right?"

"Of course!"

"Okay, good."

"Good," I agree.

"Good." She smiles.

"Good," I say.

"Good." She laughs.

"Good." I'm laughing too now.

Good.

Combinations

———◆———

A locked briefcase is far too delicious a proposition for me to let it pass me by. I've tried all the obvious number combinations I can think of, but nothing.

I give it a shake. Something rattles within.

And something rattles without as Marjie clatters through the bead curtain from the back room. "Do you want this?" She hands me a stack of paper held together with a pink paper clip. The title page says, "All the Ghosts of Newquay—First Draft, September 1987."

"Do *I* want this?"

"Yes, you know, for your collection."

I must make a face of terror because Marjie laughs.

"Eddie," Marjie says, putting her hand on my hand, "I know you take things from the shop."

"What? You do?"

"Of course." She laughs. "Nobody's jackets are *that* crunchy."

"Oh. Crikey. I can explain."

"It's okay, Eddie. I trust you."

"You do?"

"Of course. I don't doubt that what you're taking has no monetary value."

"It doesn't, I promise."

"It's okay," Marjie says, as though I'm being silly and she wants me to calm down.

"Are you sure?"

"I've always believed," Marjie says, "that as you know what it feels like to search for an item lost to charity, that whatever you're doing is probably very kind."

She passes the crinkly stack of papers towards me. It looks like a first draft of a novel, typed by hand on a typewriter, and I remember what it felt to hand my publisher the manuscript for my book. These pages are littered with hope.

When I finally get the briefcase open, it is filled with hundreds of tiny paper cranes.

Pushkin's in Love, Part One

———◆———

I get a ping on my phone and for a moment I think that it is Eunice.M_1952 replying to the message I sent her on Platinum Singles before I put my account on "hiatus," but it is not.

It is even better than that.

> Hi, my name's Jenny and I'm looking for a home for my skinny pig, Flora. I've got to move to Canada for work. She's very comfortable being handled, she's flea treated and her nails are done. Happy to drop her off anywhere in Birmingham. All the best, Jenny x

There's a picture attached. And if Pushkin is the floofiest guinea pig you can imagine, basically a hairpiece with teeth, Flora is the opposite. She looks like one of those sphynx cats; there's not a hair on her body.

I reply as fast as my thumbs will let me. Though I want to ask Jenny if she's quite sure it's a guinea pig she owns and not a short snake in disguise, instead I ask her if she would be willing to bring Flora to meet my boy. I include a photograph of Pushkin, his ginger hair freshly brushed, looking his very best. Hopefully, opposites attract! I write.

How's Saturday? Jenny replies almost immediately.

I will be meeting Marjie's new boyfriend over brunch in the morning, but the rest of the day is free.

Let's get these guinea pigs together! I reply.

Oliver Bennett

—◆—

May 1987
University of Birmingham, Lecture Theater 3

Dr. Eddie Winston isn't anything like Oliver Bennett imagined. He's hilarious, though unintentionally so. He's also very warm. Skinny. A bit of a shambles of a person. He has all the parts of a serious lecturer and he must be nearly in his fifties, but he looks like he's masquerading as something he's not. Like a goose in a trench coat pretending to be a human.

Dr. Winston trips over the cord of his own projector several times during the lecture but the content is good. There's humor in there and Eddie's way of describing some of the more technical concepts of literary linguistics make perfect sense to Oliver, even though Oliver's degree is in biochemistry and he dropped English as soon as he could at school (much to his father's dismay).

As the other students climb the shallow steps to the door at the back of the lecture theater, Oliver swims against the stream and makes his way down to the lecture table.

Dr. Winston is stacking his notes, which appear to have been inexpertly ripped from a spiral-bound notebook. And the handwriting is rather haywire. It reminds him of a poem his mother has framed in the conservatory.

"Er, hi," Oliver says.

Dr. Winston looks up and beams. "Hallo there."

. Oliver has gone off script. He isn't meant to be at the lectern. He isn't meant to be in the lecture at all. His mother would kill him if she knew. All she asked was that he "pop over" to the English department at some point once he was settled. Just to see if "Eddie" was still there. And if he found him, Oliver Bennett was meant to simply report back to his mother how her "old friend" was and not to speak to him directly.

She has never asked Oliver for a favor like this. And as such, he was instantly curious about who this man might be. And why his mother, after nineteen years of never mentioning him, happened to need to know if he was all right when Oliver started his studies at the University of Birmingham.

Oliver realizes that he has nothing to say to this man, who has paused, halfway through stacking his notes.

"I, er, really enjoyed the lecture," Oliver says because it's the truth and Oliver likes to deal in truth.

"Thank you very much, Mr.—?"

"Bennett. Oliver Bennett." If the name means anything to Dr. Winston, he doesn't show it.

Oliver could just tell him. Tell this man who his mother remembers as "a good friend." Tell him that his mother is thinking of him, that she cares for him enough that she has inconvenienced her son just to find out if he is well. But that wouldn't be fair to his mother, so Oliver asks about the lecture's conclusion.

"So, the parallelism?" he asks. "Is it used in all writing, not just fiction?"

"Once you've noticed it, you'll see it everywhere. It is how we make echoes."

"I'll look out for it."

"Parallelism is a surprising thing. Parallelism is really everywhere."

Oliver smiles and Dr. Winston beams on, seeing that Oliver has got his little joke. It seems as though Dr. Winston is about to ask Oliver a question when there is a cough from an irritated professor standing at the top of the stairs, wanting to set up for the next hour's class.

"Oops." Dr. Winston scoops up his notes. "Just leaving!" he calls.

"See you next week." Dr. Winston smiles at Oliver as he begins to ascend the stairs, and Oliver feels a twinge of guilt that Dr. Winston won't be seeing him next week, because next week he'll be in his biochemistry lecture over in the Aston Webb building, where he is supposed to be right now.

But onwards Oliver goes, up the stairs, past the uptight man with his box of photocopied handouts, and into the fresh air. When he gets to his bedroom in the halls of residence, he telephones his mother, to tell her that Dr. Winston is alive and well, but she doesn't answer.

Pushkin's First Date

I've brushed Pushkin's fur, I've cut up crudités for their main course, I've put a pink Livingstone daisy in a vase on the table and I've given Pushkin a pep talk about first-date etiquette, focusing primarily on the advice that it is best not to bite your date upon meeting her. He seemed as though he understood. He's as ready as he can be.

We wait, two bachelors with jangled nerves, as Jenny and Flora ascend in the lift to the top floor to find us.

Jenny bustles in, cooing over Pushkin's fluffiness, and places Flora's cage next to Pushkin's.

Flora is sitting in the corner of a red carry cage, looking like someone shaved a hamster.

Pushkin becomes very still. Then he scuttles to the bars of his cage. He sniffs the air, and looks, beady eyed, at her. Flora holds her ground, looking back.

He squeaks.

She replies.

Both guinea pigs press their noses against the bars of their cages, trying to get closer.

"I think it's a match." Jenny smiles.

For my cavian daughter, only one name will do.

I rechristen her Alora Flora Winston.

Ham and Cheese, Part Three

———◆———

Crispin Wilkerson III, a.k.a. Chris, a.k.a. Ham and Cheese feels a fizz of adrenaline in his stomach when he sees Sainsbury's Girl approach the table outside the cocktail bar where he is having a cigarette for luck. This cigarette is no different from any of the other fifteen cigarettes he smoked today, except for the fact that he is smoking this one before his date with Sainsbury's Girl, so he is hoping it will be lucky. He had an extra ham and cheese sandwich before getting ready, also for luck. As he chewed, he could hear his therapist's voice in his head, *"What happens if we tell ourselves that objects have no bearing on our fortune?"*

It is already dark and the patio heaters are aflame. She's wearing a black velvet dress with stars on and little star gems in her hair. Her black Doc Martens are making her walk in a slouchy way, like they're far too heavy for her. She sees him and smiles. Ham and Cheese is wearing a big faux-fur coat that makes him look like a bear who has wandered out of the woods and into the city so he can try a cocktail or two. Beneath that, he's wearing a black silky shirt and black jeans ripped at the knees, which, if his father ever saw, would make him stutter at the ridiculousness of buying clothes already damaged. Ham and Cheese has his hair in a half-up bun and he hopes that he doesn't look like a posh person pretending to be cool, which is what he feels like most of the time.

"Sainsbury's Girl," he says with a nod as she sits down. He doesn't actually know her name because her staff badge is pinned to her chest, right above her left boob, and he hasn't found a subtle way to learn her name without it appearing that he is leering. She is saved in his phone as S.G.

"Ham and Cheese." She sits down. "You can just call me Bella."

"Bella," he says with a smile, trying the name out. "You hungry?"

"I already ate," she says, "but you go on."

"I ate too," he says.

"What did you have?"

He pauses. To tell the truth or to lie.

"Was it ham and cheese?" She's laughing, but she's not judging him.

They have a table reserved inside but it's so nice out here, watching the people and the buses pass by. And also, he can smoke. Ham and Cheese wonders how many of his life's decisions revolve around where and when he can smoke and trying to increase the locations and the frequencies of those opportunities.

They order a cocktail each; he asks for an Old Spanish and Bella has a Blue Lagoon. The Old Spanish is very strong. Ham and Cheese feels it wrap around him like a warm blanket. With the fur coat, his cheeks are really warm. They have discussed films, music, and what they would name a dog if they were to get a dog tomorrow (a question Ham and Cheese always uses as an icebreaker).

"Okay, I have to ask," Ham and Cheese says, turning towards her. "The gentleman with the bow ties."

"Yes?" Bella asks as though she can't possibly think what Ham and Cheese might be about to ask. As though her association with Eddie is totally normal and du jour.

"Okay, first I need to know where he got that shirt with the leopards on."

"They're cheetahs."

"Are they? What's the difference?"

"Cheetahs are slinkier."

Ham and Cheese can't help but laugh.

"I have to know where he bought it. It's amazing."

"He got it from the charity shop on Corporation Street. He works there."

"Damn. It's fantastic. I was going to try and get one for myself."

"I'll tell him to keep his eyes peeled for another. The idea that you two might have matching shirts will probably thrill him."

The waitress comes over and they order again. Bella requests a Pornstar Martini while Ham and Cheese deliberates and goes for a Tequila Sunrise. When he taps his debit card against the reader, Bella frowns. "Crispin?"

"Don't," he says, "I know."

"I can see why you stuck with Ham and Cheese. Much less embarrassing."

"Have I told you about my brother, Prawn Mayonnaise?"

She laughs, and he can feel himself relaxing into the evening. But still, he says, "I have to know. Is he your grandpa?"

"What? No. He's far too old."

"Then how do you know him?"

"He's just a friend," she says. "His name is Eddie."

"Good, he looks like an Eddie."

"And you look like a Ham and Cheese."

Ham and Cheese waits. She sighs. "If you really want to know how we met?" she asks.

"Every time I see you together, I want to know."

"Are you sure you want to know?"

"One hundred percent."

"Okay," she says, taking a deep breath and looking Ham and Cheese right in the eye. "I met Eddie Winston because my boy-friend died."

"Oh," Ham and Cheese says. "Shit." And then remembers what you're meant to say in this sort of situation. "I'm sorry."

"I was donating his stuff to the charity shop, and there was Eddie."

"God. I'm. I— It's—" he stumbles, his stomach twisting from the awkwardness. He has ruined the date. "I shouldn't have asked. I'm so sorry."

"It's okay," she says but doesn't say any more than that. And Ham and Cheese's mind goes blank. He's unable to think of another thing to say. He puts a cigarette to his lips just for something to do, but he can't get it lit in the breeze. Bella leans across the table and holds her hands over the end of the cigarette, making a little igloo so he can ignite. Perhaps all is not lost.

"I would imagine Eddie has a lot of wisdom to share," Ham and Cheese says, blowing the smoke off to the side so it doesn't go in her face.

"A lot less than you'd think," Bella says.

There's a pause and Bella tries to take a sip of her drink even though there is nothing left in her glass.

"I really am sorry," he says again.

"It's really okay," Bella says. "I was just trying to avoid talking about it because I thought it might be a bit of a depressing topic for a first date."

He nods.

"If this *was* a date," Bella says quickly, undone for the first time. "I wasn't sure."

"I'd like to think it is," Ham and Cheese says. "How about you?"

"Go on then," she says with a grin. "It's a date."

There's another pause but this one isn't so unbearable.

"Your jacket is amazing, by the way," Bella says.

"Oh, thank you. It's from *The Nutcracker*."

"It's 'from *The Nutcracker*'?" she repeats.

He nods.

"Is that a place where clothes come from?"

Ham and Cheese laughs. "My flatmate, Terrence, is a costume designer at the Hippodrome. When they rejigged *The Nutcracker* a few years ago, a lot of the old costumes went up for auction. He bought me this to make up for his boyfriend ruining our living room carpet. I think it was for a bear originally," he tells her. "Not real fur though, don't worry."

"I used to want to be a costume designer," Bella says.

"Used to?"

"I had to do English at uni."

"Had to?"

"The only way I could afford uni was to get a scholarship and my highest marks were always in English."

"Which uni did you go to?"

"Oxford."

"That's impressive."

She shrugs. "It's not such a fun place to be when you're poor."

"I can imagine," Ham and Cheese says, though he really can't.

"I was supposed to go into some sort of graduate job, but then Jake—"

She stops herself as a waitress comes out and asks if they'd like anything else.

"What would you recommend?" Bella asks.

"The color-changing cocktail," the waitress says. "It's a little bit of magic."

"One for each, please," Bella says and hands over her debit card before Ham and Cheese can reach for his. "Technically, I should have been paying for all of these, since I asked you on this . . . date," she says.

Ham and Cheese puts his wallet away. "A stickler for etiquette," he says as the waitress heads off inside. "Interesting."

"Oh, if one doesn't have etiquette what does one have?"

"So, *Sainsbury's*?" Ham and Cheese asks. "I don't mean that how it sounds, it's just. How did you end up there?"

"When Jake died, I wanted to burn the world down."

"Understandable."

"But it was too hard to do, so I just burned my life down instead."

Their magical cocktails arrive, consisting of a martini glass of blue liquid and a conical flask of something clear.

"Enjoy," the waitress says, heading back inside.

Bella picks up the clear flask and pours it into her blue cocktail and they both watch as it slowly turns from blue through dark purple to a bright red. Ham and Cheese is mesmorized, like a child for a moment. He almost claps his hands but he manages to stop himself.

They clink their glasses together and then after the first sip, Ham and Cheese says, "If you ever feel that you might be ready to stack your last ham and cheese sandwich, I might know of something . . ."

Feedback

———————◆———————

"He's a good egg," Bella says, sitting on the bench beside me, "but he's not my egg."

I sigh.

"No, no, it's good," she says. "It was still a really good date. You know when people say 'we are better off as friends' and it's usually bullshit? I actually think we might be friends now. He invited me to see him in an improvised musical version of *Love Actually.*"

"Are you sure you're not his enemy? Because that sounds terrible."

She laughs.

"He wants you to come too," she says.

"He does?"

"He's fascinated by you, he said."

"It's the cheetah shirt. It does that to people."

"He said he wants one of his own."

"I bet he does. But he'll have to pry it out of my cold dead hands."

Bella laughs.

"Are you all right, though?" I ask.

"I'm really good," she says, and she is. The words match the smile she's smiling at me.

"Good," I say.

"Good," she agrees. "Oh, and by the way, I have a new job."

Flowers

———◆———

Oliver stands beside the grave and thinks of his mother.

His father, who really ought to be the concern of the day, is there in a peripheral way. But it is his mother whose smile, whose easy kindness towards him all his life, whose voice on the other end of the phone as a constant, is all he can think of.

Was he a good enough son to her? Did he notice her yearning for someone who was out of reach? Why did he never call his father out on the easy cruelty, on the indifference he showed her?

Oliver winces at the thought of his teenage years when he tried out his father's indifference towards his mother to see if it fitted. To see if that was what he was supposed to do as a man. But all it did was hurt. Nobody's mother was like Oliver's. Nobody's mother was as warm, as cuddly, as soft at the edges. Other mothers competed against one another, to show they were the best wife, to prove that their child was better than all the other children in the class. Bridie seemed indifferent to all that. She seemed to exist in her own orbit. But in the evenings, when he would trudge down the stairs on his way out to an empty park to go drinking in with his friends, he would spot her in the living room, alone except for the cat and the cast of *Coronation Street*, and he would notice that she was so lost. That she was so still. But he didn't know how to fix it and his friends were waiting, but now he wishes that he had. Or that he had at least tried. Why do we spend so much money on flowers for the dead but barely ever buy them for the living?

He wishes he had bought her more flowers when he was growing up, as the vicar concludes the funeral.

"We turn him over to Jesus's hands," the vicar says as Oliver wraps his arm around Bridie and looks down at his father's open grave.

Farewell

Bridie Bennett stands at the graveside of her husband and becomes Bridie Brennan again. Just like that. She takes too much of the earth to throw at him. And it sticks to her damp palm. She wipes the wet mud on her coat, smearing it by the pocket. An inelegant goodbye.

Oliver puts his arm around her. She wonders if he is also using her coat to un-mud his hands but when he gives her shoulders a squeeze, she realizes he is trying to comfort her. To be strong for her.

Some of them came, some of them didn't. The women. A few were bound by common courtesy, having been colleagues or friends' wives. Those that didn't come she likes a little better. Most of them hadn't bedded her husband in twenty or even thirty years, but still, knowing that they were in attendance at his funeral was the final humiliation.

The priest concludes the committing of the body and people begin to turn to their cars. Off to The Hound for the wake, to turn dry sausage rolls over in dry mouths. The Hound isn't a nice pub, but it was hard to find a function room near the church on a Wednesday and they had to settle for what they could get. Bridie wants to get there late. People will presume she is dealing with something at the graveside, but in truth she is ready for the day to be over.

It is supposed to happen on a gray day, isn't it? A funeral. Lightly spitting rain and overcast skies for the end of your life, for your sad mourners. But today is a glorious hot summer's day. Bridie is boiling in her coat, but she keeps it on because being encased in it makes her feel safe.

The people gathered around the grave begin to leave. Oliver heads off to bring the car around for her. She watches her son walking away in his smart suit. Oliver is fifty-five this year and he is beginning to look it, little flecks of gray in his dark hair. He has always been a good boy, a child who had a natural truth to him, a kindness that was absent in his father. From the day she met him, Bridie has not once regretted the existence of her son. He always tells her the truth. Admitted to her when he smoked his first cigarette as though she were his personal confessional. He has always looked out for her, checked on her. He brings his daughters to visit even now that they are in their late teens and have much better things to do than visit their nan. All the best parts of her and all the best parts of Alistair are combined in him. And as he disappears around the corner now it is just Bridie and Alistair and the box.

She pauses, wondering if she might finally cry. It was embarrassing not being able to cry at her own husband's funeral. She touched her tissue to her eyes a few times just in case anybody was looking. She cried when Ferris passed. She cried for weeks.

Well, goodbye, Alistair, she thinks. And goodbye to Bridie Bennett too. She is relieved that she has this slender opportunity to be Bridie Brennan once more, to begin again, unburdened by being Alistair's unloved wife.

As if sent by Saint Expeditus himself, a blackbird lands at the side of the wide-open grave. It pecks at the ground. *You kept your promise*, it reminds her. *Even if he didn't keep his.*

Cras, the bird says. *Cras.*

Flames

It's meant to be a ceremonial burning of Bella's Sainsbury's uniform fleece, but it quickly turns into an almost fire on Ham and Cheese's balcony.

He dashes in from the kitchen with a mini fire extinguisher. It looks travel-size, for any tiny fires one might encounter on the bus.

The metal bin we put the fleece in and then poured vodka on is still smoking even when the fire is out.

The smell of burning plastic is strong. "Jesus"—Bella flaps her hand in front of her face—"what the hell was that thing made of?"

Ham and Cheese toes the bin as close to the edge of his balcony as he can. "Try not to breathe it in," he says. I think he might be a secret posh person. His flat is palatial, for one thing. High ceilings, beams, those black industrial windows, but a sparkling new open-plan kitchen that looks like it will all be operated by a touchpad subtly secreted somewhere. There are hockey sticks and framed black-and-white photographs on the walls. Despite his long hair and whimsical nature, I would bet money that this boy went to Eton.

"Sorry," Bella says to Ham and Cheese, and he smiles at her. I believe he still holds a candle for my girl.

"That'll be two tickets for *Love Improvised, Actually*, then, to make it up to me."

Bella rolls her eyes. "If there's audience participation, I will genuinely run."

"I'll tell them not to pick on you. How about that?" She eyes him as though that is not nearly enough of a promise to get her to watch a three-hour improvised retelling of *Love Actually*. It was bad enough when they had the lines written down ahead of time.

The smoke slows eventually and I peer into the bin. The charred black fleece is still in the shape of a fleece, but it's no longer burgundy and the word *Sainsbury's* is gone.

"Poor fleece," I say.

"They're going to charge me for not returning it," Bella says, accepting a glass of champagne from Ham and Cheese. He pours his into a *Coronation Street* mug. "I only have two champagne glasses," he says, looking sheepish. Oh, what would his governess say?

"We have a lovely selection at the charity shop, if you don't have any qualms about secondhand glassware," I tell him.

"I'll have to check it out."

"You certainly will," I agree.

The smell of burning fleece is gently lifted with a breeze. From Ham and Cheese's balcony, we can see out across Birmingham; I can even spy the spotty Bullring building in the distance.

"To new beginnings!" Ham and Cheese says, holding out his mug, which has Roy and Hayley on it, in their matching rain cagoules.

"To the incredibly low-paid job of costume assistant's costume assistant!" Bella cheerses her glass and a bit of champagne slops over the edge onto the balcony.

I take a sup. It is very horrible, as all champagne is, but its extra horribleness makes me think it must be expensive.

"Will you miss it?" Ham and Cheese asks Bella.

She thinks about this. "I will miss the free food."

"Free? Was your discount that good?" Ham and Cheese asks.

"No," she says, as though Ham and Cheese is being particularly naïve.

"Oh," Ham and Cheese says as it dawns on him.

I must look aghast because Bella says, "Wait, Eddie. Did you think I'd been *buying* all the food we've been eating in Pigeon Park?"

"I presumed there was some staff discount at play. But yes."

"It's the five-fingered discount," she says, waggling her fingers at me like she's the Artful Dodger.

"Good God. I've been eating stolen food!"

"Yes, sorry, I'll um . . ."

"I'm a criminal!" I say.

"A fugitive," Ham and Cheese agrees.

"We are living outside of the law!" I exclaim, rather energized by the prospect of having committed and got away with crime.

"Shh, they'll hear you," Ham and Cheese whispers. "We're going to have to get you a disguise."

"It's not really *stealing*," Bella says. "They were paying me a pittance for a job at which I was spat at by strangers. So really, *they* owe *me*."

I take a sip of my champagne. This is life in the underworld then, drinking champagne on fancy balconies, my tummy full up with stolen food.

"I'm sorry for roping you into the murky world of crime," Bella says.

"It's quite exciting."

"But I do promise," Bella says, turning to Ham and Cheese, "that I won't steal anything from Terrence or the costume department."

"Don't say that," Ham and Cheese says. "How do you think I really got my faux-fur coat?"

"Seriously?" Bella says, laughing.

"No, I'm kidding. Please don't steal from Terrence, he'll never forgive me."

"Promise." She holds out her pinkie finger and Ham and Cheese offers his own pinkie to seal the pact.

We book to see *Love Improvised, Actually* for the Friday matinee and the Saturday night, because my subterranean Cupid senses are telling me that there might be something here, actually, after all.

Pushkin's in Love, Part Two

———◆———

I think she was always meant to be yours, Jenny texted this afternoon after I sent her a photo to show her that Pushkin and Alora are now sharing a cage, each of them crunching on cucumber as happily as any married couple having lunch. I hope they have many happy years together, she said.

Me too, I replied.

It is late at night now, well past my bedtime, but I can't resist checking on how they are getting on.

I creepy-creep into the living room using my phone as a light. There they are, side by side, both completely asleep. Pushkin and Alora. His floof keeping her warm in the sawdust. Totally at ease, happily odd, perfectly wrong for each other, perfectly right.

And my boy is no longer alone.

Morning

———◆———

It is a perfect summer morning. The sun is illuminating Corporation Street and I watch through the window as people walk about blessed by the light.

It has been a quiet morning in the shop. Marjie is taking the day off and there's been a customer or two. I'm listening to the radio and wondering what I shall read to pleasantly pass the day away.

And then Bella comes through the shop door wearing a yellow sundress. It is unlike anything I have seen her wear before.

In she walks, shoulders level, hair pinned back in a neat bun. I have never seen her hair like this.

Something quiet and melodic is playing on the radio.

And Bella walks up to the till, takes a deep breath, looks me in the eye, and says,

"I'm ready."

We go to our favorite bench in Pigeon Park. It seems to be a fitting place for the handover. Among all these birds and departed souls.

I wrote "Back in a tick" on a scrap of notepaper, stuck it to the door of the charity shop, and closed up, which was definitely not what I was supposed to do, but *this* is what I was supposed to do. I was always meant to reunite Bella with Jake's things when she was ready. I've been keeping his notebook and his shoes in the staff room cupboard lately, because I had a little hope that together we might find this day.

Bella sits down beside me on the bench.

"You're sure?" I ask her.

"I'm sure," she says.

I hand her Jake's notebook. Bella's face lights up. She turns the crinkling pages.

"I didn't read it," I assure her.

The photographs slip out from the back page.

"God, my hair!" she says, pulling out the top photograph. Jake looks so happy in it, standing with his arms wrapped around Bella's shoulders outside a pub.

She smiles as she carousels through the pictures. "I remember this day," she says, of a photograph of them in school uniforms beneath a staircase. "We were skiving off Music."

She crinkles through to the final pages of Jake's notebook, which have "the end" written in his frantic black biro. She closes the book.

"Thank you, Eddie."

"Of course, my dear. Next is a little something from me," I tell her, and I hand her the shoebox I bought on Etsy. It's a black shoebox with a hand-drawn, swirling pattern of white stars. Just the thing to keep his shoes safe from dust or damage. Up on a high shelf or deep within a cupboard. And this way, she can look at them anytime she wants to—pull them out when she is lonely and think of him. That's what I would do.

She smiles. "Thank you, Eddie," she says, "this will be perfect."

And then it is time.

Holding them as carefully as I can, I place in her hands the white Converse trainers covered with all the words of love she once wrote. So that he would have love wherever he went.

"Hello, old friends," she says with a smile. A tear slips from her left eye and she lets it fall without batting it away. There are smudged letters from where he must have stepped into water. Scuffs from places he traveled, gray stains on the laces. These shoes were well loved. Bella traces her finger over the letters on the back of the heels that say so clearly, "Bella and Jake Forever."

"He wore these every bloody day of his life," she says, another tear falling. "Except for prom when he had to borrow a pair of his dad's work shoes and they looked so weird on him. Too smart. Way too shiny."

They're still set to the shape of his feet and she runs her finger along the outer edge. Hers again. A reminder of Jake to look at whenever she wants. To keep nestled in the pretty box.

Except, she reaches down and unstraps her white sandals at the buckles that hold them to her feet. And it is her sandals that she puts into the shoebox I have gifted her.

Then she takes Jake's left shoe, pulls gently on the laces, opens it wide and slides her foot inside. She begins lacing as I watch in quiet wonder.

Oh, she is a mighty woman, this one.

"I always said these would fall apart one day," she says as she laces up Jake's left shoe. "But I think they'll have to fall apart on my feet, instead of his."

"Are you sure?" I ask as she laces up the right shoe. "They might never be the same."

She nods. "Where I go, he goes."

"I think that was true anyway, my dear."

I stand and offer her both my hands. She takes them and she rises.

"Come on, Eddie," she says, gathering up the notebook and her sandals, now safely stored in the pretty shoebox.

And she begins walking.

Jake and Bella Forever, her heels tell the shining paving slabs and all the pigeons who are nipping at the ground and anyone who cares to look. And onwards she walks.

And she will have love, wherever she goes.

Searching

———◆———

On the first anniversary of Alistair's funeral, Bridie opens her laptop and gives a furtive look behind her as though Alistair's ghost might be watching.

The only ghost Bridie has ever welcomed is Ferris after he ascended to the great fairground in the sky. She loves Jessie, the one-eyed ginger cat currently curled up asleep on her favorite spot on the sofa, but Ferris was the first cat who saved her. And you never forget your first. When Jessie gets the zoomies after mealtimes, thundering up and down the stairs and meowing, Bridie likes to believe she is playing with Ferris. And she leaves a little extra food in Jessie's bowl so that Ferris knows he's welcome. So he knows that she wants him to stay.

She has thought about doing this many times. But now that her wedding ring is in her jewelry box. Now that her mourning period is over. Now that she has given Alistair's clothes to charity, just as he gave her locket to the Salvation Army, not intentionally but because he was not looking at what went into the box, now that Oliver seems okay. Now that all those things.

She can look for Eddie.

Bridie can't remember how old he was when she met Eddie Winston. She can barely remember her own age, save that she is only a few years from a telegram from the king, but he can keep his telegrams. It is accidental, not an achievement to be this old. It is a falling apart of things.

Now that she is not bound by the covenant of marriage, Bridie feels both free and afraid. The rules were the only thing keeping her weighted to the ground. Now she might just float away.

She types slowly. Eddie Winston Birmingham UK.

It is the third result, after an advert for family tree research software and the statistics of a footballer from the 1960s.

And her whole body becomes very still as she reads that Eddie Winston died in Birmingham on Wednesday.

She doesn't breathe in, doesn't breathe out.

She waited too long.

It is too late.

Black

———————◆———————

Bridie, dressed in black, waits for the Uber to take her from the train station to the funeral. Such a modern thing to summon a driver from the sky, for the oldest practice in the world of saying goodbye to the dead.

It feels as though time has stopped. It is a play, her mother used to tell her. Whenever you are afraid, tell yourself that you are in a play and you are an actress who knows her lines by heart. Her mother never once set foot on a stage, but she could have. She had a sunniness to her, and despite her plump figure, she drew you in. She could have been an actress, if there had been time.

Adil S. drives his pristine car in complete silence. No radio, no chatter. Even the engine of the car is barely making a noise. Bridie keeps her hands folded in her lap. "The Birdlet," written by Alexander Pushkin in 1888 and then rewritten by Eddie Winston in 1968, sits within her black bag. For all the years she kept it in a frame in the conservatory, Alistair never wondered about it, he never asked. She had to use a butter knife to prize the clips from the back of the glass frame this morning to return his words to her. So that she might return his words to him.

And it is only now that Eddie Winston is dead that she realizes she has always, always counted on them meeting again. Has always presumed that there would be more. And how absurd to think that he might live so long. To think that *she* might live so long. The impossibility of them both being alive is not lost on her now that she is realizing how foolish she has been in the year since Alistair's death not to seek him out quicker. Not to run down the streets of Birmingham calling out his name.

The streets of Birmingham slide past the window and she does not call out "Eddie Winston." The car smells faintly of leather and a too-sweet fruity air freshener and the combination of all the left and right turns and the smell and sitting in the back has made a wave of nausea rise up in Bridie's throat. She squints at the phone on Adil's dashboard but the text telling her the remaining time of their drive is far too small for her to read.

Bridie is relieved when the gray church spire appears through the windscreen. Adil's car is so clean, he would likely not have thanked her for vomiting in it.

Outside the church they have gathered. Eddie's family. She knows the obituary by heart now, Eddie's son and his husband, Eddie's daughter and her three children. They are probably adults themselves, the grandchildren. She wonders if they will look like him. She doesn't have a photograph of Eddie, because why would she? There was a departmental staff picture taken in '61 but Eddie isn't in it. Alistair is, face screwed up into the sun, standing at the bottom of the bleachers and holding the sign—the star of the show. She couldn't forget Eddie though. Some things are fading in her memory but not those eyes.

Adil pulls up and, seeing that it is a funeral, he says very quietly to her, "I am sorry for your loss." He offers her help getting out of the car but she assures him that she's slow but steady.

There are quite a few people at Eddie's funeral in bright colors. A shock of a red dress on a blonde woman, a bright green suit on a man with a shining bald head, an orange scarf draped over the shoulders of a woman with silver hair. It is as though they are defying the somber and frightening show of death that is expected and saying, *Eddie was fun, his funeral should be also.* But the rest are in black and Bridie joins the infestation of beetles scuttling towards the church.

She sits at the back. At the first pew she comes to. She barely knew him. She loved him for most of her life. Both of these things are true. And both of them compete with exactly how close to the coffin she should be, as though being closer to the coffin proves one's importance to the deceased. The front row for the performance.

She finds she can't look at it. At the box where Eddie is lying, so she looks out at the congregation, at the women with black hats, the teenagers looking gangly and awkward in borrowed suits, at the couples holding hands, and she thinks, *He had a nice life.* Look at all these people who loved him who want to say goodbye. Some people are already dabbing tissues to their eyes and the thing hasn't even begun. On the other side of the church, a few rows ahead, a young woman with pink hair is wearing a headband with a black net across her face. She looks very chic. For a moment, the man beside her morphs himself into Eddie Winston—all old and crinkly, but the same bright eyes, same slight frame, the same smiling face even when he is not smiling. Bridie blinks once, twice, and the man leans to talk to the girl with the pink hair. His granddaughter, she must be. Bridie looks away. Her eyes are miraging Eddie where he is not. Where he cannot be. He is in the box. She must remember that. There cannot be two Eddie Winstons at this funeral.

The vicar appears before the congregation looking somber. He too could be an Eddie Winston from this far away. But if there can't be two Eddie Winstons at the funeral, there certainly can't be three.

After Alistair died, Bridie saw him everywhere, his sharp shoulders ahead of her in the queue at the supermarket, his wispy white hair on a man sitting on a park bench. It is the same now—grief overpowering all her senses. Her heart pulling too tightly on her eye strings. The eyes are the puppet of the heart; they can make a plain person beautiful so long as they are loved.

The vicar manages to call for quiet without speaking a word. An affable-looking man with glasses and slightly too tall for his robe. He's the kind of vicar Bridie would have liked, if she still went to church.

"Let us pray," he begins. "Let us talk to God before we talk to each other." Nobody joins Bridie on her pew right at the back of the church. And she finds within a few words of the Lord's Prayer that she is crying. And she did not think to bring tissues.

To be told of Eddie's life will be a gift. An answer to all the questions she has answered in her own mind with various different options. Sometimes, she answered the question as to his marriage with him being married twice, sometimes thrice. Sometimes he was alone and sometimes he was happy about that. Sometimes he missed her, sometimes he forgot all about her. But now she is hearing of his life. The answers to the questions come. They make it neither easier nor harder. He is gone and that is all there is.

When the six family members are shouldering Eddie with some difficulty, Bridie whispers, *Goodbye, Eddie.* She wishes funerals would allow for the gathered to actually say goodbye all at once and, within that goodbye, all the luck and love for the journey he is about to take.

Bridie had intended to leave Eddie's final words to her, Pushkin's poem, nestled unseen between the flowers of his graveside, but she cannot bear to see him lowered into the ground, committed to the dark, damp earth.

So she places "The Birdlet" poem, kept sacred all these years, in his messy, guilty, energetic writing, on the pew. And she begins the long journey home.

Late

To my great surprise, it turns out I died last Wednesday.

I uncrinkle the newspaper across both of our laps.

"You read the obituaries in the *Birmingham Post*?" I ask Bella, unable to hide the judgment from my voice.

"I read everything," she replies.

And there he is.

> Edward "Eddie" Winston is remembered lovingly by his son, James; son-in-law, Ralph; daughter, Georgia; and his three grandchildren, Emma, Alexander, and Sophie. He is remembered too by friends from the Rotary Club with whom he spent many happy hours of his retirement fishing. A service of thanks for his life will be held at Saint Hope's Church, Edgbaston on Monday, August 11 at 9:30. No flowers, please. Donations gratefully directed to the Myton Hospice.

"Poor Eddie Winston," Bella says.

"Poor Eddie Winston," I agree.

"*Is* it Edward? Your real name?"

I am about to reply when a man comes up to us with a flyer for an improvised comedy show. "It's free," he says and hands us both a piece of lime-green paper. "If you don't laugh, you get your money back." He seems much more amused by this than we are and then he pulls more flyers out of his beige messenger bag and heads off to the next bench.

"I doubt I'll have a newspaper obituary when I die," I say as Bella pulls out a Tupperware pot of tomato pasta from her backpack. She brings her lunch from home now that she's working at the Hippodrome.

"Why not?" Bella asks.

"There'd be nobody to write one. I'm not remembered lovingly by my son, my daughter, *or* my three charming grandchildren."

"It didn't say they were charming."

"No," I say sadly, "but I bet they are."

"Would you even want one?"

"A grandchild?" I ask

"An obituary."

"A little etching of my name in the history books of this great city?"

"Is that what you think an obituary is?"

"I—"

"The announcements section of a local paper is just Facebook for people who don't have Facebook." She scoops a forkful of pasta into her mouth and pulls a face; it doesn't smell too appetizing.

"I'd still like to be remembered though."

"If I outlive you, I promise to publish an obituary when you die."

"You can embellish a little if you like. Make me sound more fun."

"'Eddie Winston is remembered by his turtles, his sixteen great-grandchildren, and the Munich Male Voice Choir.'"

"Perfect. I look forward to it."

Hello, Goodbye

———◆———

The ring of the church bell feels particularly ominous as we stand dressed in black among the headstones. Bella is wearing an elegant net fascinator in her hair and that, combined with her black lace dress and gloves, makes her look like a character from a film noir who will eventually be revealed to be the villain. There are easily a hundred people gathered here already, dressed in black against the gray sky. I am drawn to the one or two who are wearing color. This Eddie Winston must have been a hoot.

We are saying hello to him. And we are saying goodbye.

Once we are seated inside the church and the organ begins to play, it feels evident we have made a mistake. It is somber and scary and there's a body in that box. We had thought it might be fitting to have this Eddie Winston say goodbye to another, but now it feels all wrong, as though we are crashing a party to which we were never to expect an invitation.

But my guilt is eased during the eulogies, of which this Eddie Winston has three, one from his son, one from his son's husband, and one from his daughter. It seems that he liked practical jokes, parties, and fishing, and made friends everywhere he went. "I'd be surprised if even Dad could identify everyone here today," his daughter said to a ripple of laughter. Perhaps he'd have liked it, then, to know that another Eddie Winston who read himself dead has come along to say goodbye.

Though the late Eddie Winston does indeed sound like he was

a hoot, the hymns are slow and so sad. Bella and I don't know the words or the tunes of course, but enough people do that the words rise up into the cold old arches of the church.

Do not be afraid,
For I have redeemed you
I have called you by your name
You are mine.

I give Bella's hand a squeeze and she squeezes back. And that is when I notice that she's crying, the tears falling down her face faster than she can wipe them away.

I take the pocket square from my pocket and hand it to her. It has mallards printed all over it (£1.50 and a total bargain at twice the price). She gives me a half smile.

It is all so terribly sad. Bella's tears. These beautiful words to this sad tune. I let a few tears fall. For all that can be. For all that can't. For the late Eddie Winston and the people who loved him. For the kiss I tried to find. For Bella and for Jake. For her healing heart.

When Bella notices that I'm crying too, she silently hands the mallards back to me. And we cry together for a while.

Once the late Eddie Winston has been carried by family and friends out to where the open mouth of a grave is waiting, the rest of the congregation files out, politely letting one another go ahead, to the sad improvised tune of the organ. But Bella and I stay seated. Eventually, it is only us two left in the church. The organist ends her improvisation with a minor chord flourish and we hear the creak of a key cover being pulled to protect her notes and then a door closing.

The church is cold and quiet.

"Are you all right?" I whisper.

"It feels wrong to be crying about Jake at someone else's funeral," Bella says.

"Don't feel bad, dear, everyone is crying for multiple people today."

"Are they?"

"Some people will be crying for Eddie, some for his children, some for his grandchildren. At a funeral, people are reminded of all the people they have lost before. Lots of people will be crying for other loved ones who've already passed. I have thought about my mother since we've been here. But funerals remind us that we too will die one day, so we are crying for ourselves as well. You're not restricted in who you cry for."

She nods.

"We can sit here for as long as you want."

She sniffs. "I'm okay."

"It's all right if you're not, though."

She nods and sighs. "I think I need some fresh air."

"Go on, I'll catch you up," I tell her, and she slips off and down the aisle and into the gray day, her high heels making a satisfying clacking sound that echoes around the church as she goes.

I sit for a moment more, taking in the heavy air of sadness in this place.

I gather myself. It is time to go back out into the world. As I rise in the pew and make my way down the aisle, I spot a discarded service pamphlet on the floor. I pick it up. It would be rude to leave the church in disarray. From the front of the service pamphlet, the late Eddie Winston is smiling up at me in sunglasses next to a green and lush riverside, fishing line at rest beside him. He looks happy. I place the pamphlet carefully on the pew at the back of the church, in case someone wants to keep it.

Only . . .

It cannot be.

It absolutely *cannot* be.

That is my handwriting. I would know it anywhere.

But it cannot *be*!

A square piece of paper with my handwriting on it.

Just sitting on the pew.

I pick it up, my hands shaking.

When spring, Nature's Beauty,
And the burning summer have passed,
And the fog, and the rain,
By the late fall are brought,
Men are wearied, men are grieved,
But birdie flies into distant lands,
Into warm climes, beyond the blue sea:
Flies away until the spring

How?

How?

Though I believed this church to be built on land, it reveals itself to be on water. The Gothic arches rise up on the crest of a wave and the floor dips down low, and I have to hold on to the pew so that I do not fall. The candles flicker as we rise up on another wave, though I am certain this church rests upon concrete, surrounded by grass.

I feel quite sick.

We dive downwards for another wave, and I hold on tight to the poem I wrote for her when she was flying away.

My Birdie.

She was here.

Seek and Ye Shall Find

———◆———

I feel as though I am full of electricity.

I pace my flat.

Bella is stroking Pushkin on her lap, which is astounding in itself because until he met Alora, Pushkin made it very clear (via his sharp little teeth) that he strongly disliked being picked up.

"She was there." I'm aware I have said this seven or eight times now.

"I'm going to be honest with you, Eddie," Bella says. "I always assumed Bridie was dead."

"What? Did you? Why?"

"You know, with the whole sending birds as a sign and stuff. I just assumed she was sending them from, you know . . ."

I gesture for her to continue.

She whispers, *"Heaven."*

I can't help but laugh. "It is ridiculous that we're both still alive, let's get that out of the way first." I take another lap of the living room.

"I don't know," Bella says thoughtfully. "Sometimes you hear of people holding on when they have something to do. When my grandad was dying, my mum was on a flight in from Germany and her plane was delayed, but my grandad held on until she got there and said goodbye."

"That's beautiful. But. Oh God, do you think we'll both die the moment we meet?"

"No, I just . . ." She's distracted as she realizes that Pushkin is nibbling the tassel on one of my sofa cushions (£6.50, with a pop art diving illustration).

She wrestles the tassel from Pushkin's mouth and says, "I think perhaps it was meant to be."

"But what do we do? What do *I* do?" I pace again to the window and look out at the registry office, the tiny strip of canal.

"What do you mean, *what do we do*?" Bella asks. "We've got to find her!"

A Ringing Phone

———————◆———————

The landline is ringing. It is the toss of a coin whether she will answer. Oliver always calls her mobile. Only salespeople call the landline. And yet a ringing phone demands an answer. She recalls Alistair's brother's penchant for ringing the landline thrice to announce his safe arrival from wherever he had been traveling home from. He's long dead now. Anthony barely spoke to Alistair by the end. It made Bridie less envious, less sad to be an only child, seeing how their relationship eroded over the years. There were no siblings to disappoint her.

It has been a quiet day. It might be nice to hear someone else's voice. Even if it is a salesperson. Sometimes Bridie goes to the shops even when she doesn't need anything, just for the opportunity to talk to someone, to use her voice for the first time that day.

"Hello?" she asks.

"Oh. Hi. Hello." It is a young woman's voice on the other end of the phone. Then it sounds as though she has covered the phone with her hand to say to someone near her, "She picked up!"

"Hello?" Bridie says again.

"Hi, um, am I speaking to Bridie Bennett?"

She sounds like she might be a salesperson, but an inexpert one, because Bridie detects nerves there. Nobody has called her Bridie Bennett in a year. She changed her name back to Bridie Brennan once Alistair was gone—changed everything, the deed to the house, the bills, her passport, everything. Becoming Bridie Brennan again felt like coming home.

"Yes," Bridie says; she supposes she will always also be Bridie Bennett too. "How can I help?"

"It's a bit of a strange one," the young woman says. It's hard to place her age with her voice alone, but she can't be beyond her twenties, a slight Brummie accent. Bridie is intrigued. This is already the most interesting conversation she has had in months.

"Go on," Bridie says.

"Did you work at the University of Birmingham in the 1960s?"

"I did," Bridie says, holding the phone a little tighter. Perhaps this young woman is a researcher working on an article about the history of linguistics, perhaps she is a journalist writing about women in academia in the 1960s, perhaps she is a scammer and is about to tell Bridie that her bank account security has been breached and she needs to move all her life savings into a new account. There are so many perhaps. But Bridie is not ready for the next question that the young woman asks.

"And did you know a young man named Eddie Winston?"

"I did," Bridie says, feeling the strange pain of his death again. Now she understands. The university is writing an obituary for Eddie and asking for quotes from colleagues, though there can't be many colleagues left. She wonders what she should say. There are no secrets to keep now.

"He's looking for you," this young woman says.

"Looking?" Bridie asks. "But. He died."

"Eddie Winston is sitting opposite me," the young woman says. "And he'd really like to see you."

Bridie drops the phone.

A Ringing Phone, Part Two

He is not dead.

They will meet the next morning.

Her hands are shaking so much she pours herself a glass of sherry.

He is not dead.

They will meet the next morning.

Good God.

Bridie feels as though she is filled with helium.

Circles

———————◆———————

This cannot possibly be real. I am going to see her. Bridie. She is willing to see me. She is a widow now. She thought I was dead. It is too many new pieces of information for my brain to comprehend.

"Hop in!" Bella shouts, pulling up in front of my flat.

We are to meet on the university campus tomorrow afternoon, beneath the Old Joe clock tower.

There is much to be done. I need to scope out how the campus is laid out now, I hope there will be a place for us to share a cup of tea.

Then I will swing by the barbers for a quick tidy-up of what is left of my hair. I want to look my best. Then I must invest in a new aftershave. I must keep busy. I must do something with my hands to calm my nerves.

English summer rain comes from nowhere, doesn't it? It batters the car, as Bella's windscreen wipers swoosh at a panicked full tilt. But the rain just keeps coming, huge waves of it smattering down on the glass.

We are driving through the new built-up area of Selly Oak. It certainly didn't look like this when I worked here; there's a huge Sainsbury's and so many new apartment buildings. It looks so . . . *vast*.

"I cannot believe this," I say to Bella for perhaps the third time since I got in the car.

"Less than twenty-four hours to go now," she says, tapping the clock on her dashboard. Her dashboard turtle nods along.

The rain is splashing up from the smooth tarmac.

Less than twenty-four hours until I get to give Bridie Bennett back her heart.

"I'm so happy for you, Eddie," Bella says, notching the windscreen wipers into a greater frenzy as her windscreen becomes temporarily opaque with the rain.

"Thank you, dear," I say to her. "For everything."

Her brakes are screeching as we approach the descent to the roundabout. She hits them harder.

"Shit, shit" she says, pressing hard on the pedal, but it is too late.

And there is the bus. And there is the beeping.

Open the doors.

And there are the people.

Elizabeth

And now, unfortunately, I'm dead.

It was all going far too well for the second Eddie Winston, I think as I drift.

It is not uncomfortable, it is not painful, there is just a gentle movement, like floating on a Lilo inflatable on top of the water. I must have said my thought out loud because one of the angels attending me replies, *What was going well, Eddie?*

She's dressed in blue. I had expected white. But the blue suits her nonetheless and she smiles.

Oh, it was love, you see. And now I'm dead.

You're not dead, Eddie.

Is it a limbo situation? I ask her. I must right a wrong before I can get into heaven? Not to presume that I would, of course, I wouldn't want to seem presumptuous.

This is Queen Elizabeth.

Goodness. Your Majesty. I thought you were . . . well, it makes sense that you're here. But I thought you'd have insisted on some sort of segregated, upper-class heaven. I'm surprised you're slumming it here with me and the blue angels.

She smiles again and says, *Sharp scratch.*

What an odd thing to say. Perhaps it is a code. I ought to have read more of the Bible, really, to know what to expect. I wonder if there will be some sort of orientation for nonreligious folk such as myself. What is the first one? The first book? *Is it Deuteronomy?*

Sorry? The angel asks.

Is it Deuteronomy?

Sorry, Eddie, I'm not sure what you mean, she says. You would think she would know.

I wonder where her wings are. They must be very small that I can't see them peeping out from behind her back.

And Bella. Oh Bella. If she is here too, I will never forgive myself.

Your friend is just fine, the angel tells me. She must have a portal where she can watch the goings-on of earth. *It's you we're worried about, Eddie,* she says. *Can you tell me what happened?*

Oh, can I!

But I find that I can't. There is nothing there, so I tell her the first image that I see—the clock tower.

Another angel I cannot see tells my girl in blue that the head brace can be removed. That's nice. I wonder who he's talking about.

And then my angel asks me to stay still.

I want to be obedient to show how grateful I am that I have ended up in heaven and not hell. So I stay very still and there is an incredibly loud noise, like being inside an airplane engine. My ears, if I still have ears, must surely be bleeding. The angel, whose voice sounds tinny and distant now, commends me for managing to stay as still as I am, though I don't believe I *could* move, even if I wanted to. The whirring is incredible. It hurts my ears, but I don't want to be quarrelsome, so I let them get on with it. If only I'd read Deuteronomy, I'd know what they were up to.

And I find myself drifting again, on the top of the water, only the occasional thought of how loud the sound is. My angel pleads with me to stay awake, but oh, it is so comfortable.

IV

◆

I wake up to find Bella standing at the foot of my bed, looking aghast. Her hand that isn't in a sling is holding a potted plant with a gift wrap bow stuck on it.

"Hello, you," I think I say.

"Eddie, I'm so sorry," she says.

"It's okay, dear."

"I—the bus and my brakes . . . I couldn't."

"It was an accident," I tell her. I remember it now. I remember the rain. Her brakes failing. "All is forgiven. But you're okay?" I point to the sling.

"Just a fracture," she says.

I lean forward.

"What?" she asks. "What's wrong?"

I'm trying to see Jake's shoes.

They're on her feet. None the worse for the adventure.

I lean back with a sigh.

"I'm so sorry, Eddie," she says. "I could have killed you."

I wave my hand. "I'm a tough cookie."

She places the potted plant on my bedside table. It's an olive tree.

"Wait," I ask her. "What day is it?"

"It's Friday," Bella says, looking concerned for me.

"Bridie!" I cry and peel the covers off my hospital bed, not stopping to check if I am clothed first. Fortunately, I am wearing a very fetching NHS gown.

"It's okay," Bella says, putting her hand on my arm.

"I have to get to her!"

"Hold your horses," Bella says. "They've got another few hours of obs to do."

"'Obs'?"

"Yeah, your hot doctor told me. She points to the cuff on my upper arm. That will be taking your blood pressure every thirty minutes for a few more hours and they're monitoring your pulse." She draws my attention to a gray clip on the tip of my finger.

"Oh God. I'm dying, aren't I?"

"Actually, they said your scan was clean but they want to monitor you because you lost consciousness and were, and these are their words, 'talking a lot of nonsense.'"

"And because I'm ridiculously old?"

"Well, they didn't say that, but that was pretty much the vibe."

"I can't wait that long. You have to get me out of here, I have to see her! What if one of us dies before I get to see her? We're both so bloody old!"

"Eddie." Bella sits beside me and puts her non-slinged hand on mine. "It's okay. She's coming. You just have to get these tests done and you'll be a free man."

"She's coming?"

"She's coming."

"She's coming *here*?"

"She's coming here." Bella's tone is very calming.

"She can't see me in a hospital bed."

"Okay, we will see her somewhere else, I promise."

Time is crawling. Each minute feels like it hurts. The gap between when the arm cuff inflates to check my blood pressure, slowly deflates, and then inflates again, stretches out for many weeks.

Bella is a patient and dutiful friend and she sits with me, forces me to play Scrabble. And then when she sees how bored it makes me, gets out the Mouse Trap she bought from the charity shop that is missing its boot piece. We are midway through travel Monopoly when I notice that Bella has been secreting the tiny £500 notes into her sling straight out of the bank. That rascal.

"Not long now," one of the nurses says as my arm band inflates again and she notes down what it says on the screen. "Everything is looking really good, considering."

A Prayer for the Day

———————◆———————

Bridie Bennett wakes every morning at seven and says a prayer for the day. This morning she wakes and cannot remember ever feeling more excited, perhaps except for the day when Oliver was due to be born. She cannot quite believe that this is happening. It is as though reality has let her peek between his curtainy folds and she is in another world. She gets ready, taking extra care to add some blusher, some lipstick, some mascara. They just about do the trick.

Just two weeks ago, Adil S. in his perfectly pristine and silent car escorted Bridie from the train station to Eddie's funeral, and now Johan W. is escorting her to see him. The risen Eddie. It makes him all the more precious that she thought she'd lost him and just yesterday afternoon nearly lost him again. *Don't you see how precious he is?!* the universe is screaming.

They are getting closer and closer. Bridie can feel her insides swirling with adrenaline. Her phone pings. It's Oliver. **Good luck, Mum x.** Oh, how she loves that boy.

Would Eddie recognize her son now, she wonders, all tall and gray and sensible? Father to a stunningly intelligent pair of daughters and still surprisingly close to his ex-wife. She's often hanging about in his kitchen when Bridie is invited over. Bridie often wonders if he and May will ever reunite. She would like that for him, so he's not alone when she goes.

The landscape is changing from residential homes to the out-of-town shops, a big *Sainsbury's*, and then there it is. The Queen

Elizabeth Hospital. Goose bumps shimmer onto Bridie's arms. Though she was dressed in black for Eddie's funeral, she is dressed in her brightest colors for his resurrection.

What will happen next is an entirely unknown thing to her. She has imagined it only up to this point. To them reuniting. She has never imagined the practicalities of it. Who will speak first, what they will say, whether she might be able to touch him by the hand, whether he will smile.

The roads around the hospital are quiet; it is the early evening in late August, the sun all golden and warm. Autumn is coming and the earth is ready for it.

It is a little heavy-handed that there are birds, two pigeons, pecking around the discarded food in the taxi drop-off point, and yet Bridie cannot help but smile. She has sent him birds. Whenever she has seen a good one. *Go and see Eddie*, she's told them in her mind. She hopes some of them have reached him. Have taken wing to the wild and found him. The ones with magnificent beaks, the ones with a missing wing, the ones with beautiful plumage, with bright darting eyes. It is not far from Cambridge to Birmingham, really. They might have found him.

"Thank you," Johan W. says as he comes around to open the door for her. She thanks him; she will text her son and tell him to award him the maximum number of stars. All the stars in the digital sky. Because he has brought her here.

Bridie makes her way through the doors, and the high, bright atrium of the hospital is as quiet as the roads outside. It is as though everyone can feel autumn coming too, and they are out in their gardens, on warmed pavements, in pretty parks, soaking up the last of the summer. There is not a person around

except one.

There he is.

And it is as though all the music has stopped.

There he is, waiting for her.

Sitting in a wheelchair, he is wearing a hospital gown but with a black bow tie at his neck, beside him an IV drip is standing sentry, wiggling into a vein on the hand that is resting on his knee, and what is left of his white hair has been neatly, carefully, thoughtfully combed to one side.

Though he is sitting in the wheelchair and he has the drip in his hand, he does not look ill. When she allows herself to look upon his face, she sees that he is smiling. Not smiling—gleaming. He is illuminated, and the unbelievable thing is that he is looking at her, Bridie. It is she who has caused the smile to raise upon his face. She upon whom he looks and sees something worth smiling about. Something worthy. The years have not changed the essence of him. She hopes the same is true of herself as she walks across the sun-drenched floor towards him.

And it is now that the thought, full of grace, comes to her:

It is not too late.

She kneels beside Eddie Winston's wheelchair and she is not tentative nor afraid to place her hand on his hand. Even where the IV burrows within.

His smile is beyond anything anyone has smiled at her before.

And then he speaks.

"Hello, Birdie."

Eddie

———◆———

There she is. My girl.

Finally, finally, finally, my body sings.

"Hello, Birdie," I say, when I manage to speak at last.

"You waited," she says, and she seems saddened by the thought.

"I waited," I tell her, and it sounds like a song.

The light of the hospital window ignites her hair and everything glowing metal around her.

She smiles again.

Eddie, her smile says. *It's time.*

And so

I take her perfect face in my hands

and she leans in close

and I close my eyes

and it begins.

Acknowledgments

Eddie came to visit me on a summer's day in 2021 when I was deep into full-scale panic about book two and horizontal with morning sickness. I was listening to a song that I'd played hundreds of times while writing *Lenni and Margot* (*The Ramblin' Rover* by Andy M. Stewart) when a lyric I'd heard countless times ignited something in my brain, and there was Eddie and we were off.

I am forever grateful to my fantastic and endlessly supportive agent, Sue Armstrong at C&W, for her wisdom, her guidance, and her belief in my writing throughout this journey. Thank you to Jane Lawson, my marvellous editor at Doubleday for her enthusiasm for Eddie even in his early days when he was just a one-sentence pitch. I'm grateful to both Sue and Jane for the patience they showed me when I kept trying to write books during lockdown and they kept getting worse. To everyone at Doubleday—the editors, proofreaders, design, marketing, and PR, I'm so grateful for all your work. Thank you also to the translation team at C&W for your wizardry at sharing my writing with the world.

Thank you to Alexandra Machinist, my agent at ICM, for the amazing things she's done for me and Eddie, and to the wonderful Sarah Stein, my editor at Harper Perennial, for putting her faith in me a second time, which meant so much. Thank you to the whole team of editors, designers, proofreaders, PR, and marketing at Harper Perennial for their enthusiasm for sharing Eddie's story and the incredible things they achieved for Lenni and Margot too.

Thank you to the family and friends (old and new) who have cheered me on during the writing of *Eddie* and to those who showered me with kindness and love (and requests for signed copies) when *Lenni and Margot* went out into the world. It made me feel like a real writer and it meant so much to me.

You don't realise how much you need your mum until you become one yourself, and I'm extra grateful to mine for the weird and wonderful weeks she spent with me and my newborn daughter— her shoutout in *L&M* was when Humphrey declares he's "as cold as a witch's tit"—I'll let you come to your own conclusions about what shoutout is hers this time around. I'm grateful to my nest of siblings for their sage cover advice, for such rousing compliments as "it's not bad, is it?" and for keeping me up to date on Richard Osman's continued publishing achievements.

I'm also grateful to my headshot photographer for patiently taking photos of me that I don't hate and for having unfounded levels of optimism for everything I do.

And to the readers, reviewers, booksellers, and bookstagrammers who have championed *Lenni and Margot* and made this deeply anxious soul willing to go on social media once in a while—thank you.

As with all great works of literature, there are plenty of animals to thank. Firstly, of course: Puffin. My giant, FIV-positive, dining table–destroying cat—he'll probably never get around to reading this, but he always knows when I need a boop. Ferris's taillessness was inspired by my sister's two beloved felines. They were degloved too. Let's not think about it. And last but not least, Pushkin was inspired by a guinea pig named Pigwig and a guinea pig named Alan.

And finally, the most important thank you: thank you to my daughter for being a constant surprise, for making the world new and exciting again, and for teaching me everything I need to know. I said I'd never dedicate a book to anyone

and then you came along.

About the Author

———◆———

Marianne Cronin was born in 1990 and grew up in Warwickshire. After gaining her PhD in applied linguistics, she worked in academia until becoming a writer. Her first novel, *The One Hundred Years of Lenni and Margot*, published by Harper Perennial in 2021, was short-listed for a Goodreads Choice Award for Fiction, and received the American Library Association Alex Award. She lives in the Midlands with her family and her cat.